OFFSHORE

DON CORACE

EMERALD INK PUBLISHING

SECOND U.S. EDITION 2005

Published in the United States by Emerald Ink Publishing.
ISBN 0-9760426-0-6

10 9 8 7 6 5 4 3 2

PRINTED IN THE UNITED STATES OF AMERICA

To Ammi

for all your love and support…

in calm and rough seas.

ACKNOWLEDGEMENTS

I cannot fully express my gratitude to all those in the offshore oil industry for helping me with my research and giving me their support: Loren Sheffer; Robert G. Burke; all the wonderful people at Global Santa Fe (both past and present) including Jon Marshall, David Herasimchuk, James McCulloch, Tom Morrow, Jack Downing, Thomas Johnson, Alexander Krezel, and the April 1999 Captain and crew of the drillship Glomar Explorer.

Many thanks to Roger Olien for the historical perspective on the West Texas oil patch, Don Evans for hiring me as a roughneck, my late friend and Midland mentor, Al Dillard, and his widow Jane, who introduced me to Texas hospitality, and to my brother, Dick Corace, for his support.

A special thanks to Barbara Malone for her skillful editing and keen marketing sense, Bryant Ewing for his artistic guidance and enduring friendship, Dick Price for his sage advice on publishing and printing, and Chris Carson for his steadfast optimism.

And last, but not least, to my children Natalie, Brandon, and Erik, who never let me take myself too seriously.

CHAPTER 1

Clay Drummond wished he had been the one to die...

"I should have brought the rig in hours ago," he said to his brother, Dirk, in the passenger cabin of the helicopter.

Dirk didn't respond and reached for a life preserver under the seat in front of him.

A flash of lightning lit the night sky. Heavy winds rocked the chopper back and forth violently. Rain pelted it like machine gun fire. The cabin lights blinked on and off.

Clay turned to Tito Martinez who was seated across from him and added, "The storm turned sooner than I thought."

Tito shook his head, frowned, and looked out the window.

Clay noticed Tito's knuckles were white from gripping the arm rest so tightly.

"There she is!" said the pilot through his headset.

Everyone looked out the window.

The helicopter's search light swung around on the jack-up rig below.

The rig's three steel column legs, which rested on the ocean floor during drilling, had been retracted and now extended two hundred and fifty feet above the deck. Waves washed across the main platform. One rescue capsule had been launched. Crew members were boarding the other two capsules. Heavy drill pipe had broken loose and was rolling around the deck. Men were in the water, maybe a dozen or more.

One tug boat's tow line was still tied to the rig. It struggled to hold the vessel in position. A second tug was trying to reach it, but every time the boat seemed to gain ground a swell tossed it back. The third tug was nowhere to be seen.

Clay told the pilot to hover over the rig for a better look. And just as he was about to say to stay clear of the rig's jacking columns, a sudden gust flung the chopper to the left.

Clay saw the rotor blade shatter. Sparks flew. The chopper's nose dropped. They hit the side of the rig nose-first and plunged into the heavy seas.

Total darkness. And the muffled sound of screams, screams he would never forget...

"Sir," said the doorman at the Houston Omni Hotel. "Are you checking in?"

Clay managed to bring himself back to the present and looked at the young man.

The female taxi driver turned around and asked, "You okay?"

Clay reached into his pocket, handed her a fifty and got out of the cab. He looked at his watch: eight-ten. Kate, his sister-in-law, was supposed to meet him in the lobby lounge at eight-thirty. Good, he thought to himself. I'll have time for a drink. I need one.

He checked in at the front desk, asked for his bags to be taken to his room, and then walked into the lounge.

There were around a dozen people sitting on leather couches and high-back chairs having cocktails. He found a table next to the large picture window overlooking the pool and waterfall.

Shrubs cut in the shape of swans and dolphins were up-lighted and except for the trees being much larger, it was how he had remembered it on his wedding day in nineteen eighty four, exactly twenty years ago in two weeks.

He sat down and ordered a double vodka-tonic with a lime from the waitress.

Clay looked at the lawn area beyond the pool and recalled how the helicopter had brought him and Heather, his ex-wife, from the wedding reception at the ranch. What a party that was.

The Gatlin Brothers Band played all night. The old man enjoyed their music, but he especially liked the fact they had grown up in Odessa and had worked as oilfield roughnecks before they got their big break. George Bush, who at the time was Vice President, and his wife Barbara, were there. And the who's who in the Texas oil industry and politics.

It was a period in Clay's life when he loved the excitement of working in the family business. Every day brought new challenges. And he had earned the respect of the close-knit oil community. But there was one stark reality: He had been unmistakably in the shadow of his legendary father, D.L. Drummond. And Clay hated him for it.

———

Kate Drummond, Dirk's widow, arrived at the hotel at eight forty-five. Normally, the two margaritas at Happy Hour with some of her staff at Drummond Offshore would have taken the edge off. But she was both anxious and apprehensive to see Clay again. Why, she thought to herself, after four years, had he decided to come back? To see his dying father? To help the family from losing control of the company to its second largest shareholder, Ramsey Croft?

Kate walked into the lobby. She noticed Clay staring out the picture window and wondered how many drinks he had had. She felt her heart beat faster and she thought about going to the ladies room to get a grip on herself, but Clay turned his head and saw her. He smiled nervously and stood.

She walked toward him and said, "Sorry I'm a little late."

"I just got here."

Kate noticed Clay's dark tanned face had more lines. He had put on a little weight. And there was a slight trace of gray in his brownish-blonde hair.

Clay said, "As usual, you look great." He gave her a hug.

Kate felt his thick, sinewy arms grip her tightly and his chest press against her breasts. Strangely, she felt herself slightly aroused. And for those few seconds she felt a bond, a closeness, she had not felt since the last time Dirk had held her in his arms.

They exchanged kisses on the cheek and sat down.

Kate was not surprised to see Clay drinking his customary vodka-tonic.

Clay motioned for the waitress and asked Kate, "How 'bout a drink? Still scotch and water?"

Kate nodded to the waitress. She looked at Clay and hoped she was sitting with the old Clay. The Clay she had known in college. The Clay she had known before his divorce. The Clay before all the gambling and drinking. She asked, "So how are things in the Bahamas?"

Clay avoided eye contact at first and answered, "Good, real good."

"You still have that scuba diving operation and lodge?"

"Yup." He took a swig of his drink and asked, "How are the kids?"

Kate realized he wanted to change the subject and replied, "Brock is working as a hot shot geologist in the Exploration Department. His wife, Haley, is pregnant with a boy and due in five weeks. They're naming him Daniel Lloyd, after Dad. And Kendra is going to start working for me in Investor Relations in a couple of weeks."

"That's great. Good for them."

"Have you gotten my letters?"

"Yeah, thanks. I'm just not much of a letter writer."

"A phone call once in a while would be nice. Just to see how you're doin'?

Clay's face twitched and he said, "I should've."

The waitress returned with Kate's drink.

Clay raised his glass and said, "Here's to you, Kate."

Kate raised her glass and replied, "Welcome home."

Clay paused before drinking, looked at her, and then drank.

Kate glanced around at the people in the room and Clay looked at a young couple embracing in the pool.

Clay broke the silence by asking, "So how's the old man holdin' up?"

"He still refuses to go in for chemo or radiation."

"It's in his lungs?"

"And lymph nodes," Kate said in a weak tone of voice. "The doctors give him a month or two, at the most."

"I'm sorry to hear that."

Kate didn't know if Clay was sincere, but sensed there was an opportunity to turn the discussion toward the plight of the company. She asked, "Remember the agreement Dad signed that as long as he was Chairman he had to provide medical reports every six months to the board?"

"Yeah, after he had the by-pass."

"Well, we just found out he falsified them and hid the fact he has cancer."

Clay shook his head and asked, "The board doesn't know?"

"Not yet. And the attorneys are telling us he can be sued for securities fraud since the medical exams are mentioned in the shareholder reports." She frowned and added, "As if we didn't have enough to worry about with Croft and everything else."

Clay's face was expressionless.

Kate said, "He's really glad you've come back," and looked closely for his reaction.

Clay looked out the window and replied, "I bet he is."

"He's missed you, Clay. He wants to see you."

Clay smirked and shook his head.

Kate was hoping time had made Clay less bitter toward his father. Did his resentment stem from the way Dad constantly second-guessed Clay's management decisions after Dirk's death? She recalled how, at times, D.L. had belittled Clay in front of some of the other executives. But in her father-in-law's defense, he had still been trying to cope with the death of Victoria, his wife of forty-nine years. Clay should have been more understanding.

Kate was, however, certain Clay still blamed himself for Dirk's death. According to one of Kate's friends, a psychologist, the fact that Dirk and Clay were fraternal twins may have made the loss even more difficult for him.

She asked, "Have you been keeping up with what's going on at the company?"

"Enough to know that the value of my shares has dropped by over thirty percent in the last month."

"Have you read the reports I've sent you?"

Clay nodded and asked, "Why is the company drilling such deep and risky wells, especially with the financial shape it's in?"

"Dad is insisting on it."

Clay grinned and replied, "I suppose he's saying," he lowered his voice to mock his father, 'We've got to earn our way out of this'."

Kate nodded reluctantly.

Clay added, "And I assume all the dry holes aren't making the banks real warm and fuzzy."

"That's putting it mildly."

"Has the board turned on him?"

"The Mercers seem to be holding everyone together so far."

He chuckled, "The Mercers?"

Kate was surprised by the sarcasm and replied defensively, "They've been very supportive."

"Yeah, I bet they have."

Clay took a long draw on his drink.

Kate asked, "I thought you and Arlen were friends."

Clay smiled and replied, "Arlen and his father are only *friends* if they want something from you."

Kate was not in the mood to delve into the Mercers' motivations for wanting to help the company. In a way, she didn't want to know. As politely as she could, she asked, "May I ask why you've decided to come back after all these years?"

Clay finished his drink and looked for the waitress as if he needed another one before answering.

"Well?" asked Kate.

Clay looked at her, blushed, and replied, "I'm broke."

Kate's heart sank.

He asked, "That isn't what you wanted to hear, is it?"

"I was hoping you came back to help us through all this. So was Dad."

"I didn't create the mess you're in."

Kate tried to regain her composure. She took a sip of her drink and asked, "So you'll be going back after you see Dad."

Clay nodded.

Kate tried to gather herself. Her hopes that Clay would help the family through its crisis were dashed. But Clay was, after all, her brother-in-law. And despite his shortcomings, she still loved him. If nothing else, she thought, I can at least make him feel at home. She said, "I arranged for you to play golf with Arlen and Rex tomorrow morning at the club. I thought you'd like to see 'em again."

"Ol' Rex Novack. How's he doin'?"

"He's fine." Kate didn't want to tell Clay she had been seeing Rex for a few years and then asked, "Do you want me to cancel it?"

Even though Clay didn't seem too keen on the idea, he replied, "No. I'll play."

"Then I'll pick you up afterwards and take you out to the ranch to see Dad."

Clay nodded.

Kate tried not to show her disappointment. She sipped her drink and said, "I'm sorry I jumped to conclusions, Clay."

CHAPTER 2

The next morning, Clay directed the driver of the hotel van to pull around to the bag drop area at the Houston Country Club. He had not slept well because of his concern that the old man wouldn't bail him out of his financial problems and hoped a round of golf with Arlen Mercer and Rex Novack, friends from high school, might help him relax.

He tipped the driver and climbed out. Typical August morning, he thought to himself. The humidity is already a hundred percent.

Arlen Mercer and Rex Novack were on the practice green. They noticed Clay, smiled, and walked toward him.

Rex said, "We hope to hell you brought a lot of money."

Arlen added, "We've got just the right set of clubs for you," and pointed to an old leather golf bag on the back of a golf cart.

Clay walked to the cart and pulled out a wooden driver. The steel shaft was badly bent and the irons were covered with rust.

"Very funny," replied Clay.

The men exchanged handshakes.

Rex's hair was grayer since Clay last saw him and he was still slim. Arlen, on the other hand, had ballooned to probably two hundred and thirty pounds. He had also lost quite a bit of hair and was obviously self-conscious about it because he rubbed his head and said, "I'm about ready to get one of those two-pees."

Clay chuckled.

Rex turned to Arlen and said, "You need a hell of lot more than that." He then turned to Clay. "You look good. Caribbean life agrees with ya."

"It's okay."

"I heard you've got a boat," said Arlen. "When you gonna invite us down to do some fishin'?"

Clay smiled and replied, "Whenever you want."

A pudgy, middle-aged man with a flat top haircut approached.

"Clay," said Rex, "this is Mike Sidowski. He's with Tel-Sat Communications. He's doin' a bunch of stuff for you guys right now."

Sidowski shook Clay's hand and said, "Nice to meet you."

"Clay," said Arlen, "you're riding with me."

"I need to hit a bucket of balls. I haven't picked up a club in almost two years."

"No time. We're up."

A pair of golf shoes and a new bag of clubs were brought out by the assistant pro.

Clay climbed into the passenger side of the cart and the foursome made their way to the first tee.

Arlen slapped Clay on the knee and said, "Its good to see you, ol' buddy. Things have been kinda dull around here."

"So what's new?"

"Well, for starters, Rex and Kate are gettin' pretty serious."

"What? I didn't even know they were going out?"

"Yeah, for a couple of years now. Hell, I think the little weasel is gonna propose."

Clay was surprised Kate would fall for the former disc jockey. He always considered Rex a bit feminine.

Arlen added, "I guess he's selling his radio stations to some Canadian outfit and then he plans on takin' her on some trip around the world."

They pulled up to the tee.

"How's your Dad?" asked Clay. "I heard he remarried."

"Yup, number four. She's some young thing. He says she has an un-limited budget... and exceeds it!"

Clay laughed. He climbed out of the cart and pulled out a Titleist driver from his bag.

Rex asked, "What's your handicap, Clay?"

"He's a six," replied Arlen.

Clay shook his head and said, "That was over four years ago. I think I've played maybe three times since then."

Arlen looked at the others and said, "Six is good enough for me, huh, boys?"

Rex and Mike grinned and nodded.

Arlen continued, "I'm an eight. Mike's a twelve, and Rex's handicap is golf."

"Real funny, smart ass," replied Rex. "I'm a twenty."

"On a good day," said Arlen.

———

After everyone ribbed Clay about lowering his handicap since he hit his drive over two-hundred and eighty yards in the middle of the fairway, he climbed into the cart with Arlen.

Arlen stomped on the gas pedal and they made their way down the fairway.

Arlen asked, "So, what do you think about all this stuff with Croft?"

"I haven't really paid too much attention."

Arlen grinned and said, "You Drummonds never change. A bunch a tight-lipped sonofabitches."

"You still with the Mineral Service?"

"Yeah, but I don't know how much longer. They got me headin' up some new task force in the Gulf to check rigs for safety violations."

"When they start that?"

"A few months ago. Some bureaucrat back in Washington tryin' to justify his existence got the bright idea. He figured since the service sells offshore leases they should also make sure contractors and operators maintain better safety programs."

"Has there been a rash of accidents?"

"Nope."

Clay never understood why, after Arlen and his father sold their marine service company to one of Croft's investment groups, he chose to work for the service. The old man once said it was so he could get pay-offs.

Arlen added, "It hasn't been a real popular program."

"I wouldn't doubt it," said Clay.

"It's an experimental sort of thing for a year. I'm sure they're not gonna keep it goin'."

———

After the round, Clay climbed out of the golf cart and followed Arlen, Rex, and Mike to the club's bar and grill. He had won a hundred and thirty dollars in bets, but his back ached and his clothes were soaked with sweat from the oppressive heat and humidity.

There were nearly two dozen, mostly retired, men in the grill. Many of them, Clay recognized, were acquaintances of D.L. and they greeted him in such a way as to make him feel he had never left Houston. Good ol' Texas hospitality was alive and well, he thought.

As he walked from table to table, Clay tried to avoid talking about what seemed to be on everyone's mind: Croft. This group of old-guard oilmen didn't think very highly of Wall Street bankers and weren't bashful to say so. Clay tried to keep his composure and not engage in name calling. But when one of D.L.'s old poker buddies said, "It's good you're back to teach that sonofabitch a lesson." Clay almost replied by saying, "You bet your ass I will!"

Arlen ordered a pitcher of beer and the four of them raided the buffet.

Clay was glad the round was over, not only because of his aches and pains and the heat, but to get the hell out of the cart with Arlen. Since they were kids, Arlen could never shut up. And it seemed he had gotten worse with age.

Clay had been cautious not to talk about the company, although Arlen kept probing for information on what moves the old man planned to make with regard to Croft.

After Clay filled his plate, he sat next to Mike Sidowski at a table and asked, "So what's your company doin' for Drummond?"

"Quite a bit. We're up-grading all your telephone systems and IP networks using satellites."

"IP?"

"Internet protocol. We're connecting all the corporate networks so anyone in the company can communicate with anyone else, whether they're on land or at sea, anywhere in the world."

"Huh, it probably took awhile for the old man to spring for that."

Rex joined them and added, "What is it, Mike, a seven million dollar contract?"

Mike nodded and added, "We've also developed a satellite system on one of your drillships to transmit all navigational, drilling and eventually production data in real time."

"Which one?"

"Global Explorer."

"I'm a little surprised. My father hasn't always *embraced* new technology."

"Get this," said Rex. "Kate told me he's made a donation of twenty million for a Stanford research project on global warming and alternative energy sources. They're spending something like $225 million over the next ten years. Exxon/Mobil, General Electric, and Schlumberger are in on it, too."

Clay felt a hand on his shoulder. He turned around. It was a retired executive with a rival drilling company.

The man pointed to Arlen, who was still standing in line at the buffet, and said, "Watch out for that sneaky bastard, Clay. Especially since you guys are drillin' more and more in deep water."

"Why?"

"He's still in bed with Croft."

———

D.L. Drummond sat in his study later that morning at his ranch west of Houston waiting for Tito Martinez to arrive by helicopter. He reached for the Gulf of Mexico offshore oil and gas lease map and rolled it out on his desk. The blocks the company owned were numbered and marked in yellow against a blue background.

He picked up his reading glasses and found Block Nine-Forty-Seven. Above it was written, 'Seahorse Canyon'. Water depth contour lines between fifty-nine hundred and sixty-five hundred feet criss-crossed the block. Toward the southerly end of it, there was a notation: 'Narrow Trench 10,990'.

This could be the one, D.L. thought to himself. It has to be.

———

D.L. heard Ramona, his housekeeper, greet her son before he walked into the study.

"How've ya been, boy?" D.L. asked Tito Martinez and motioned for him to have a seat. At six foot-six, two-hundred and fifty pounds, Tito easily filled the chair.

"Fine, Sir."

"Your Mom cook you up some food?"

Tito's eyes rolled.

D.L. said, "You better eat it or there'll be hell to pay."

Tito smiled.

"Clay is in town."

Tito's face turned serious. He replied, "I've heard."

D.L. knew Tito wouldn't be overjoyed to see his son again. Even though he had a plan to get the two of them to reconcile, his first priority was Seahorse Canyon. He asked, "Where are we with Ocean Explorer?"

"We're disconnecting the riser this afternoon and should be on the BP and Chevron location within a few days."

"What about Global?"

Tito exhaled and replied, "We're having problems with the new thrusters. I'm going to Brownsville to check it out after I leave here."

"What the hell is the problem?"

Tito blushed and said, "Wiring, we think. Since it's a new system, no one has a lot of experience with it."

"We've got to be on Block Nine-Forty-Seven within a few days."

"We'll try, Sir."

D.L. pointed to a spot on the map.

Tito stood and looked at it.

D.L. cleared his throat, coughed, and said, "We're going to drill this trench. But I want you to use the coordinates in the six thousand foot water depth in all the drillin' reports."

Tito looked at D.L. and then stared blankly at the map.

D.L. added, "This needs to be between you and me for right now."

Tito sat back in his chair. With a stunned expression on his face, he replied, "How do you expect me to keep a lid on this? Over ten thousand feet! It's a record depth!"

D.L. knew the fines from the Mineral Management Service would be hefty once they discovered the information was falsified. He said, "It will just be an honest mistake, Tito. That's what we'll say."

Tito was speechless.

D.L. said, "And I know it won't be easy drillin' either."

Tito looked at him and said, "There's bad loop currents and mud slides in that area. The rig isn't ready for those conditions. It needs an overhaul."

"She can handle it."

"I'm not so sure Ricci will go for this."

A few years ago, D.L. had flown to Rome to steal Captain Salvatore Ricci from an Italian oil company. He was confident Ricci would jump at the chance to break the world water depth record and said, "I'm sure he'll go along with it." He cleared his throat again and added, "This well could mean the difference between this company surviving or not. Do you understand that?"

Tito nodded.

"I'm counting on you, son." D.L. leaned forward and added, "Just like you and your family have counted on me for all these years."

CHAPTER 3

It wasn't two minutes after Kate picked up Clay at the country club in her black Mercedes that he asked, "What's this about you and Rex?"

Kate blushed and replied, "We've been going out."

"Arlen says it's pretty serious."

"We're just good friends," she said defensively.

For the next half hour, as they drove west of town toward Simonton, what little conversation there was centered around how Westheimer Road had become so developed over the years. Occasionally, he would look out the passenger's side window and then glance back at her. She was a beautiful woman.

Kate had aged very little from their days at The University of Texas. She still had that long, thick auburn hair. Her high cheek bones and full lips were the envy of most women. And those sparkling hazel eyes. He wondered, as he had done so many times before, what their lives would be like if they had married.

Once they reached the small town of Simonton, Kate turned right on *Four Oaks Lane.*

Clay recalled that it was exactly three-eighths of a mile from the main road to the ranch gate.

As a teenager, he'd try to drive to the entrance in less than thirty seconds, which meant that he'd have to do seventy miles per hour. He would then open the gate with a remote controller without stopping and slow down at about the twentieth pecan tree down the driveway so that no one at the main house would see him speeding.

They approached the red brick entrance.

Kate slowed to a near stop. She pushed the button on her remote. The heavy iron gate, inscribed with the name *Four Oaks*, creaked open.

As they started down the driveway, immediately to their left, was the large lake where some of the old man's prized Longhorn cattle were watering. The lake was low, no doubt due to a persistent drought. The scene reminded him of an incident one summer when he and Dirk were in high school.

Clay had run their ski boat up onto the shore to impress Dirk and two of their buddies. But one of the bulls didn't take too kindly to the intrusion and charged him. To avoid being gored, Clay had to dive into the water.

The boys, sitting under the oak, broke out in laughter. But then the angry bull turned and charged them. Clay remembered how comical the situation was as they frantically climbed up the rope hanging from the tree.

They drove down the driveway toward the main house.

The canopy formed by the huge pecan trees lining the driveway had always made Clay feel as if he was driving through a tunnel, especially at night. He remembered how he would turn off the headlights half-way up the road to avoid waking anyone. But no matter how late it was, Mom always mentioned the exact time he got home the next morning.

They approached the circular driveway in front of the house.

Despite the thousand acre ranch being covered with pecan trees, "Four Oaks" was a perfect name for the place. The red brick, two-story, Southern Colonial style home was surrounded by four sixty-foot Live Oaks and always gave Clay the impression of permanency, of strength.

Kate came to a stop at the front steps.

Clay's stomach felt queasy. He took a deep breath and exhaled. His first priority was to get a loan, he thought to himself. Forget about any notion of coming back to Houston. Forget about being a part of the family again. Those things didn't matter. And if the old man says 'no' to a loan, I'll just have to pick myself up again and go on. I'll get out of this mess. I don't really need him or his money.

He climbed out of the car.

About six or seven mixed-breed dogs slowly emerged from the shade. They approached Kate because they knew she'd pet them, but they were leery of Clay.

The front door opened and Ramona walked onto the porch. She had put on weight and looked much older from when Clay last saw her. And as expected, she was wiping her eyes with a handkerchief.

Clay smiled and started up the steps.

Ramona extended her arms and they embraced.

"Ramona, it's good to see you."

She sniffled, wiped her eyes and said, "Your father will be glad to see you, Clay."

The old man would never admit to it, he thought.

Ramona said, "I hope you haven't eaten lunch."

Clay was pretty full from the beer and sandwiches at the club, but he dared not tell her. He replied, "Of course not. I figured you'd run me off if I had."

Ramona looked into Clay's eyes and whispered, "Try not to look shocked when you see him."

"Okay," said Clay. He looked over her shoulder and saw his father. He was pale and had lost a lot of weight, and he shuffled his feet slightly as if he was too tired to pick them up.

D.L. smiled and said, "Welcome home, boy."

Clay extended his hand, but D.L., unexpectedly, gave him a bear hug.

Ramona patted Clay on the shoulder.

D.L. said, "Let's get out of this damn heat."

They walked into the hallway.

Ramona rushed toward the kitchen and told them lunch would be ready in fifteen minutes.

Kate grinned and followed her.

Clay looked around. The same English antiques Mom had bought in England years ago were still there. The same pictures on the walls. And a large vase of yellow roses on the table in the middle of the hallway. Nothing had changed.

D.L. walked beside him and said, "You look good, son. A little skinny, but Ramona will fix that."

Clay smiled and said, "How ya' feelin'?"

"Ah, I guess some days are better than others, and the goddamn heat doesn't help much."

"I noticed the lake was pretty low."

"We've had to drill a few water wells for the cattle just to be on the safe side. We'll also have a pretty bad pecan harvest because of shuck disease." D.L. grinned and said, "And other than that sonofabitch Croft circlin' like a vulture and me dying of this damn cancer, things couldn't be better."

Clay managed a grin.

D.L. said, "How 'bout we go into the study?"

Clay nodded.

They entered the wood paneled office.

Clay looked at the large oil painting of his mother riding her white horse.

D.L. noticed and said, "You know, I think about your mother more and more every day." He walked to the wet bar and added, "I really miss that English accent of hers. I guess that's the sort of little things you think about when you're dyin'."

Clay was surprised by his father's demeanor. First, the hug and the admissions he was dying. That was uncharacteristic of him. *He's trying to make me feel sorry for him. He's up to something, I know it.*

D.L. dropped ice cubes into two glasses, filled them with scotch and said, "The doctors say I'm not supposed to drink, but the hell with 'em." He handed Clay a glass, sat behind his dark mahogany desk, and motioned for Clay to sit down across from him.

"So, how's things in the Bahamas?"

Clay knew the old man would be direct, but he was not ready to bring up his troubles and replied, "Everything is fine."

D.L. asked, "I suppose Kate has been keeping in touch with you about what's going on at the company?"

"You mean Croft?"

"Croft and Manhattan Commerce."

Clay replied, "She hadn't said anything about the bank."

"Schultz is now the Chairman."

"Isn't he the guy that you always thought had side deals with the Crofts?"

D.L. nodded and replied, "He's gonna try to make us stop the deepwater drillin'. Hell, I've got another meeting with him tomorrow at nine. Damn bankers love to have meetings." He leaned forward and looked into Clay's eyes and said, "We've got to *earn* our way out of this, ya know."

Next, Clay thought to himself, *he'll say, "We've got to tighten our belts".*

D.L. added, "And we've got to tighten our belts."

Clay sipped his drink.

"The bank is pressurin' us to come up with a plan to get back into the black," said D.L. "But don't kid yourself, Croft is pullin' the strings. I'm sure of it."

Even though Clay was reluctant to talk about the company, he hadn't mustered up enough courage to ask for a loan and asked, "What about asset sales?"

"We sold a lot of our shallow production two years ago and invested heavily in deepwater."

"What about the rigs?" Clay asked and then realized he'd been really sucked into conversation.

"We've been talking with Transocean and Global Santa Fe, and others, but we'll never get the price we want."

Clay said, "You may not have a choice." He noticed D.L. blink his eyes and shake his head slightly and asked, "You okay?"

"Yeah, I just get dizzy spells once in awhile." D.L. took a sip of scotch and said, "We could use some help coming up with a plan, son. I just don't have the energy."

Clay was surprised by the weakness of D.L.'s voice and said, "I've been away too long."

"Hell, you could get up to speed in no time. Just look into things and see if there is a way out of this mess we haven't thought of."

"I'm not going to come up with any magical solution."

D.L. grinned and said, "You don't know that until you get your feet wet."

Clay was surprised he was getting the full-court press so early in the conversation and replied, "I've got commitments back in the Bahamas."

D.L. took another sip and replied, "Don't you have people to run things?"

"Yeah, but I've got to be there."

"I'm not asking you to jump back in the saddle and take over everything, son. Just for your opinions, that's all."

Clay knew now he was definitely being set up.

D.L. said, "Then you can go back."

Clay looked into D.L.'s bloodshot eyes and said, "It won't work out, you know that."

D.L. frowned.

The lull in the conversation made both of them uneasy.

Clay figured this was as good a time as any and said, "My business isn't doing so hot."

"What's the problem?"

"More competition mostly. And the collateral for the loans is my stock. And since the value has gone down, they're threatening to call my loans."

"Have you ever turned a profit?"

Clay nodded and said, "This is just a temporary thing."

D.L. looked at him and asked, "How much do you need?"

Clay gulped before answering, "Around a hundred and fifty. It would strictly be a short-term loan."

"How much debt is on the place?"

"Total?"

D.L. nodded.

"Around four-fifty."

"Why don't I just pay the whole thing off?"

Clay was caught off-guard by the offer and replied, "I wouldn't want you to do that."

"Would you rather owe it to the damn bank or me?"

Clay didn't know how to respond.

D.L. said, "I'll tell you what. I'll have Kitty wire the money to your bank first thing in the morning if you give me a couple of weeks to look things over and tell me what you think."

Clay paused before answering. The old man was making this easy. He replied, "I'll pay the same interest I pay the bank."

"That'll be fine."

Clay said, "No other strings attached."

"Nope."

Clay paused and said, "I understand you've made Al Rosenberg President. He won't like me sticking my nose into everything."

"Ah, don't worry about Al."

Clay knew he was being railroaded, but what choice did he have? He said, "Okay, but only two weeks."

"Fine," replied D.L. with a grin. "So be at the office by six-thirty tomorrow morning. I'll have Al set up some meetings with the staff."

CHAPTER 4

"Good morning, Mr. Drummond," said the parking lot attendant at Drummond Offshore headquarters. "You can park in your father's space."

Clay said, "Thank you."

"And welcome back, sir."

Clay pulled the black Lincoln Navigator he borrowed from the ranch through the entrance, made a right, and noticed there was no nameplate over his old parking spot. It used to say, 'C. Drummond.'

Before Dirk's death, he was the Senior Vice President of the company's exploration division. Back then, of course, his title was not his true job description. He managed the exploration department, but he also oversaw drilling operations on some of the company's leases in the Gulf of Mexico, the North Sea, and in South America. And during times when the exploration budget had been cut back, Clay was put in charge of rebuilding certain rigs. Those were the days when he had to be a jack-of-all-trades.

He pulled into his father's space. At six-fifteen, the parking lot was nearly deserted. In the old days, this was the time he usually got to the office, not only to avoid rush hour traffic but to review drilling reports before his day had begun.

He climbed out of the truck and walked across the lot. When he reached the crosswalk outside the parking structure, he looked up at the gray fifteen-story building the company had bought in the early seventies. It had never been an attractive building, especially compared to the new, shiny skyscrapers that had been built downtown. But as the old man always said, "It's paid for."

Clay recalled when he and Dirk proposed selling the building and moving to a new location on the west side of town where most of their suppliers were located. They also thought the old man would be in favor of it because it was close to the ranch, but the idea was shot down immediately. "We don't need to impress anyone with fancy offices," he told them.

Clay crossed the street. The magnolia trees in the planters around the perimeter of the building had grown. The bushes that had been between the trees had been replaced with beds of flowers. And new wooden benches had been added near the main entry to the building. He figured Kate had something to do with the changes.

Clay walked up the steps and entered the building. He immediately recognized the slim, elderly African-American man behind the check-in desk. Aaron Banks must be at least seventy-five by now, he thought.

A wide smile appeared on Aaron's face. He walked around the counter and said, "Well, Mr. Drummond, it is good to see you, sir. It truly is."

They shook hands.

"How's the family, Aaron."

"Fine, just fine. You remember my son, Cliff?"

Clay nodded.

"He's one of them full professors now over at Rice, and he's an assistant coach of the track team."

"Good for him. Tell him I said hello."

"I'll do that." With a twinkle in his eye, Aaron said, "It's good to have you back."

Clay walked to an open elevator and pressed the button for the fifteenth floor.

The elevators had been refurbished. The cream-colored floor tile had been replaced by dark, green carpet and the light brown wallpaper with dark wood paneling.

The doors closed and the elevator began its ascent.

Clay assumed many of the office staff on the fifteenth floor would be the same, but he knew many of the managers he would be meeting with later were new. Kate had written in a letter several months ago that the company had gone through a management reshuffling. Many of the old timers whom had been with the company for years either retired or were forced to take early retirement. The board felt new blood was needed, especially with all the rapid changes in technology.

According to Kate, however, the old man hired some former employees back as part-time consultants to make their transition into retirement easier. He probably figured he owed it to them after all their years of service. But the board was not happy with his charitable gestures.

The all male nine-member board had also changed. They were no longer the old cronies the old man used to play cards with over at the Petroleum Club. Most of them, with the exception of Croft's lackey, were former CEO's from some segment of the oil industry, either drilling companies or oilfield suppliers. And, as it has always been, the board sided with D.L. on major decisions. But considering the company's recent problems, and especially when they find out the old man failed to disclose his cancer, that could change.

The elevator opened onto the fifteenth floor. Above the empty reception desk was the company's logo: a silver seahorse inside a circle with a dark blue background.

Everything was new: the dark wood paneling; a stylish, curved receptionist counter to replace the old desk; the sitting area with new high-back leather chairs and a coffee table.

But the photographs of the company's first rigs still hung on the walls, including *The Victoria*. There were also three glass cases containing models of the company's newest generation of rigs. There was a fourth generation jack-up, a third generation semi-submersible, and a replica of the *Global Explorer*, the company's state-of-the-art drillship which Clay had been in charge of rebuilding in Stavanger, Norway.

He walked to the right and down the hallway toward the executive offices.

Kitty Carver emerged from a cubicle directly across from his father's corner office. Underneath that gentle, grandmother-like appearance was a highly professional and intensely organized woman who had kept the old man pointed in the right direction for nearly thirty years.

She said, "Well, aren't you a sight for sore eyes," in a thick Texas accent.

Clay embraced her, kissed her on the cheek, and said, "It's good to see you, Kitty. Been holding down the fort?"

"I'm sure as hell tryin'." She looked into Clay's eyes and added, "But it hasn't been the same without you. And your father...well, it's been pretty tough," she said with a strained voice.

"I know."

Kitty held back tears, straightened up, and said, "But now that you are back, everything will go back to the way it was, won't it?"

Clay smiled.

Kitty asked, "Coffee?"

"Sure."

"If its okay, you'll be using your father's office for now."

"That'll be fine."

Kitty walked toward the kitchen, turned and said, "Your father mentioned something about a wire transfer to a bank in the Bahamas."

Clay felt himself blush and said, "I'll get with you on that later."

"And just so you know, you're scheduled to fly to Brownsville tomorrow morning."

"Why Brownsville?"

"Your Dad wants you to look over the *Global Explorer*. It's in the yard."

Clay entered D.L.'s office. Not unexpectedly, nothing had changed: the old, battered metal desk; the pictures of the old man with several Presidents; the Remington sculptures on his credenza; and several framed photographs of the family.

Clay walked around the desk and noticed a photo on the credenza taken of him and Dirk on the floor of a land rig in Midland when they were sixteen. That was the summer they had been officially initiated into the business.

They had been around rigs since they could walk, but to actually be working as a roughneck was a big step. And, of course, there was a lot expected of them.

He recalled how both he and Dirk figured the driller and fellow roughnecks would go easy on them those first few days. Boy, were they wrong.

"Good morning," said Al Rosenberg holding two coffee cups.

Clay turned and replied, "How ya' doin', Al? It's been a long time."

Rosenberg placed Clay's cup on the desk and they exchanged handshakes.

Clay was surprised at how tired Al looked. He had dark circles under his eyes and sensed the pressure was taking its toll on him. After all, Al was now in his mid-sixties.

Al had been the old man's lawyer before he started Drummond Offshore. He helped form the company over thirty years ago and eventually take it public. He had always been pretty feisty, Clay recalled, especially in the courtroom. But to put him in the hot seat with the responsibility of stemming the company's losses while at the same time trying to anticipate Croft's maneuvers was probably more than he could manage.

Clay said, "Congratulations on becoming President."

Al frowned and replied, "I got it by default. No one else wanted it. And now I know why." He sat down and asked, "How're things in paradise?"

"Not bad."

"Well, things haven't been paradise around here."

Clay grinned and sat behind his father's desk.

Al said, "Your first meeting this morning will be with the exploration division. I told them to bring you up to speed on the current drilling program and what prospects are in the works."

"I understand Manhattan Commerce wants to throttle you back."

Al's face reddened and he said, "Frankly, I don't blame 'em. Your Dad and I are meeting them at nine."

"He told me." Clay sipped his coffee and asked, "Do you think Croft and this Schultz are workin' together?"

"We're sure of it. But can't prove it."

Clay leaned back in his chair and asked, "How many shares does Croft control?"

"As it stands today, around twenty-four percent."

"What about the Mercers?"

"They're hanging in there with us so far."

That could change, Clay thought to himself.

Al added, "They have over one percent themselves, but they could sway at least another three or four. It's not a rosy picture by any means."

Clay realized now that things were much worse than Kate had let on and said, "From the last quarterly report, it seems the drilling division is doing pretty well."

"They're holding their own, but we have been spending too much money on rig up-grades, especially on the Global Explorer. That's why your father wants you to go down there."

"Where is it?"

"The Haddock Yard."

The memory of being in the yard's office with Dirk and Tito when the distress call came over the radio four years ago flashed through his mind.

Clay asked, "What's being done to it?"

"I'm not sure. But the only chance we have to get out of all this, Clay, is to agree to the bank's demand to halt the deepwater program."

"And the old man won't."

Al nodded and said, "He thinks we'll be playing into Croft's hands."

"I take it finding another bank isn't going to be easy."

"Almost impossible," replied Al. "We're too far in the red."

"What about selling the rigs? The market should be pretty good right now."

"Croft will put up enough roadblocks to delay it for a year or more."

"While the company bleeds to death."

"Exactly. And we've got nine days before the shareholder's meeting and still have the cancer issue to deal with."

"Does anyone on the board know?"

"No, I'm gonna have to tell them sometime this week."

Clay was glad he wasn't going to be the one to break the news.

Al added, "Croft has us by the nuts." He leaned forward in his chair and said, "I know your father means well about wanting to bring you back in, Clay, but"

"Wait a minute, Al. I'm just here for a couple of weeks to give him my opinion, that's all."

"Well anyway, I think it's too late for miracles. It'll only be a matter of time before Croft gets control. And, unfortunately, time is on his side, not ours."

"So what are you saying?"

"For the family to negotiate the best deal it can for its shares before the price drops much more."

Clay pondered the idea, but he knew his father would never do it and asked, "Have you mentioned this to the old man?"

Al paused and said, "I was hoping *you* would."

CHAPTER 5

After five hours of meetings, Clay retreated to D.L.'s office and closed the door. He was exhausted. His short talk with Rosenberg earlier had only scratched the surface.

The company's operations were falling apart. Morale was terrible. Managers had even openly criticized one another in some of the meetings. And it would only be a matter of time when key employees would start to leave. Clay had seen this when the Crofts tried to gain control in eighty-six. But this time there was a big difference: The old man is not at the helm.

Clay knew there was no way to turn things around and fight off Croft's attacks at the same time. It was an impossible situation. And he wouldn't want to shoulder the blame after Ramsey Croft takes over and people lose their jobs as he sells the company off in pieces.

He sat down and started to go over what had transpired to make sure he wasn't just being paranoid. After all, he had been bombarded with so much information that it was hard to sort everything out.

His last meeting with the Chief Financial Officer was the most shocking revelation. Clay was told the former CFO had resigned because of the pressure D.L. was putting on him to inflate the drilling division's income. Every drilling company tries to recognize revenues sooner by reporting to auditors that contracts were more complete than they actually were. There was always some room for fudging. But the old man tried to push it too far. And if Croft somehow found out about it, he would use it to his full advantage.

The drilling division was profitable, at least on paper. But after meeting with the managers, including Tito Martinez, it was apparent that they had deferred too much rig maintenance. Several rigs needed to be upgraded and there were concerns among the staff that the Mineral Management Service would shut down operations on two, possibly three, rigs operating in the Gulf.

The estimates on how much the maintenance would cost were grossly underestimated, at least by thirty to forty percent, which meant the division was actually losing money. But the most unsettling thing about the meeting was seeing Tito again.

Clearly, Tito still blamed Clay for the deaths of Dirk and eight other crewmen. The fact that Tito testified before the National Transportation Safety Board against Clay, especially since they had been like brothers, still made him mad. Clay could never forgive him.

Then there was the meeting with the exploration division. Clay could tell that the head of the division, Estaban Hernando, was more of a technician than a manager. He also seemed to be overly cautious about what prospects to drill and Clay sensed he was the type who studied geological data to death.

He kept looking at Brock, Kate's son, during the meeting, who was not overly thrilled that Clay was there. But beyond that, Clay sensed his nephew was frustrated with Hernando's management style, or lack of it. The Brazilian definitely had a big ego, and he was the type of person Clay would have cut to shreds in the old days.

Even though Hernando and some of the exploration staff seemed tentative, Clay sensed there may be some merit to their cautious approach. After all, the prospects the old man wanted them to drill were in ultra-deepwater, five to six thousand feet. Not only was the geological data sketchy in some instances, but to justify the cost to produce a field at such depths made it necessary for them to discover fields with at least five hundred million barrels of oil reserves. None of the fields the company had discovered had ever exceeded two hundred million.

This was a whole new ball game. The old man was pushing the envelope, even beyond the limits Clay would. And considering the financial condition of the company, it was reckless. It was apparent that his father wanted 'to go out with a bang' and recalled how D.L. always told him how much he wanted to discover a giant offshore field.

Some of his first attempts were in the early seventies. The timing was right because the Arab oil embargo sent oil prices soaring.

The company agreed to become partners with Shell in Indonesia and Western Australia to drill some wildcats in twelve to thirteen hundred feet of water - record depths back then.

Cyrus Croft, Ramsey's father, was a board of director at the time and opposed to any deals where the company would reduce its contract drilling rates in exchange for earning interests in exploration deals. But when the old man proposed reducing its rates *and* investing, Croft went ballistic and did everything he could to stop it. He believed the company should focus on drilling, not exploration. Nonetheless, D.L. won approval from the board and went ahead with the deals.

All six wildcats were dry holes. The company lost over thirty million dollars and Croft tried to oust D.L. as Chairman of the Board and President. In order to stop in-fighting among board members, D.L. was forced to withdraw from Shell's *Cognac* prospect, which became one of the largest oil fields ever discovered in the Gulf of Mexico. Naturally, the old man was bitter.

Then, Clay recalled, in eighty-six, when he had been promoted to Senior Vice President of Exploration, oil prices collapsed. Soon after, the Crofts and their New York investment partners made their move to take over the company.

One of Croft's biggest beefs was a series of dry holes the company had drilled. So, in order to stem its losses, Clay was forced to back out of several deals, including the deepwater wildcat known as *Coulomb MC 657-1.*

Coulomb was not only drilled in at record water depth of seventy-five hundred feet, but it was also a major discovery. Another lost opportunity.

It was ironic, thought Clay. Again, while under the threat of a take-over, the company was being forced to curtail its drilling in deepwater. But this time all the cards were stacked against them, especially since the old man was on his deathbed. And there was no way Clay was going to fight a hopeless cause. Rosenberg was right: The only solution is to sell out to Croft.

But the old man had set up his estate to discourage the sale of the family's stake, he recalled. Ninety percent of the profit will be donated to The Victoria Drummond Charitable Trust. But based upon a price of, say, twenty-five dollars a share, the payoff for the shares I own outside the Trust should be around three and a half million. That should take care of me for awhile.

———

Ramsey Croft cut short his luncheon with a group of investment bankers at River Oaks Country Club after his office called telling him the meeting between Manhattan Commerce Bank and Drummond Offshore had concluded. Luckily, he had reached Schultz from his car phone before the banker's jet had taken off from Bush Intercontinental Airport. Croft wanted to hear every detail of the meeting. Drummond must be scrambling, he thought. If that old bastard thinks the bank is tightening the noose, wait until he sees what I have in store for him.

Croft parked his BMW outside the hangar where the bank's Lear jet was parked and looked around to make sure there was no one who could recognize him. Schultz had insisted over the phone they not meet, but, as usual, Croft got his way.

A jet was making its way to the runway. There was a mechanic working on a single engine Cessna two hangars away. And a little farther beyond, Croft's new Falcon was being fueled for his trip to New York City.

Ram climbed out of his car and was immediately assaulted by the hot, humid air. It was over a hundred degrees for the fifth straight day.

He walked briskly toward the jet so he wouldn't be exposed to the hot air too long. He had already come down with one of those dreadful colds caused by going back and forth from the outdoors and air conditioning this summer. He hated this time of the year.

Croft looked at the cockpit window and didn't see the pilots. Undoubtedly, Schultz had them disembark so they didn't witness the meeting. What a paranoid.

The doorway opened, and Schultz's head popped out. He nervously surveyed the area before giving Ram a less than genuine smile.

Croft entered the cabin. He made his way toward the back of the plane as Schultz closed the doorway. No one else was on board.

Ram noticed a bottle of Beefeaters Gin and a glass that was half full on a table and sat down across from it. Must have been a tough meeting, thought Croft. Either that or old Russy-boy is back hitting the sauce again. How can anyone drink that stuff?

Schultz was trying to maintain his composure, but when he reached for the glass, Ram noticed his hand was trembling.

Schultz said, "This isn't such a good idea, Ram. We shouldn't be seen together."

"Don't worry about it, Russ."

Schultz chugged the gin and replied, "I thought we agreed to go through your attorney, Nugent, on all this. We have to be even more careful now than before."

"We *are* being careful."

"You don't understand, I've got a lot at stake."

Ram grinned and said, "And what about me?"

Schultz poured himself another drink and replied, "I can't be doing this sort of thing anymore."

"Sit down," said Ram firmly. He didn't want to totally demoralize the guy by saying, "Who do you think put you where you are?" or remind him of the dirty little secrets that Ram knew about him. That wasn't necessary. Not yet.

Schultz sat down.

Croft asked, "Now tell me what happened"

"There isn't much to tell."

"Humor me."

"The meeting only lasted a few minutes."

"Was Kate there?"

"Kate?"

"The old man's daughter-in-law."

"No."

Ram wondered how she was. It had been over a year since he saw her at some charity ball. He tried to talk to her, but she avoided him. Even though she broke off their secret affair two years ago, he still had feelings for her.

Ram asked, "How did Drummond look?"

"Not very good, now that you mention it. He was pale and kinda tired-looking. And oh, by the way, D.L. confirmed that his son, Clay, is back."

"They must really be desperate. He's nothing but a drunk."

"I don't know about that. He's pretty..."

"Go on."

"Like I said, there wasn't much to tell. I repeated what was in my letter, that they were in technical default of their loan, and that we were not inclined to renew the line of credit."

"Not inclined?"

"Listen, Ram. Drummond is into us for over eight hundred million. We have to tread lightly."

Croft frowned.

Schultz added, "We don't want to push too hard. They may file bankruptcy."

"Drummond's ego is too big. He'd never do that."

"Maybe, but we can't take that chance."

"What did you say about the deepwater program?"

"We told him he was to cease and desist and said there wasn't enough oil or gas reserves to justify the investment."

"What did he say to that?"

Schultz paused and replied, "He...said the bank couldn't find oil on a garage floor."

Ram couldn't help from grinning.

Schultz continued, "Drummond said he didn't understand why the bank was panicking because they've never missed a payment. I said, 'not yet,' which really pissed him off."

Ram said, "Then he started in on his good ol' boy routine, didn't he? About how he always pays his bills. How he's made money for the banks and shareholders and built *his* company from scratch. Well, let me tell you something. He wouldn't have a company if it hadn't been for my father. He'd still be out in West Texas running a couple run-down rigs and drilling dry holes." Croft's heart was pumping. He felt perspiration on his forehead and sensed Schultz was amused that he had lost his cool. "What else?"

"I told him the bank has to take whatever actions it deemed appropriate. Rosenberg tried to say something, but the old man stopped him.

They got up, walked toward the door, and then Drummond turned around." Schultz took another drink and added, "He said to tell you that you don't have the guts to take him on."

"He said *that!?*"

"And, he said that at least your father knew when to quit."

Ram had an image of his father slumped over his desk after he shot himself in the head. His face tensed and said, "Well, we'll see who's left standing this time."

CHAPTER 6

Kate asked Kitty Carver, "Is he in?"

Kitty nodded from her desk.

Kate knocked on D.L.'s office door, opened it, and saw Clay standing at the window.

He turned around.

Kate asked, "I guess you've had a pretty busy morning?"

Clay managed a grin and said, "Nothing like jumping in with both feet."

"So what's the prognosis?"

Clay didn't reply immediately and then simply said, "Bleak."

"Ah, come on, it can't be that bad," she said trying to ease his tenseness. "How about some lunch?"

Clay nodded and followed her into the hallway.

Kate could see that Clay was distracted and the tense look on his face made her wonder if there were more problems than she had been made aware of. Both D.L. and Al had come to rely on her over the years, but she knew there were certain things they didn't tell her.

They walked to the elevator.

Kate noticed an attractive woman, perhaps in her early thirties, smile at Clay.

"Hello, Clay," the brunette said with a Scottish brogue, "I heard you were back."

Clay was surprised and said, "Morgan? How've ya been? It's probably been five or six years!"

They embraced.

Clay asked, "Are you working here now?"

"No, I'm still in Aberdeen. Just here for a few more days."

Clay turned and said, "Kate, this is Morgan Prosser. Morgan, this is Kate Drummond, my sister-in-law."

"How do you do?" replied the Scot.

Kate noticed the woman was not wearing a wedding ring.

Clay said, "You're probably running the office over there by now."

Morgan grinned, "Not yet."

"You look great," said Clay. He turned to Kate and said, "Morgan was working her way through night school when I was opening up the Aberdeen office."

It was probably grade school, Kate thought to herself.

Morgan said, "I heard you've been living in the Bahamas."

"About four years now."

"Are you back here for good?"

Clay glanced at Kate before answering and then said, "I'm not sure yet." He looked back at Morgan and asked, "Why don't we get together for dinner?"

Morgan perked up and said, "I'd love to."

"Where are you staying?"

"At the company's townhouses on Allen Parkway." She reached into her purse and wrote a phone number on the back of her business card.

Kate sensed Clay and Morgan had been more than just friends.

Clay said, "I'll give you a call. "

"Great!" Morgan turned to Kate and said, "Nice meeting you, Mrs. Drummond."

Kate grinned and said, "Likewise."

Clay pushed the button for the elevator.

Kate said, "Was she one of your earlier conquests?"

Clay chuckled and said, "Just a friend."

"Robbing the cradle, weren't you?"

Clay frowned, shook his head and said, "Still looking out for me, huh?"

"Someone has to."

The elevator doors opened and they walked in.

Clay asked, "How's your day been?"

"Pretty shitty, thank you. I've been trying to arrange meetings with the shareholders who have the largest remaining blocks, but it looks like Croft has already gotten to 'em."

"Have you talked to Arlen?"

"I have a call into him. I'm sure we can count on him."

Clay paused before answering and said, "I wouldn't be so sure about that."

Kate was surprised by the comment and replied, "What makes you think that?"

The elevator stopped on the tenth floor and several people boarded.

Kate wondered whether Clay knew something she didn't. The Mercers have been friends of the family for years, she mused. Surely, they wouldn't turn their backs on us.

The elevator was stopping on nearly every floor since it was the lunch hour. Kate kept looking at Clay as if the answers to her questions were written on his face.

Some of the employees greeted Kate. She knew a few of them had been with the company when Clay was running it. They smiled at him, but for some reason he tried to avoid their stares. One woman, who Kate was almost certain had worked in the exploration division when Clay was Senior Vice President said hello to him. Curiously, he simply smiled and avoided making eye contact with her. Why not say hello, she thought? Why not at least acknowledge he knew her even if he didn't remember her name?

There was an eerie silence inside the elevator. It seemed every time she rode it these days, she got the distinct feeling that company morale was getting worse.

At first, she thought it was the heat wave that was getting to everyone. But it was much more. The articles about the company's troubles were taking their toll on everyone. But aside from the media coverage and the rumor mill, both inside and outside the company, there were all kinds of doom-and-gloom stories circulating.

Kate thought about the memo she had received from the company's personnel director a few days ago. He was pleading with her to convince Rosenberg to hire some personnel counselors to help employees cope with the crisis the company was going through. She had discussed it briefly with Al, who, not unexpectedly, dismissed the idea. "We've got enough things to worry about," he had told her.

In a way, Al was right. The company was in crisis mode. This was survival in its purest form. So, if certain employees couldn't hold up to the pressure, maybe it was better they left.

But when Kate put herself into their shoes, coming to work every day and wondering if they would be laid off, she felt more compassion. The employees were dependent upon the company to support their families. And no matter how much she tried to block their plight out of her mind, she just couldn't. Damn Croft!

The press was hanging on his every word. And Wall Street was listening to one of their own. Wall Street, what heartless bastards! They don't give a damn about the company or its employees. Earnings. That's all they were interested in. Not how Dad built the company from scratch. Nor how Dirk and Clay had helped it get through some of its most trying times. No, they didn't give a damn about any of that. She hated them. She hated them for what they stood for. She hated Croft.

She turned and looked at Clay who was staring at the numbers above the door. Maybe it was asking too much of him to help pull the company out of this mess. Everything has gone from bad to worse. How can she, how can anyone, expect him to solve all its problems *and* keep the company in family hands?

———

Clay had suggested they go to the Spindletop Restaurant on the thirtieth floor of the Hyatt Regency instead of the Petroleum Club for lunch. He was not in the mood to field questions from oil people about what he has been doing for the past four years or if he was back to stay.

His mind was made up. He would report back to D.L. that the best option was to sell the family's shares to Croft. Now it was time to break the news to Kate.

They were escorted to a table next to the window.

He could see by the anxious look on Kate's face that she wanted to hear why Clay thought the Mercers may not support the family in its fight with Croft. She had asked him as they walked through the underground tunnel from the office, but he told her he would explain when there were fewer people around.

A waiter asked for their drink order. Kate ordered iced tea, but after Clay ordered a vodka on the rocks, she changed her mind and decided on a scotch and water.

Kate asked, "Now, what's this about the Mercers?"

"There's always been a kind of unholy alliance between them and Croft."

"Because they sold their company to him?"

Clay nodded and said, "The old man always suspected they got kick-backs after they got their shareholders to sell out."

45

"What makes you think they would do that sort of thing to us?"

"Money, and I suppose revenge."

"Revenge?"

"Back in ninety, the Mercers were short on cash and the old man bought about three hundred thousand shares from them at around twelve dollars a share. Then, about two months later, we announced the company would buy back a bunch of shares. The stock almost doubled in value, and the Mercers felt they got screwed."

Kate shook her head and said, "Oh, this is just great."

"And remember when we bought four rigs from Oceanic Drilling?"

Kate nodded.

"Arlen kinda brokered the deal. The old man found out he was getting a hidden fee and confronted Arlen, Sr. during a board meeting. It got pretty ugly."

Kate sat back in her chair and sighed.

The waiter brought their drinks and asked, "Are you ready to order?"

"Not yet," Clay told him. He sipped his drink while Kate stared out the window. He realized she must have pinned a great deal of hope that the Mercers would stay on the family's side and said, "You need to know where all the skeletons are buried, Kate."

"Why didn't Rosenberg tell me all this?"

"He should have."

Kate took a drink and said, "So how is the company faring?"

"From an operations side, it seems that the drilling division is on track. There may be a couple senior people who are dead wood that should go, but the core operations people, toolpushers and drilling superintendents are the same people who got us through hard times ten, even fifteen, years ago." Clay finished his drink and continued, "As far as exploration goes, this Hernando guy is more of a high-tech nerd than a manager. But I agree with him that this deepwater program the old man embarked on is too ambitious. I also get the impression he and some of the other staff are ready to jump ship."

"Brock has said the same thing."

"It doesn't take a financial genius to figure out that the old man's deepwater program is bleeding the company dry, Kate."

She put her elbows on the table and began massaging her temples with her thumbs.

Clay put his hand on her shoulder and said, "I have to tell you: I think the old man has lost it. I'm sorry. I wish I could do something."

"What are you going to tell him?"

"To sell out to Croft."

Kate's eyes widened. She said, "He'll never do that."

"What other choice does he have?"

"How about selling our shares to another drilling company?" "Who would want to be in bed with Croft knowing that his objective would be to eventually break up the company and sell it off. C'mon, Kate. I realize it's like admitting defeat, but Croft is the most logical buyer."

Kate stared blankly out the window and said, "It would be so humiliating for Dad."

"The longer we delay, the more the stock price will drop."

Kate's face turned serious. In a harsh tone of voice, she asked, "Is that your biggest concern? What you would get for your stock?"

Clay didn't respond.

She added, "Then I guess you'll get what you came for, won't you?"

"Listen, if I didn't care, why did I put myself through all this?"

"Because Dad said he would pay off your debts if you did."

Clay looked out the window.

Kate added, "He's going to pay them off, isn't he?"

Clay fidgeted in his chair.

"So now that you've seen how bad things are, you can go on back and wait for Dad to die and collect a big fat check."

"It's over, Kate. Deal with it!"

"So, you're just going to throw in the towel, huh?"

"I didn't create this mess, the old man did."

"So that means you can just turn your back on everything?"

"You have no goddamn right to talk to me that way!"

"I have every right!" Kate rose from her chair, grabbed her purse and said, "Go ahead, go back and hide from the world! We'll go on without you!"

Clay scoffed and said, "You don't have a chance in hell against Croft."

She leaned over the table and said, "At least I'm not going to give up without a fight! The Clay Drummond I used to know wouldn't have either!"

CHAPTER 7

"In conclusion," said Ramsey Croft, "we expect crude oil prices to move sideways from current levels before recovering in the fourth quarter. Thank you for coming. Please enjoy the Happy Hour buffet."

The crowd of Wall Street investment bankers seated in the ballroom of The Four Seasons Hotel in New York applauded. Croft shook hands with other members of the energy industry panel.

He stepped down from the elevated podium area and recognized three business reporters. They jostled for position to interview him.

A man from *Fortune* magazine asked, "Mr. Croft, how do you plan to restore shareholder value at Drummond?"

Croft replied, "I hope the company's management has gotten my message that my fellow shareholders and I expect changes to be made that are in our best interests, not just in the best interests of the Drummond family."

A woman from *The Wall Street Journal* asked, "There have been reports you are accumulating large blocks of Drummond stock to mount a takeover bid. Is this true?"

"I can't comment on that. Croft & Company takes positions in stocks for both its own account and the accounts of other investors looking for undervalued opportunities in the energy sector."

The man from *Business Week* asked, "Could this be a repeat perform-ance of what you and your father attempted back in eighty-six and eighty-seven?"

The question caught Ram off guard. He was especially irritated that the seasoned reporter, who may have covered the story back then, was grinning.

Croft responded coolly, "I look to the future, not the past."

All three reporters smiled.

Ram looked at his watch. "I'm sorry. I have an appointment that I'm already late for. Excuse me."

Ram shook the hands of several investment bankers on his way to the door. There were exchanges of business cards, a lot of "let's do lunch," and "give me a call."

Ram knew most of the men and women. Many of them were around fifteen years ago when Ram had taken his fall. They had abandoned him then, he thought. But now, now they're all kissing my ass.

He was back on top again. He knew it. They knew it. This time he was going to do it right.

Ram walked through the lobby, grabbed a few celery sticks from the buffet, and caught an elevator to his room on the fifty-second floor.

He had left a key to his room at the front desk for Marty Nugent. If any of the investment bankers downstairs or the pesky reporters got wind that Croft had retained Nugent, it would ignite rumors that could boost the price of Drummond shares. At this point in his plan, that was the worst thing that could happen.

McCann, Fishman, Nugent, and Kline was the most aggressive cor-porate takeover firm in New York, if not the country. And Marty Nugent had the reputation of being their most ruthless top gun.

Croft looked at himself in the mirrored wall of the elevator. He straightened his blue silk tie and slicked his gelled dark hair back.

The elevator door opened. He walked down the hallway and slipped the key card into the door

As expected, Nugent was there. He was sitting on a white silk couch sipping a martini with a lemon twist.

Nugent stood, offered a handshake and asked, "How did it go? They ate it up as usual, didn't they?"

Ram grinned and shook Nugent's hand. It was the hand of a physically powerful man who had found his calling in the legal profession after a decorated career as a Marine Colonel during the Vietnam War. The intense look in his eyes and completely shaved head reminded Ram of Marlon Brando in the movie *Apocalypse Now*.

It was the first time Croft had hired Nugent and his firm. Jonas Truesdale, his father-in-law, had arranged for the two of them to meet a few months earlier. Truesdale was a longtime client of the law firm and had retained them for many of his shipping and real estate acquisitions.

Jonas, the control freak, wanted Nugent to be his watchdog on the Drummond deal. But what neither Nugent nor Truesdale knew yet was that Ram had decided to do the deal on his own.

Ram grabbed a Perrier out of the ice bucket. He walked over and looked at a signed Kandinsky on the wall.

Nugent said, "That piece of crap is probably worth big bucks."

Ram turned to him and asked, "I take it you're not a fan of abstract impressionism?"

By the look on Nugent's face, Ram figured he didn't know what the term meant.

Nugent replied, "I like wildlife paintings."

"You're a hunter?"

"Big game, mostly." Nugent sipped his drink and added, "Jonas tells me you're quite a marksman yourself."

Ram said, "I don't hunt animals, only companies." He sat down and asked, "How did your meeting with the pension funds go?"

"I met with all three. We have a deal except they all insist on selling their shares within thirty days."

"I need more time. At least ninety days."

"Jonas is ready to go."

"I'm not."

"I'm sure he'll loan you the money if you can't raise your share."

"Go back and tell them we need another sixty days," Ram said finally.

Nugent paused and asked, "Have you discussed this with Jonas?"

"I don't need to," Ram said firmly.

"I recommend you do."

Croft glared at Nugent and replied, "Just do it, or I'll find another attorney who will."

"Okay," said Nugent raising his hand. "I'll see what I can do. I'm just trying to cover your ass, that's all."

"I can manage that myself."

Ram knew he could raise the money through banks to acquire the nineteen percent stake held by the funds. The tricky part, however, was going to be buying out Truesdale. He didn't know how he was going to swing that yet. Even though their agreement said he could buy out Truesdale at a premium, that didn't mean he would agree to it. The bastard has broken agreements with me before.

Nugent leaned forward and said, "The Drummonds aren't going to go down easily."

"I'll have all my bases covered."

"I'm sure you will," said Nugent with a grin. "But just to give us a better edge, I've got a suggestion. An old Vietnamese buddy of mine is an expert on bugging offices."

Ram looked into Nugent's eyes and asked, "What are you suggesting?"

"We would know every move they plan to make."

The idea intrigued Croft, but he didn't think he had to risk being caught. He had the Drummonds where he wanted them. It was only a matter of time.

Nugent added, "At least give him a call and meet him. His name is Lee Tran. He does a lot of work in Houston." He reached into his pocket and tossed a business card on the end table. "He's very discreet. Believe me."

"You've used him?"

Nugent simply grinned and then asked, "Are you going to see Jonas while you're here?"

"I'm leaving early in the morning."

"I guess that means no."

Ram nodded.

"Listen," said Nugent, "I don't feel comfortable about saying this, but he's concerned about you and Monique."

"Are you playing marriage counselor, too?"

"I've been divorced three times," chuckled Nugent. "Seriously, he'd just like to see the two of you patch things up, that's all."

Ram stood and walked to the window overlooking Central Park. The Upper West Side and the George Washington Bridge were in the distance. With his back turned to Nugent he said, "Let me know what the pension boys have to say about the ninety days."

Nugent paused and said, "Okay, I'll call you."

Ram heard the door knob turn and then Nugent said, "I'm on your side, Ram. I want you to know that."

"I'm sure you are."

Ram wondered if his eventual divorce from Monique would make as big a splash in the New York gossip columns as his mother's and father's had more than twenty years ago. Monique, in many ways, was similar to her socialite mother. The sooner he could rid himself of her, and Jonas, the better. And at the same time, he'll make the Drummonds pay for what they had done to him and his father.

Ram had been at the top. He had been on the path of becoming an icon in the Wall Street community - until he and his father decided to take a run at Drummond in eighty-six.

Oil prices had collapsed. Drummond Offshore's stock lost nearly half of its value within three months. And Ram and his father quickly raised money from their wealthy group of investors and borrowed from banks to buy large blocks of Drummond shares. It became a media event: Cyrus and Ramsey Croft, Wall Street financiers, versus an ex-roughneck, high school dropout and his twin sons.

The Drummonds mounted a series of legal defenses and counter attacks. The fight was drawn-out for almost a year, Ram recalled. Then, just when he had thought they had the Drummonds on the ropes, came the October eighty-seven stock market crash. The downward spiral had begun.

Banks began calling their loans. Drummond stock plunged further. The Crofts' backers wanted to take their losses and get out of the deal. But what Ram didn't know was that his father pledged the investors' holdings for more loans without their authorization. It was a clear case of fraud.

Ram remembered when his father called a meeting with the investors to confess what he had done. He provided proof that Ram had nothing to do with it and assured them he would pay them back and came up with a plan. Knowing they would not get their money if he was behind bars, the investors reluctantly agreed to a deal.

The first step of the plan was to sell their shares of Drummond. And the most likely buyer was the Drummond family.

The meeting with D.L., Clay, and Dirk did not start off well, he recalled. There was a great deal of mistrust. Heated arguments continually erupted. But after hours of intense negotiations, an agreement was finally reached for the Drummonds to buy back the shares, at least that is what Ram and his father had thought.

As the documents were being drawn up, D.L. issued a press release that Drummond would buy Delacroix Engineering, a rig building company heavily in debt. Drummond Offshore's shares plunged on the news. It was a shrewd move.

D.L. lowered the price he would pay for the shares. Ram and his father had no choice but to accept it, even though they couldn't fully repay the investors.

There were lawsuits and indictments. The Crofts were going to lose everything. The 'scorched earth' strategy of the Drummonds had worked.

Ram would never forget the day it all came crashing down. He was sitting in his office wondering how he would be able to salvage his reputation.

His secretary interrupted him and said a police detective was calling. Ram took the call. The detective told him his father had committed suicide. It had been with a pistol Ram had given him for his birthday a few weeks earlier.

Ram looked at his watch. Five-forty five. He figured he should join the others downstairs and walked toward the door. He looked at the business card on the end table and picked it up. Maybe Nugent is right, he thought. Maybe I need a little added insurance this time around.

CHAPTER 8

Clay lay down on the bed in his hotel room. He was exhausted from the day's events. No matter how many vodka and tonics he had drunk, he couldn't stop thinking about his argument with Kate. She expects too damn much, he thought.

It was time to think of himself now. Why didn't he have Kitty wire the money to the bank this morning? After all, he agreed to the old man's proposition to hang around for a few weeks. They had a deal. No strings attached.

But when he had stepped foot in the company's offices, things took on a new dimension. There were moments during the morning meetings that Clay felt he had never left. He felt in control. He was able to quickly assess each department's problems without getting bogged down in details. Just like the old days.

But the company was in deep trouble, probably the deepest trouble it had ever been in. He wanted to find ways to turn everything around. And with the old man out of the picture, this could be his time to shine. This could be his opportunity to take the company in the direction he always wanted. But who was he kidding? Croft has thought of everything. He has been planning this raid on the company probably since the day his father blew his brains out. This is more than money to him. This is pay-back time.

Clay thought of Dirk and what it would be like if the two of them were running the company again. If there had only been a way to find a happy medium, an arrangement where they could have both shared equal standing at the company.

He remembered them discussing it, at least before the old man made his famous declaration that only one of them could lead the company. But it probably wouldn't have worked out anyway. As Kate had said, 'It's the Drummond stubbornness and a big dose of male ego.'

She desperately wants the old man's legacy carried on and she wants to see Brock and Kendra run the company someday. But the situation is hopeless. It won't happen.

I've got to get Kate to convince him to sell out to Croft. With the shares from Dirk's estate, she and the kids would be well off.

Clay's head was spinning. He needed another drink.

He got up from the bed and walked to the mini-bar. He fumbled with the ice, poured himself a vodka from three small bottles and walked to the window overlooking the pool.

He remembered swimming in the pool with Heather on their honeymoon and how they had clung to one another. He would never have that feeling again. That was for the young, not forty-somethings with a lot of rough miles behind them.

The phone rang. His first impulse was not to answer it, but it could be Kate. He picked up the receiver, "Hello."

"I'm down in the lobby, and I have a hankerin' for whisky, ol' boy." Despite the mock Texas accent, Morgan Prosser's thick Scottish brogue could still be detected.

Clay laughed and said, "I'll be right down."

———

Kate was driving west on Woodway Drive and reflecting on her day. Rosenberg had poked his head in her office late in the afternoon while she was cajoling one of many shareholders who had called asking about the emergency shareholder meeting. After she finished the call, Al said she was beginning to sound like a politician. Normally, she would find the remark amusing.

She had been bombarded with calls from reporters and investment bankers all day. And then her fight with Clay. It had been one of those days that pushed her to the brink of just walking out the door and never coming back.

She knew the shareholder meeting would only get things rolling. The legal battle would start after that and, of course, Croft would continue his assault through the media. When would it all end? According to Clay, the end wasn't too far off.

She could kick herself for what she said to him. He was right, she had no right to talk to him the way she did. She wanted to see him again, if he hadn't already left for the Bahamas. She wanted to explain how much stress she was under, how hard everything has been.

Kate debated whether or not she should stop by the hotel. Since Clay hadn't come back to the office all afternoon, he was probably stone-drunk.

The left turn into the hotel was just up ahead. Maybe it would be better to see him in the morning, she thought to herself, when both of them had had time to think things over.

She slowed as the road curved and then decided to make the left turn into the main entrance. This could be a big mistake, she thought.

Why am I apologizing for what I said? Its clear he doesn't give a damn what happens to the company. He's just concerned about the price of his stock.

She pulled into the covered parking area instead of leaving her car with a valet. She had too many important papers in her briefcase. Then it dawned on her how paranoid she was becoming.

She parked her Mercedes and turned off the engine. She put her hands on the steering wheel, took a deep breath, and then exhaled.

Why, she thought, am I making such a big deal of this? And then she remembered how Clay had held her when they met in the lobby a few days earlier. She remembered how protected and aroused she felt. She couldn't dismiss the fact that she still cared for him. Not like a brother-in-law. It had always been like that. It had always been more.

It was hard to characterize how she felt about him. In a way, she felt sorry for him because of everything he had been through. She wanted to help him, but it seemed as if he had given up hope, not just on the company and the family, but on life. He must feel so alone.

But when Kate saw Clay in the hotel lounge that day, she felt something she had not felt in years. He carried himself the same way Dirk did. His mannerisms were the same. The way he wrapped his hand around a glass when he drank. The expressions on his face.

She climbed out of the car and walked toward the hotel lobby. Two well-dressed, middle-aged couples were getting out of a stretch limousine. They were carrying glasses of champagne and no doubt had dinner reservations at *La Reserve*.

She recognized one of the men, but couldn't remember his name or where they had met. It was probably at some charity function or a shareholder meeting. Luckily, he didn't look her way. She wasn't in a sociable mood anyway.

A bellman held the door open. Kate thanked him and walked into the lobby. Then it dawned on her who the man was: Tyler Baldwin, one of the heirs to the Baldwin estate. He and the others were probably celebrating their stock sale to Croft. Christ, of all places for them to come. What a day.

Kate walked through the marbled lobby. She looked in the lounge in case Clay was having a drink. There were only a couple of people sitting on leather couches and chairs.

She looked toward the far end of the room. Clay was sitting on a couch facing the window overlooking the pool with his arm around a woman. The light was low, but she could see that it was the woman who they had bumped into at noon.

She was kissing Clay on the neck. It was obvious they were too preoccupied with one another to notice her.

He hasn't changed a bit, thought Kate. He hasn't grown up.

He's still a drunken playboy.

She turned and walked briskly toward the front door. He can rot in hell!

CHAPTER 9

The loud, shrill sound of the telephone woke Clay. He rolled over, reached across Morgan, and picked up the receiver.

Kitty Carver said good morning before Clay was able to clear his throat and speak. In an instant, he remembered he was supposed to be at Hobby Airport at seven o'clock to catch the company jet and fly to Brownsville.

He asked, "What time is it?"

Kitty replied, "A few minutes after seven."

"Damn." He knew with morning rush hour traffic, it would take him at least an hour to get to Hobby.

Kitty said, "A helicopter should be there in a few minutes."

"You're a dear."

"Have a good trip."

Clay hung up the phone.

Morgan turned her back to him and moaned. She had no intention of waking up.

Clay kissed her on the shoulder and crawled out of bed. At first he felt fine, but after taking a few steps his head began to throb and his stomach felt queasy.

As he walked toward the bathroom, he heard the faint sound of the helicopter and realized he wouldn't have time to shower and shave.

He quickly dressed, grabbed his electric razor and briefcase, and rushed out the door.

———

Thanks to coffee and donuts, Clay's hangover was beginning to subside by the time the company jet began its descent to Brownsville. He tried to read some accounting reports, but was distracted by a question that kept coming to mind: With all the problems the company has, why would the old man want me to make a special trip to Brownsville to see the *Global Explorer?*

Making a decision to continue the ship's upgrades was easy. The company couldn't afford it, especially since the rig was not under contract with an oil company. And why didn't it have a contract? Demand was high for rigs capable of working in deepwater. Maybe the old man thought this would somehow motivate me to stay and help the company through its crisis. But, hell, nothing could do that at this point. There's no way. I won't fight a losing cause.

Clay looked out the window as the jet smoothly touched down on the runway. Even though it was only half past eight o'clock, heat radiated off the tarmac and blurred the view of the terminal in the distance. It'll probably get up to a hundred degrees within a few hours, he figured.

The jet taxied along the runway. It slowed as it approached the section of the terminal reserved for private aircraft and came to a stop next to a white pick-up truck with the company logo emblazoned on its door.

Tito Martinez climbed out of the driver's side.

What is he doing here? Being in the meeting with him and the rest of the drilling department yesterday was unsettling enough. This is going to be awkward.

Maybe the old man arranged this trip so that Tito and I would bury the hatchet. That sure as hell won't work. I'll never forgive him for testifying against me.

Clay recalled the confrontation with Tito after the National Transportation Safety Board hearing. Five or six men had to hold both of them back to avoid a fist fight.

That was the last time Clay and Tito had spoken to one another. It was a shame. We had been such good friends.

Clay recalled the summers roughnecking in Midland. He and Dirk worked alongside Tito on one of the two rigs the old man kept in operation after he had sold all his West Texas production.

Tito had come from a long line of oil field workers. His grandfather had worked during the early West Texas booms and busts, and his father had been a driller for the old man before dying of leukemia. The Martinez clan was like family, especially Tito. Mom often referred to him as her third son.

Clay also remembered those long nights when he, Dirk and Tito drove to shanty towns along the Mexican border. The bars. The women. The gambling. The fights. Then, with little or no sleep, they would start their shift at five o'clock in the morning. Ah, to be young again.

———

The drive from the airport to the shipyard took only fifteen minutes, but it seemed like an hour. Clay made an effort to start conversation and asked Tito about his wife and his two girls. Aside from saying his daughters were good softball players, Tito was pretty closed-lipped.

Clay realized he wasn't going to break the ice, so he pulled some drilling reports from his briefcase and began to read.

Tito kept glancing over to see what Clay was reading.

They pulled into the shipyard parking lot.

Clay was surprised the drillship was in the bay and asked,

"Isn't it supposed to be in dry dock?"

"They're probably testing the new thrusters."

Tito parked next to the metal building that housed the shipyard's main office.

Clay climbed out of the truck and looked around. Except for a few additional metal buildings and three more tower cranes, the yard was as he remembered it.

Tito shouted, "We'll take the chopper," over the noise of a tractor trailer driving by them carrying a large load of drill pipe.

They walked toward the helipad.

Clay immediately saw that the helicopter was the same model that he, Dirk and Tito had taken out to the jack-up rig six years earlier. He and Tito glanced at one another, then climbed in the back seat and fastened their seat belts.

The woman pilot turned around, greeted Clay, and gently lifted off.

It took only a few minutes to reach the drillship.

Clay looked out the window. The *Global Explorer* was as impressive as ever. At six hundred and twenty feet in length and a hundred and sixty feet in breadth, the vessel had been the largest drillship in the world until Amtex Petroleum and Oceanic Drilling built their ultra-deepwater drillship, the *Deepwater One*. She had also held the deepwater record of 9,845 feet until Transocean's *Discoverer Deep Seas* went to 10,011 in November 2003.

Clay recalled when the company bought the moth-balled, former ocean mining vessel from the U.S. Navy in seventy-four. Not only was the price right, but the hull was, and still is, the strongest of any drillship in the world. The reason was due to the wide, heavy steel claw that was used to retrieve nodules of minerals on the sea floor. As a result, the moonpool, the opening in the center of the ship above where the derrick stood, was exceptionally large and could accommodate the huge risers needed to drill ultra-deep wells.

Over the years, the ship had gone through several expensive upgrades. Clay had been in charge of the latest one which had cost over seventy-five million dollars.

The helicopter approached the ship from the stern-starboard side, but began to circle since another chopper was parked on the helipad.

Clay noticed the two-hundred-and-fifty-foot derrick had been modified. More metal reinforcing braces and railing had been added. The four cranes, two aft and two on the bow, were new, larger Seatrax models. The deck, which used to be painted a drab gray, was now bright orange and was a stark contrast to the white pipe racks, yellow railings, and black hull. And the four orange rescue capsules, which hung by thick chains near each corner of the ship, appeared larger than he had remembered.

The helicopter passed the ship and banked sharply to the left. It approached the stern, slowed, and then hovered port-side while the chopper on the helipad prepared to take off.

Below, a supply boat carrying several metal containers labeled 'Drummond Offshore', was maneuvering alongside. The boom on one of the cranes began to lower. Considering the ship was going through a six-month upgrade program in dry dock, it struck Clay as odd that so many containers were being loaded.

There were also more crew members scurrying around the deck than Clay expected. Normally, when a drillship was testing its thrusters, only a skeleton marine crew, those people responsible only for the supply and maintenance functions of the ship, were on board. But there were men on the drilling deck and around the drill pipe conveyer system which meant there was drilling personnel aboard. Why? Something didn't add up.

Clay turned and looked at Tito, who intentionally avoided eye contact and glanced out his window.

The helicopter on the pad lifted off and headed toward shore. The chopper moved forward, hovered over the pad, and began its descent.

Suddenly, a gust of wind shook the craft, but the pilot maintained her composure.

Clay looked at his hand gripping the arm rest. His knuckles were white and the veins of his forearm were bulging.

Images from the night of the rig accident flashed through his mind. The sparks flying in the air from the rotor hitting the jack-up leg. The chopper crashing to the deck. The muffled screams underwater...

The chopper touched down. The pilot turned and gave them a nod, and they climbed out.

Clay followed Tito to the door that led to the aft control room of the vessel. They entered a hallway, passed the captain's quarters and office to their right, a row of lockers on their left, and then entered the control room.

Seven or eight men stood mesmerized in front of the display console used to monitor the ship's dynamic positioning thrusters.

A short, balding man, in his late fifties or early sixties, turned and walked toward Clay and Tito.

Tito said, "Sal, this is Clay Drummond. Clay, Salvatore Ricci, our Captain."

The two men shook hands.

Ricci, in a strong Italian accent said, "Welcome aboard, Mr. Drummond."

Clay nodded and said, "Please call me Clay."

Ricci smiled. He then turned and motioned to a tall, thin man in his early thirties wearing wire rim glasses and said, "This is Auburn Puckett, the company's techno-whiz kid."

Puckett frowned, shook Clay's hand and said in a slight Cajun accent, "It's a pleasure meeting you."

Clay couldn't help but notice the nervous quiver in the young man's voice.

An agitated technician who sat in front of the console operating a joystick summoned Puckett.

Puckett leaned over the console and glanced at the instruments and gauges. He then looked at the color monitor which depicted an aerial view of the ship's hull with the location of the six submerged thrusters plotted on a grid.

Puckett turned to Ricci.

The Captain nodded.

Puckett said, "Switch to back-up."

The technician punched a few buttons.

The room grew silent. Everyone stared at the monitor.

A minute passed.

Puckett said, "It looks like she's holdin' on location."

"It's about time," replied Ricci.

Suddenly, an orange and red light began blinking on and off.

Everyone's eyes were fixed on the monitor. The ship was drifting slowly off-course.

Ricci shouted, "Goddammit!"

Puckett looked up from the console, turned to the Captain and said, "I just don't understand it."

Ricci frowned and shook his head. He turned to Clay and said, "We installed two new thrusters, and they haven't been responding when we go to backup power. We can't move to the location until we get this straightened out."

Clay turned to Tito, who avoided eye contact, and then back to Ricci and asked, "What location?"

"Block Nine-Forty-Seven," Ricci replied with a confused expression on his face.

Tito turned and walked toward the Radio and Chart Room behind them.

Clay said to Ricci, "Excuse me for a minute."

Ricci and Puckett looked at one another. Then Ricci asked, "When do you want the five-cent tour?"

"In a few minutes."

Clay followed Tito into the room and said, "We need to talk."

Tito nodded. He took a rolled-up chart a crewman handed him, walked back into the control room, and then proceeded through a door that led outside onto the bridge deck.

Clay followed him around the corner, around a stairwell, and past a lifeboat. He asked, "Now can you please tell me what the hell is going on? What's this about moving out to Block Nine-Forty-Seven?"

Tito began unrolling the chart and replied, "Your father decided to put off the repairs." Tito gulped and said, "He wants to drill Nine-Forty-Seven."

Clay looked at the map. Water depth lines between fifty-nine hundred and sixty-five hundred feet criss-crossed the block. The area was labeled 'Seahorse Canyon.'

Clay's eyes widened.

Tito said, "I'm just following orders."

Clay looked at the chart again. He knew the spot.

After the company leased the block ten years earlier, the Mexican Government contended the company would drain oil from its territory and demanded a major share of the profits. It was all a ludicrous situation.

First of all, back then no one dreamed it was possible to drill in six thousand feet of water. Secondly, there was no geological basis that production could be found.

Tito looked at Clay and said, "He wants to drill deeper than six thousand feet." He pointed at the southwest corner of the block and added,

"It's not on this map, but there's a narrow trench in this area that goes to a depth of over ten thousand feet."

Clay was speechless.

Tito continued, "He had me file a Plan of Exploration showing that our location would be shallower."

"Do Ricci and Puckett know about this?"

Tito looked aimlessly out to sea and said, "Not yet."

"And when were you planning to tell 'em?"

"Once we got out there."

"Jesus Christ, Tito!"

"Your Dad said he'd handle everything."

Clay chuckled and said, "It's not his ass on the line, its yours. Besides, he won't be..." He caught himself before he mentioned D.L. was dying. "You can't go ahead with this."

Tito looked into Clay's eyes and asked, "Could you talk to him?"

Clay paused, "Give me one good reason why?"

Tito leaned up against the railing and looked down.

Clay added, "I guess I'm supposed to forget everything that has happened, huh?" He turned and walked away.

——————

Clay poured himself a cup of coffee in the mess hall and walked toward Captain Ricci and Auburn Puckett who were seated at a table in the corner of the room. During the tour of the ship, Clay could not help wondering why the old man didn't tell him about the plan to drill Seahorse Canyon. Why would he want to spring the whole thing on him this way?

Clay recalled his research on Seahorse Canyon. There were only small patches of source rock on Block Nine-Forty-Seven, and they were too far apart to establish a meaningful geological trend. Besides the whole idea of drilling in a ten thousand foot canyon that probably was no more than five hundred feet wide was insane.

Clay sat across from Ricci and Puckett and asked, "Is the ship ready to move on location?"

Ricci and Puckett looked at one another.

Puckett looked over Clay's shoulder to make sure crew members seated at other tables wouldn't overhear what he was about to say. He replied, "We'd really be pushing the envelope. We not only need to work out the kinks in the new thrusters, but there's something wrong with the new backup generators."

Ricci added, "The only reason we would have to go to backup power would be if our main system fails for some reason."

"In other words," said Clay, "if the computers shut down."

Ricci nodded and said, "It used to be that the crew technicians could fix just about any electronic problem. But with all these fancy computers if something goes haywire we're shut down until techs come out to fix it."

Clay grinned when he noticed Puckett roll his eyes.

Puckett said, "He's exaggerating a bit."

Ricci looked at Puckett and asked, "What happened at Atwater Banks then?"

Puckett blushed, adjusted his glasses, and said, "That was an isolated situation." Puckett looked at Clay and added, "We lost our up-link to GPS and had to go manual on our thrusters for about two hours."

Clay asked, "While you were drilling?"

"Yeah, but it was no big deal."

Ricci asked, "What would have happened had we been in rough seas?"

Puckett said, "Well, we weren't, were we. It was a freak accident."

Clay asked, "What caused it?"

Puckett replied, "It all came down to a faulty wiring job to the satellite dish. There was nothing wrong with the onboard computers."

Ricci said, "All this new technology and it couldn't even identify a loose wire."

Puckett's nostrils flared.

Clay intervened and asked, "What do we know about the drilling conditions at Nine-Forty-Seven?"

Ricci said, "From what I can gather, it's some of the most difficult drilling in the Gulf. Shell and Chevron drilled northern parts of Seahorse Canyon a few months ago and encountered severe loop currents. And I hear Conoco is going to delay their drilling."

Puckett added, "Mud slides are a bigger problem. I don't know the exact location of the well, but there are a lot of unstable ridges and trenches that could be real trouble."

Clay wondered if the old man knew about this. Probably not.

Puckett added, "I'm no geologist, but it appears that the further you move south, the worse the conditions get."

Clay remembered looking at Tito's chart. The well location was near the southern boundary of the block.

CHAPTER 10

D.L. ended his phone call with Tito. Clay had taken a chopper from Hobby Airport and was coming out to the ranch. And, he was extremely upset.

D.L. knew Clay didn't agree with his decision to drill the Seahorse Canyon well. Maybe he should have told him before he sent him to Brownsville, he thought. But then he probably wouldn't have gone.

I've got to make him see things my way. I've got to make him realize that finding a major oilfield is the only way we can gain the support of shareholders and beat Croft at his own game.

———

Clay climbed out of the helicopter and walked briskly toward the front door of the house. A few of the ranch dogs barked and then approached him wagging their tails. When they sensed he was in no mood for affection, they retreated to their favorite spots under the large oak trees surrounding the house.

He climbed the stairs and burst through the front door. He was met by Ramona and asked, "Where the hell is he?"

A frightened Ramona pointed toward the study.

Clay rushed past her.

She asked, "What's wrong, Clay? What happened?"

Clay entered the study.

D.L. was seated at his desk and looked up at him.

"Seahorse Canyon?" shouted Clay. "Have you lost your goddamn mind?"

D.L. didn't respond.

Clay added, "This is the same kind of crap you pulled on me before I left. You don't want my advice! You're just going to do whatever you damned well please, aren't you?"

D.L. cleared his throat and said calmly, "Let me explain."

"Who else in the company knows about what you're tryin' to pull?"

"Sit down," said D.L. in a raspy voice.

Clay remained standing and said, "Answer me!"

"Just you and Tito so far."

"And I suppose you thought you could keep it under wraps until the rig got to location?"

D.L. nodded and said, "That was the plan."

"What happens when Mineral Management finds out Tito falsified the reports? What do you think they'll do then?"

"We'll say it was done by mistake."

"Mistake! To drill in ten thousand feet instead of six thousand!"

"By the time they find out about it we'll already be drillin'."

"And what happens when the bank and Croft find out?"

"We'll deal with it."

"We? I'm not going to be a part of this."

"Settle down, son."

"Aren't you aware of the drilling conditions?"

"It's nothing we can't handle."

Clay said, "And you *know* the Mexicans are going to raise hell."

"We'll work it out."

"You honestly think drilling Seahorse Canyon in ten thousand feet of water is going to solve all your problems?"

"Do you have a better plan?"

"Yeah, sell out!"

D.L. stared deep into Clay's eyes.

Clay added, "Sell out to Croft! It's the only option left."

"Never!"

"Al is in favor of it, but he doesn't have the guts to tell you."

D.L.'s face reddened, and he said, "That's bullshit!"

"It is, huh? Ask him." Clay knew he had hit a nerve and added, "When are you ever going to get it through your thick skull that Croft is going to get control? Pretty soon everybody will start turning their back on you. Even Rosenberg."

D.L. didn't respond. He stood, walked over to the bar, and poured himself a scotch.

Clay continued, "Just wait until the board finds out about this! And what about the cancer?"

D.L. took a large swig of his drink. He walked back to his desk, sat down, and replied, "So, I come out and say I've got cancer. What's the big deal?"

"Just like that?"

"Yup."

"And when do you plan to do that?"

"At the shareholder meeting."

Clay shook his head and said, "That'll certainly win 'em over!"

He walked to the bar, poured himself a drink, looked at D.L. and said, "You've really backed yourself into a corner this time."

"I've been there before, and I've always managed to get out."

"There's a big difference this time around, though. You won't be around to get out of it!"

D.L. glared at him and replied, "But you will, won't you?"

Clay chugged his scotch.

D.L. added, "What kind of life do you have, anyway? You run some two-bit hotel that's never turned a profit."

"I'm your last chance, aren't I? I'm the only one who may be able to keep the precious D.L. Drummond legacy alive. That's what really matters to you most, isn't it? I tried living up to your grand expectations after Dirk died, but you never let go! You never let me run things my way! Now you expect me to save your ass! Go to hell!"

D.L. paused and said calmly, "We've all made mistakes."

Clay grinned. He poured himself another drink and asked, "Was Heather one of them?"

D.L. looked down at the desk and exhaled a deep breath.

Clay yelled, "What kind of father screws around with his son's ex-wife?"

D.L. looked up and said, "I was drunk."

"She came to you for money, didn't she?"

D.L. nodded slightly.

Clay asked, "So, she became your whore?"

"Stop it!"

"I bet Kate would find this little tidbit interesting."

D.L.'s eyes became teary. In a strained voice, he asked, "You really hate me, don't you?"

Clay finished his drink and walked out the door.

———

Clay threw his briefcase against the wall in his hotel room and then kicked a trash can. Why the hell didn't I have Kitty wire transfer the money to the Bahamas yesterday?

He grabbed the phone and began dialing her direct line. It rang three times and then her voice mail recording began.

He was about to leave a message, but then slammed the phone down. *I don't want charity from the old man. Damn him!*

———

Dining at a greasy spoon restaurant in Houston's Chinatown was not Ramsey Croft's idea of how to spend an evening. Lee Tran, Marty Nugent's Vietnamese Army pal, had said only the address, not the name of the restaurant, on Croft's voice mail on Thursday. Now, as Ram looked at the front of the place, he understood why. Except for 'Bud Light' in the window, the partially lit sign above the front door was in oriental script.

Ram parked his BMW across the street and looked around. Most of the buildings in the area were an assortment of metal or concrete block warehouses.

He got out of the car, double-checked the number he had written on the back of Tran's business card with the number above the front door, and then crossed the street.

Ram opened the door and was engulfed in a cloud of cigarette smoke. *My sinuses are going to act up,* he thought to himself.

The only person he could see was an oriental bartender, but as he walked between tables he saw red glows of cigarette butts around the perimeter of the room.

"Over here," said a man in the far right corner.

Ram walked past a table where a man and woman were seated. They were arguing, or maybe haggling, over something. By the looks of the young girl, who could be no older than sixteen, it was probably over the price for sex.

The man, seated by himself at a small table, motioned.

Ram approached and asked, "Mr. Tran?"

"That's me. Have a seat, Mr. Croft," he said with a slight oriental accent.

Ram brushed fortune cookie crumbs off the chair and sat down.

Tran asked, "Any trouble finding the place?"

"A little."

Tran chuckled and said, "I take it you don't get over on this side of town very often."

Ram didn't reply.

Tran asked, "Want anything to eat?"

"No, thanks."

Tran shouted something to the bartender in Vietnamese, at least Ram figured it was Vietnamese.

Tran asked, "What did Nugent tell you about me?"

"Enough."

Tran reached into his shirt pocket for a cigarette. When he lit a match, Ram noticed a thick reddish scar running from the corner of his left eye to a few inches below his ear lobe.

The bartender rushed to the table with a bowl of soup, a porcelain sake bottle, and a small cup.

"First of all," said Ram, "I want you to know I'm not completely sold on this whole idea."

Tran smiled and handed Ram a large envelope.

Ram took out a sheet of paper and looked at a drawing of an office floor plan.

Tran said, "That's the top floor of the Drummond Building."

"How did you get this?"

"That's not important," Tran said as he picked up the soup bowl and began eating noodles with chop sticks. He slurped a long noodle and said, "Who is in which office?"

"I've only been to the conference room. And that was over two years ago."

"Okay, so we'll do all the suites, including the conference room, and the phones in every office."

"How can you be sure you're not going to get caught?"

"I'm not in jail, am I?"

"But what if they find...?"

"There's no way to trace them back to us."

"You're certain of that?"

Tran raised his hand and said, "Scout's honor."

"And you do all this by yourself?"

"Me and one other guy," Tran replied. He slurped another noodle and said, "This is the way it works. We listen to the conversations, edit out all the useless stuff, and send you tapes when and where you want."

"How will you know what we need?"

"I've got a pretty good sense about that sort of thing. Besides, Nugent has filled me in and he'll listen to the tapes before you receive them."

"How much does all this cost?"

"Nugent says to count on at least four to six weeks. I get ten thousand a week plus expenses. Half before I start and the balance when the job is done. Cash only."

Ram sat back in his chair.

"Listen," said Tran as he reached into his pocket, "if you don't want to go through with this just let me know. I've got plenty of other work I can do." He handed Ram his business card with a telephone number written in pen on it and added, "If I don't hear from you by midnight, I'll figure you don't want to go ahead with it."

———

Later that night, Croft sifted through the mail his maid had placed on a glass top table in the den of his River Oaks mansion.

The French country-style mansion had been one the few assets Ram had been able to salvage from his father's estate. He had gutted many of the rooms to give it a more airy feel, especially to show off his impressive collection of post-modern paintings and sculpture, and replaced his father's dark antiques that had been in the family for generations with more stylish contemporary furnishings.

Ram noticed the blinking red light on the phone recorder. There were two messages. He pressed the 'PLAY' button.

"Ram. Marty Nugent. Great news! All three pension funds are in the bag. The agreements will be on your desk in the morning. Jonas is creaming in his pants. Call me."

Ram clenched his fist and said, "Yes!" Now it was time to set into motion the class action suit and proxy fight, he thought to himself.

He needed only four percent more of the outstanding shares to surpass the Drummonds as the single largest shareholder. It was time to put the Mercers in play.

Arlen Mercer, Senior, one of D.L.'s old pals had been on the board for years. Mercer and his son owned a little over one percent, but they had influence with enough shareholders that they could sway the other four percent to sell.

The machine beeped.

"Ram, this is Al Rosenberg. D.L. would like to arrange a meeting just between the two of you. Please call me at the office Monday."

What is the old man up to now, thought Ram. We've had these face-to-face meetings in the past. He always plays the dumb, good ol' boy routine and says something like 'Let's try to meet each other half way' or 'Why don't we just bury the hatchet'. But he never budges, never. The only meeting we are going to have, Drummond, is when I rip your heart out in front of the shareholders.

Ram felt himself trembling and sat on a black leather-strapped chair. He knew he couldn't let his hatred for Drummond cloud his judgment. He looked at his pistol collection in a glass cabinet on the wall and figured he should go to the shooting range in the morning to let off a little steam. Back to business.

The Mercers are going to be the key to all this. I'll have lunch with Arlen next week and see what it would take to get him to rally the other four percent behind me. I'll have to pay him a kickback like I did when I bought Mercer Marine, but it'll be worth it. Just a cost of doing business.

What about Manhattan Commerce? Schultz? If I could get the bank to call the company's loans, it would put them in a serious cash crunch. I need to start pressuring Schultz. He'll do it. He doesn't have a choice. And the best time for the bank to drop the hammer would be a few days before the shareholder meeting.

And then there's Truesdale. He'll make a hefty profit on the sale of the pension fund's shares, but that's it. I'll buy the rest of the shares on my own. The financing is already lined up with First Nation Bank. It will be a relief to get that bastard out of my hair once and for all. Monique, too.

Tran. Why should I take the risk of wire tapping the offices? It would certainly give me an edge to know how the Drummonds plan to mount a defense. But what defense? They've dug themselves into a hole with no way out. But that is what Dad and I thought back in eighty-six.

Ram reached into his pocket for the phone number Tran had given him. He dialed the number and as it rang he thought about Kate. The image of them making love in front of the fireplace at his Aspen home flashed through his mind. Maybe there is a chance she I can be together again. But first I need to get rid of Monique and then gain control of Drummond.

CHAPTER 11

The next morning, Kate pulled-up in front of the main house. Ramona's call at seven o'clock telling her D.L. had to see her at once had shaken her.

She climbed out of the car and rushed up the steps.

Ramona met her at the door.

Kate asked, "What's going on?"

"I don't know. He and Clay had an argument last night. He wouldn't eat dinner and just stayed in the study most of the night."

Kate exhaled a deep breath and asked, "Where is he?"

"He's on his way down."

Kate walked into the study.

The office smelled of scotch, and the letters, photo albums, and news clippings that Victoria had meticulously organized over the years were scattered around the room.

She walked around the desk and noticed a broken glass on the floor.

Suddenly, Ramona screamed.

Kate rushed out of the study.

D.L. was rolling down the steps.

She ran to the bottom of the stairs in an attempt to catch him before he hit the marble floor, but she was too late.

He rolled onto the floor and landed face-up. His body was twisted, and he lay awkwardly on his right hip. Blood trickled out of the side of his mouth. His eyes were shut.

Kate screamed, "Call 9-1-1!" D.L.'s right leg was contorted. She kneeled down and pulled up his robe to get a better look. She turned and saw that Ramona was in a state of shock. "Hurry!"

Ramona rushed into the study.

Kate looked down at D.L. She knew she shouldn't move him, but feared he would choke on the blood trickling out of the side of his mouth.

She carefully gripped his jaw with one hand. She then placed her finger in the corner of his mouth and gently pulled his lip down to allow the blood to flow more freely.

The puddle of blood on the floor grew wider.

She shook his jaw slightly and yelled, "Dad! Dad!"

No response.

She pulled her bloodied finger from his mouth and placed her hand on his neck to check his pulse. It was faint.

Blood accumulated in his mouth quickly.

He coughed.

She put her finger back in his mouth to drain it. She had to turn him on his side.

Ramona was yelling to the emergency operator on the phone.

Kate pulled her finger out of his mouth and began to slowly turn his head to the right while bracing his neck.

He coughed again. A thin stream of blood and two teeth shot out of his mouth. He opened his eyes, looked at Kate, and said in a garbled voice, "Those goddamn stairs!"

Kate wiped tears from her eyes and managed a smile.

Kate was exhausted as she slowly made her way down the stairs. The morning and afternoon had been a series of highs and lows.

She was relieved, however, that D.L. was joking about what had happened even before the ambulance had arrived.

The paramedics confirmed he may have torn a ligament in his right knee, but when they began to lift him onto a stretcher to take him to the ambulance, D.L. had a fit and refused to be taken to the hospital.

She argued with D.L., but he wouldn't budge. Kate told the paramedics to ignore him. They did until Bert Glover, D.L.'s six-foot five, two hundred and fifty pound chauffeur, showed up. The paramedics immediately backed down.

Doc Bender, a retired family physician who lived a few miles away, was called. By the time he arrived, D.L. was sitting-up in bed and most of the bleeding in his mouth had stopped.

The doctor recommended he stay bed-ridden for a few days before being taken to an orthopedist. He prescribed a painkiller and said to keep the knee iced.

By mid-afternoon things began to settle down. Then Kate called Dr. Shahir to let him know what had happened. Big mistake.

Shahir had just received the results of D.L.'s latest blood tests. The cancer had become more aggressive. In fact, he said in all his years of practice, he had never seen such an acceleration. It was possible, he told her, due to his injuries and the debilitating effects of the cancer, that D.L. might never get out of bed again.

Kate reached the bottom of the stairs and walked into the dining room to join her daughter Kendra, Haley, Brock's pregnant wife, and Al.

Kendra asked, "How's he doing?"

"As well as can be expected, I guess."

Haley asked, "Is he sleeping?"

"Not yet," replied Kate. "He's still being his ornery self."

Al grinned and said, "I'm really surprised he didn't break something."

Kendra rose from her chair. She poured Kate a cup of coffee and said, "You look tired, Mom."

Kate sipped her coffee and said, "I'll be fine."

Kendra put her hand on Kate's shoulder.

Al exhaled a deep breath.

Kate wiped her eyes with a napkin and said, "Considering the fall and everything, he probably won't get out of bed again."

Al said, "Oh, I wouldn't count on that. He's a pretty tough old bird."

Kate said, "Doc Bender suggested we contact the Hospice."

Al said, "Well, he sure as hell doesn't want to be in the hospital, does he?"

Kate managed a smile and said, "Anybody heard from Clay?"

Al replied, "He's at the office. Brock told him what happened."

Ramona walked into the room and said, "Kate, Mr. Rosenberg. He wants to see both of you."

Kate and Al looked at one another, got up from the table, and walked to the hallway.

Rosenberg said, "I wonder what this is all about?"

They began to climb the steps.

Kate turned to Al and said, "Ramona told me Dad and Clay had a pretty bad fight last night."

"About what?"

"I don't know." She stopped walking and said, "Clay told me about the Mercers. The kick-backs on the rigs and when Dad bought some of their stock and made a tidy profit when the company bought back shares."

Al avoided her stare.

Kate asked, "When are you going to start leveling with me, Al?"

He was surprised by Kate's harsh tone of voice and replied, "Listen, Kate, there are certain things you don't *want* to know."

"Oh, really. Who the hell has been fielding all the phone calls from pissed-off shareholders? Who's been dealing with the media? I have a right to know!"

Al didn't respond.

"Quit shutting me out!" she said.

Al's face reddened and he began climbing the stairs.

———

D.L. was sitting up in bed. He was drowsy from the painkillers and could hardly keep his eyes open. But what he had to say to Kate and Al couldn't wait.

He cleared his throat and said, "Aside from my dumb move this morning, this cancer is takin' a lot out of me."

Kate and Al looked at one another.

D.L. added, "I need to finalize a few things." He turned to Al and said, "I want you to draw-up a proxy for the shares that aren't held by the Trusts and name Kate as my attorney-in-fact instead of you."

Kate was stunned.

D.L. continued, "Make her the sole Trustee for all the trusts, too."

In a weak tone of voice, Al said, "I'll take care of it."

"You want to know why I'm doing this?"

Al nodded.

"Clay told me you wanted to sell out to Croft."

Rosenberg looked at the floor to avoid eye contact.

D.L. asked, "It's true, isn't it?"

"It's an option you should consider."

"*Option* my ass!"

Kate interrupted, "Wait a minute, Dad. Al didn't..."

85

"No, I won't wait a minute!" He looked at Al and added, "I'll be goddamned if I'm going to let you sell the company out from under me!"

Al's face turned red, and he said, "You're going to lose it anyway, you stubborn old bastard!"

"We'll see about that!"

"So you'll just keep spending millions drilling in deepwater and hope like hell you hit something? We're not going to make payroll in a few months, for Christ's sake! And nobody's going to lend us a dime because of the situation *you've* put us in!"

D.L. cleared his throat again and said, "We'll keep drillin'."

Al stared into D.L.'s eyes. He was about to say something, but then turned and walked out the door.

There was a moment of silence.

Kate then asked, "Are you serious about this thing with the trusts and proxy?"

"Dead serious," he said with a grin.

Kate frowned and said, "I'm not so sure I want the responsibility."

"You can handle it."

"What about Clay? What will he think?"

"Don't worry about him."

"He's not going to stick around after he finds out about this, you know."

"He will."

"What makes you so sure?"

D.L. looked deeply into her eyes and said, "Because I didn't raise a son who would turn his back on his family."

CHAPTER 12

It was seven-twenty in the evening by the time Clay got back to his office. He was worn-out after meeting with four board members and then the Drilling and Exploration Departments.

It was clear the directors' patience was wearing thin and they wanted to know what D.L. planned to tell stockholders at the emergency shareholder meeting in six days. But despite their irritation with the situation, they were glad Clay was back to help deal with the crisis. He had to admit to himself it was a boost to his ego.

He walked around D.L.'s desk and noticed a financial report on the chair. The accounting people had been badgering Kitty all day to get him to look at the new cash flow forecasts. Apparently, someone made a mistake in last month's financials and had not properly accounted for some drilling department expenses. Not good news.

Clay was in no mood to read the report. He picked it up, tossed it onto the credenza, and sat down to reflect on the day's events.

No one in the drilling department or exploration had any idea about the plan to drill the location in Seahorse Canyon that was in ten thousand feet of water. Clay had asked the geologists, including Brock, what the prospects were to drill a spot in six thousand feet. Brock liked the chances. The others believed there was a fair chance they would find oil, but it was a long shot there were enough reserves to justify the cost of producing the field at such a depth.

They briefed Clay on three promising prospects in the Gulf, but reserves were expected to be slightly more than marginal. Clay knew it was a waste of money to go forward with them, but he kept his opinion to himself. Morale was bad enough.

He looked out the window and wondered if there was any merit to the ten thousand feet location. The old man couldn't have come up with this idea on his own.

———

Clay knocked on Brock's open office door and asked, "Got a minute?"

Brock looked up from his computer monitor and replied, "Sure."

Clay asked, "Anything new on the old man?"

"I talked to Ramona about an hour ago. He's sleeping it off."

Clay sat down in a chair in front of the desk.

Brock said, "Let me finish this e-mail, and I'll be right with you."

Clay looked around the room. Except for family photos and a couple of Brock's gold medals and ribbons from his college swimming days at UT, the place was more like a map room than an office. Offshore acreage maps, several long sheets of electric log graphs, and red, white, and blue seismic printouts covered three walls.

Brock looked up from his computer and asked, "What's up?"

"Has the old man talked to you about Seahorse Canyon?"

"He asked me if I thought it was a good prospect."

"When was this?"

Brock appeared curious and replied, "A few weeks ago. Why?"

"But you were referring to the northern part of Block Nine-Forty-Seven, weren't you?"

Brock nodded and said, "But come to think about it, he asked me about the southern sections, too."

"And?"

"I said we didn't have much data on that area."

Clay leaned forward in his chair and said, "He's moving *Global Explorer* to the southern tip of the block to drill in a ten thousand foot trench."

Brock's eyes widened.

Clay said, "He got Tito to issue false reports to Mineral Management that show the rig will be drilling in six thousand feet."

Brock rose from his chair and walked to a map on the wall. He pointed to Block Nine-Forty-Seven and said, "We don't have good seismic on any of that area!"

"Then where the hell did he get this crazy idea?"

Brock grimaced, turned to Clay, and replied, "Probably from the work I've been doing in Indonesia." Brock exhaled and said, "For the past two years I've been studying a series of crevices in Java that developed from all the offshore earthquake activity." Brock put the palms of his hands together. "When the tectonic plates shift during an earthquake, one plate moves up and one down." He shifted his hands to illustrate the motion. "But instead of these plates lying flat up against one another, they separated and crevices, or trenches, were formed." Brock separated his hands to illustrate a gap. "Then, over millions of years, sediments gathered and deposited in these areas. After more earthquakes, the plates shifted again, and in some isolated instances, the upper, open end of the crevices were capped off."

"So the sedimentation formed submarine fans?"

Brock nodded and turned his hand so his fingers were pointing downward and the back of his hand was facing Clay. He spread his fingers and said, "But what happened was that each one of these thin channels separated. They ran very deep, but then eventually terminated and formed a series of lobes — what we call distal lobes. Theoretically, these lobes hold huge oil and gas deposits."

"Theoretically?"

"I've identified areas where these have occurred, but the only problem is they're in over twenty thousand feet of water. It'll probably take ten to fifteen years to develop the technology to drill them."

Clay recalled in eighty-one the first deep wildcats the company drilled in Java.

Brock continued, "A few months later, this was about a year ago, Dad asked me to plot these same type of trenches in the Gulf. I did. And the only one at a reachable depth was on the very southern tip of Seahorse Canyon."

Clay rose from his chair. He looked at the map and asked, "Do you have anything at all on this trench?"

"Very little."

He looked at Brock and asked, "Do you think you could piece something together to support your theory?"

"You can't be serious about drilling it?"

"Just see what you come up with."

Brock paused and said, "I'll do what I can."

Clay said, "For now, let's keep this between you and me," and he offered his hand.

Brock nodded and shook his hand.

———

Kate watched the light above the elevator door blink from fourteen to fifteen. Coming to the office at nine o'clock in the evening after such an exhausting day at the ranch was against her better judgment. But when she spoke with Brock by phone to update him on how D.L. was faring, he told her Clay was still working. She had to talk to him. It couldn't wait until tomorrow, she thought to herself.

I have to apologize for what I said at the restaurant. I have to make him understand how much stress I'm under and that I didn't mean the things I said. But how is he going to react when I tell him I now have the authority to vote the family's shares?

––––––

Kate stood in the doorway of D.L.'s office and asked Clay, "Burning the midnight oil?"

Clay looked up from a stack of files and grinned.

She sat down and asked, "How was the Brownsville trip?"

"Okay, I suppose. How's the old man?"

"He's doing fine, considering.

Kate took a deep breath, exhaled and said, "Clay, I'm sorry for what I said the other day. It wasn't fair for me to jump on you like that."

"You've been under a lot of stress lately."

"But that's no excuse for what I said."

"Don't worry about it." He grinned and said, "We've got more important things to think about."

Kate smiled. This is a good as time as any, she thought to herself, and said, "Don't ask me why, but Dad is giving me the proxies to vote all the family's shares."

Clay's eyes widened.

Kate added, "I'm sorry."

Clay rose from his chair. He turned his back to her, looked out the window and said, "What's there to be sorry about? He made the right decision."

Kate sensed Clay was disappointed. She said, "He should have given them to you."

Clay didn't respond.

She tried to hold back her tears and said, "I don't think I'm ready for any of this, Clay."

He turned around and said, "Listen Kate, I'll do whatever I can to help."

She began to weep.

He put his hands on her shoulders and said, "Look at me."

She looked into his eyes. Tears rolled down her cheeks.

Clay said, "I'm going to do everything I can to keep this company out of Croft's hands. You can count on me, okay?"

Clay held her in his arms.

Kate's first impulse was to kiss him deeply on the mouth and then realized falling in love with him would only complicate her life more. She kissed him lightly on the cheek instead.

CHAPTER 13

When Clay arrived at the office the next morning, Kitty said Al Rosenberg needed to see him immediately.

"What's up?" asked Clay as he entered Al's office.

"Schultz called about fifteen minutes ago. He wants to see your father and me at one o'clock. It's probably about the results of their audit."

"You don't know that."

"More than likely it is," Al replied nervously as he rubbed his hands together. "I found out the auditors talked to our former CFO."

"I agree the old man got a little aggressive on booking income sooner than he should have to make the quarterly earnings look better, but I didn't think it was outrageous."

"It wasn't your father who told the accountants to do it, Clay. It was me."

"I thought..."

"I told the accountants your Dad directed me to do it."

Clay exhaled a deep breath and said, "Well, it doesn't matter who told them. What's done is done."

Al said, "You know Schultz will leak all this to Croft."

Clay knew Al was right. Over the years, Schultz would force financially strapped bank customers to accept buyout offers from partnerships or corporations that Croft was directly, or indirectly, advising. And because of the maze of legal entities involved, no one had proof of the conspiracy.

Clay said, "Aren't there a bunch of non-disclosure laws that banks have to follow?"

Al nodded and replied, "Lenders can't disclose material information about a borrower, but I'm sure Croft and Schultz have covered their tracks."

"Maybe they slipped up somewhere along the way. What would happen if we dig up something that violates banking law?"

Al shook his head and said, "We're running out of time here, Clay."

Clay leaned forward in his chair and said, "We've got to get some leverage. Don't you know any private detectives?"

Al nodded.

Clay added, "There has to be something we can use."

Al leaned back in his chair and said, "We could get someone to follow Croft and Schultz to see if they meet."

"They're not going to be dumb enough to do that. How about the Mercer Marine deal? The old man always said there was something about it that stunk. Remember how the Mercers kept trying to ward-off Croft and then suddenly gave in?"

"The final purchase price was a little less than what Croft first offered them."

"Dad suspected Croft gave them money under the table."

"I don't know, Clay. This all really seems like a stretch."

"What do we have to lose?"

"You're forgetting one important point: We're in technical default of our loans. The bank has the right to demand full payment.

"We're current, aren't we?"

"For now, but there are provisions in the loan agreements that say we have to maintain certain financial ratios, and we sure as hell aren't meeting them."

"Since when do banks call loans that are current?"

"They could."

Clay shook his head and said, "Let's see what Schultz has to say before we start jumping to conclusions."

———

As Clay walked down the hallway, he noticed a repairman wearing a Southwestern Bell uniform coming out of his office. The man made eye contact with Clay and then abruptly turned and walked in the opposite direction.

Clay asked Kitty, "What was he up to?"

"We've had some problems with the phones."

Clay looked down the hallway. The man looked at Clay out of the corner of his eye before boarding the elevator.

Kitty asked, "About your wire transfer?"

Clay couldn't believe he had forgotten to give her the wire instructions. He pulled a slip of paper from his wallet and handed it to her.

She said, "I'll take care of this right now."

"Thanks," he replied and made a mental note to call his banker to let him know the money was on its way. He asked, "Could you call Brock and see if he has a minute to come up here."

"Should I tell him what it is about?"

"Seahorse Canyon."

Kitty picked up the phone.

"Clay!" said a man walking briskly down the hallway.

Clay turned. The man looked familiar, but he couldn't put a name to the face.

"I'm Mike Sidowski. We played golf the other day."

Clay remembered he was Rex's friend who had installed the new phone and video conference system.

Mike anxiously asked, "Could I see you, please."

"Sure. Come on in."

They entered Clay's office.

Mike said, "I found one of these in the conference room." He opened his hand. It was a silver disk the size of a nickel attached to a thin wire about six inches long. "Someone has bugged your offices."

Clay was stunned. He looked at the device and said, "There was a phone repairman in here just a minute ago!"

"Was he wearing a shirt with this logo?" Mike pointed to a patch on his shirt pocket: 'Advanced Electronics'.

"No, a blue Southwestern Bell uniform. Kitty said there's been problems with the phone system."

"We installed the new system, not them! Where is he?"

"He just got into the elevator."

They rushed out of the office and down the hall.

The elevator that the man had boarded was on the tenth floor. The three other elevators were on the third, seventh and eighth floor.

Clay shouted, "The stairs!"

They ran down the hall toward the 'EXIT' sign.

Clay opened the door. He began running down the steps.

Mike trailed.

Clay took one step at a time, but by the time he reached the twelfth floor, he was leaping over three or four steps while hanging onto the handrail.

Mike was a floor behind him and shouted, "There's a Southwestern Bell van in the garage parking lot!"

Clay kept a hurried pace. It was hot in the stairwell. He felt himself perspiring. His adrenaline surged.

It took him less than ten seconds to make it from one floor to the next.

Nine.

Eight.

Seven.

Six.

He could hardly breathe. The heat was oppressive. Sweat dripped off his brow.

Five.

Four.

Clay looked back as he rounded the stairwell on the third floor. Mike was two flights of stairs behind him.

Two.

Lobby.

Garage.

Clay slammed the metal arm on the door forward. He gasped for air. He had to get to the elevators.

He ran around the corner.

An elevator door was closing. The other three were on the sixth floor or higher.

He looked around the corner.

The repairman was running toward the far end of the parking lot.

Clay ran after him. He saw a van with a Southwestern Bell sign on it.

The man kept looking back and screaming to someone in the van.

Clay was gaining ground quickly.

Suddenly, within twenty or thirty feet in front of the van, the man stopped, grabbed his chest, and then fell to the ground.

The side door of the van swung open. A short, slightly-built oriental man holding a pistol with a long silencer jumped out. He aimed.

Clay ran for cover behind a company car.

There was a spit sound. The bullet grazed a concrete column.

Clay dove to the floor behind the car. Another spit. A window shattered.

Clay looked back. Mike rounded the corner from the bank of elevators. He screamed, "Get back!"

Another shot was fired. The bullet hit the wall above Mike's head. He dove behind a column.

Silence.

Clay wondered where he would run to if the man came toward him. He peered around the car.

The gunman was dragging the other man to the van by one arm. He saw Clay. He aimed.

Clay ducked behind the car.

The shot shattered another window.

Silence.

He heard the door of the van close and looked from behind the car.

The man climbed into the driver's seat and started the engine. The van's tires screeched as it backed up.

Clay's first impulse was to run after it, but he realized how foolish that would be.

The van went forward, rounded the corner, and headed toward the exit in the far corner of the lot.

Clay got up and walked around the car. He saw the van stop briefly at the parking lot attendant's booth. Then it drove out onto the main road and sped off.

CHAPTER 14

How many did you find?" Clay asked Mike.

"This office, Kate's, the two conference rooms, and Mr. Rosenberg's office were bugged. Phones, too."

"Can you check the other floors after hours?"

"Sure." Mike reached into his briefcase and pulled out a black, nine-inch rod and said, "This is a sweeping device. I bought one the other day for a customer, and I happened to have it in the car. It's one of the best."

Al came into the room. He patted Mike on the shoulder, turned to Clay, and said, "The car in the parking lot has been sent to the shop."

"Who drove it?"

"Aaron Banks, one of the doormen. I told him someone threw rocks at it."

Mike asked, "Were there any other witnesses?"

Al answered, "Apparently not."

Clay said, "Good."

"Good?" asked Mike.

"I'll explain later," said Clay, who looked at Al and then back to Mike. "Can these things be traced back to whoever planted them?"

"I'm no expert in this sort of thing, but I don't see how. I'll check with a buddy of mine who knows about all this kind of stuff."

Clay said, "Do it discreetly, please."

Mike nodded.

Clay added, "How about coming back, say, around seven o'clock so we can check the other offices."

"Every floor?" asked Mike.

"Probably just five or six."

"I'll be here."

"And please, Mike, keep this under your hat for now."

Mike nodded, rose from his chair, and left the room.

Al asked, "Could you identify either man?"

"The repairman, yes. I didn't get a good look at the oriental guy."

"The repairman, you said he fell down?"

"At first I thought he was shot by the guy in the van, but he grabbed his chest like he had a heart attack or something."

"Give me one reason why we shouldn't call the police?"

"Croft has got to be behind this whole thing."

"Maybe, but you heard Mike."

"Let's see what happens at our meeting with Schultz."

Al's brow furrowed, and he said, "I don't see the connection."

"Schultz could tip us off by the type of questions he asks us."

———

Clay sat with Al in the reception area at Manhattan Commerce's offices. They had spent over two hours going over meetings and phone conversations they had had and concluded there were two issues that could link Croft to the bugging: D.L.'s cancer and Kate having the authority to now vote the family's shares.

Clay had retraced instances when he spoke about Seahorse Canyon and remembered his only conversation about it was in Brock's office yesterday evening. The problem was that he didn't know yet whether Brock's office had been bugged.

He knew it would be a slim chance Schultz would reveal something he could use against Croft, but he had to try. The more he thought about it, though, the more he realized how desperate the situation was.

Manhattan Commerce could legally call the company's loans, but would they do it? Would they take such a drastic step and force the company into bankruptcy? If they did, the price of the stock would surely plummet. More shareholders would then start supporting Croft. Things were definitely bleak.

The receptionist looked across her desk and said, "Mr. Drummond. Mr. Rosenberg. They are ready for you now." She pointed to a closed door to her left.

Clay and Al looked at one another and rose.

The door opened.

Russell Schultz greeted them coldly and introduced Clay and Al to three of the Houston offices' senior male bankers and a female lawyer with one of the biggest law firms in town. The female stenographer seated in the corner of the room was not introduced.

A crystal chandelier hung above a long, dark cherry conference table that was buffed to a bright shine.

Clay and Al sat down.

Al said, "I wasn't aware that a stenographer was going to be here."

Schultz asked, "Is that a problem?"

Al glanced at Clay, who shook his head.

Rosenberg said, "I suppose not, but we want a copy of the transcript."

Schultz said, "I expected to see D.L."

Al said, "His schedule didn't permit it. Clay is acting on his behalf."

Schultz turned to Clay and asked, "Is your father ill?"

Clay asked, "What makes you think that?"

Schultz paused and said, "We've heard he's got a bad case of the flu."

Clay said, "He's fine."

Schultz leaned forward in his chair and asked Clay, "Then why does he refuse to meet with us?"

"Who says he refuses to meet?"

"We have made several requests."

Al said, "I can assure you that we will report back to him."

Schultz frowned.

The female lawyer jotted some notes on a legal pad.

Al asked, "Why are we here?"

Schultz replied, "To inform you that Drummond Offshore is in technical default of its loans."

Al said, "You've already given us notice of that."

The lawyer said, "So you acknowledge that you are in technical default?"

"No," said Al, "I acknowledge that we received your notice."

The lawyer asked, "Do you contend that the company is not in default?"

Rosenberg did not respond.

Clay noticed Al rubbing his hands together.

Schultz turned to Clay and asked, "Are you an employee of the company now?"

"Just a consultant. My father asked me to review the overall operations of the business."

"For what purpose?"

"To see how we could cut costs and improve productivity."

"Does that include stopping the deepwater drilling program?"

Clay paused. He knew he had to choose his words carefully and replied, "I've only been in town a few days."

"But surely," said Schultz, "as a former President of the company, a geologist, and a shareholder, you have to question such an aggressive exploration program, especially in light of the company's deteriorating financial condition."

Clay didn't respond.

Schultz looked down the table to one of the bankers.

The banker said, "We have carefully evaluated the merits of each deepwater prospect and have concluded they are not prudent investments."

Al asked, "Since when does a bank give advice on how a customer should invest its money?"

The banker's jaw tightened, and he replied, "We are not giving advice, Mr. Rosenberg. We have simply made an evaluation and believe that our security would be further impaired should the company proceed with its exploration program."

Neither Clay nor Al responded.

Schultz said, "The bank hereby demands that the company cease and desist any and all exploration in waters deeper than three thousand feet."

Clay grinned and said, "That's impossible. The company is not in a position to simply halt its drilling plans. We've made commitments."

The banker at the end of the table looked at a sheet of paper and said, "Only one prospect the company plans to drill in water deeper than three thousand feet has a partner, Kennerly Exploration. And they only have a ten percent interest."

That was information the bank probably got through reports issued by the company or data from the Mineral Management Service, thought Clay. Did they know about Seahorse Canyon? He asked, "May I see your list?"

The banker rose, leaned over the table, and handed it to him.

Clay read through the list. Seahorse Canyon was not on it.

Schultz said, "How do you plan to finance these projects?"

Al replied, "We are currently in negotiations with several parties."

"Care to elaborate?"

Al said, "We are not at liberty to tell you at this time."

Schultz frowned and asked, "Are these *'parties'* in a position to refinance the company's debt?"

"Possibly."

"Are any of these parties interested in buying assets?"

"Yes, and the family is also considering selling its shares."

Schultz' eyes widened. He said, "It would be helpful for us to know who you are talking to and what progress is being made. Otherwise, actions we take could jeopardize those plans."

"Actions?"

"Exercising our legal rights under the loan indenture agreements."

Rosenberg's bluff was not very convincing, thought Clay. This was going nowhere. He had to somehow get Schultz to tip his hand that Croft was putting pressure on him. He said, "What assurances do we have that what we tell you doesn't get leaked to Croft?"

Schultz was stone-faced.

Clay added, "This sort of thing happens, you know." Clay felt Al's knee bump his leg. "Have you or anyone else at the bank had discussions with Mr. Croft?"

Schultz replied, "Mr. Croft's company is a customer of the bank."

"Okay," said Clay. "Let me rephrase it then. Has he approached you to finance his stock purchases in Drummond Offshore or requested any information on the company?"

Schultz paused and said, "Mr. Croft is not the subject of this meeting."

"Why can't you just answer the question?"

Schultz didn't respond.

The lawyer jotted something on her legal pad.

Clay knew he had hit a nerve and added, "It's well known that the bank has financed many of Mr. Croft's mergers and acquisitions over the years."

Schultz said, "I do not appreciate what you are suggesting, Mr. Drummond."

Al put his hand on Clay's arm and then looked at Schultz and said, "As you know, Russ, the Drummonds and the Crofts have not exactly had a harmonious relationship over the years. I think Clay is just overly cautious, aren't you Clay?"

Clay stared into Schultz's eyes and didn't answer.

Schultz straightened his back and said, "Within three days, we want a written response to our demand to cease and desist the deepwater program in addition to what plans you have to refinance the company's debt. Otherwise, the bank will take whatever means it deems necessary to protect its interests."

Clay asked, "And Croft's interests as well?"

The vein in Schultz' throat bulged. He stood and said, "Gentlemen, this meeting is over."

———

Clay could see that Al was furious as they waited for the elevator. The doors opened. They boarded. And the doors closed.

Al said, "What you just did was goddamned stupid!"

"We accomplished what we wanted."

"Oh, and what was that?"

"To send a message to Croft that we're going to play hardball."

———

Kate was on her second slice of Ramona's pecan pie when she heard Clay's car pull up to Four Oaks. She had been at the ranch since noon visiting with D.L., making calls from his office, and even managing to take a nap. She had felt a bit guilty, especially since Kendra had started work at the company two days earlier. But she had to get away from the office to clear her mind.

And then there was Clay. She couldn't stop wondering whether she was making a big mistake. What would Kendra, Brock, Haley and D.L. think about her and Clay being together? And what about Rex? She didn't want to hurt him.

Clay walked through the front door and joined her in the dining room. He seemed agitated when he kissed her on the cheek. She sensed something terrible had happened.

Ramona walked through the door from the kitchen and asked, "How about some fried chicken?"

Clay nodded and said, "And a beer, please."

Clay sat next to Kate and said with a grin, "I'm trying to lay off the hard stuff."

Kate smiled, put her hand on Clay's arm, and asked, "How come I get the feeling you haven't had a very good day?"

Clay's face turned serious, and he said, "The offices downtown have been bugged."

Kate was stunned.

Clay added, "Mike Sidowski, the guy who installed the new phone and video conferencing stuff, found them this morning."

For the next few minutes, Kate was in a state of shock while Clay explained what had happened, including the two men and the shooting.

Clay concluded by saying, "According to some expert Mike knows, there's no way to trace it back to Croft. But you know he's got to be behind all this."

"There could be a lot of people...competitors... who could do this sort of thing."

"Maybe. But who would gain the most by eavesdropping on us right now?"

Kate knew Clay had a point and said, "So what are you going to do?"

"Meet with Croft. I want to see the look on his face when I accuse him of it."

"But...what if he didn't do it?"

"He did, I'm sure of it.

Ramona came out of the kitchen with Clay's meal.

Clay looked at Ramona and asked, "Mind if you have a few house guests?"

"Who?"

"Kate, Brock and Haley, Kendra and me."

Ramona's face lit-up and she said, "Your father will like that."

Clay turned to Kate and asked, "What do you think?"

"What about Haley? She's due in about two and a half weeks."

"The chopper can take her to the hospital?"

"I suppose so."

Ramona was overjoyed and said, "I'll have to fix up the rooms." She walked back into the kitchen.

Kate whispered, "Do you think we could be in danger or something?"

"No. I just think it's better we're out here. We'll have reporters breathing down our neck after the shareholder meeting."

Clay picked up a chicken leg and bit into it.

Kate asked, "So the only offices that were bugged were yours, mine and Al's."

"And the two conference rooms. Sidowski checked most of the floors with some gadget."

Certain phone conversations Kate had had with shareholders and meetings she had had with Al and Clay flashed through her mind. She then realized that she had to stop Clay from seeing Croft. She knew Ram was still bitter about her ending the affair. Would he try to use that against her? Oh, my God. If Clay goes to see him, Ram might tell him everything.

CHAPTER 15

This can't be happening, thought Croft, as Tran told him what had happened.

He looked into his rearview mirror at a car that pulled up behind them in front of the Vietnamese restaurant and said, "How could you be so stupid? Now you and the other guy can be identified."

Tran grinned and said, "They'll have trouble finding him at the bottom of the ship channel."

"What?"

"He had a heart attack in the parking lot and croaked about an hour later."

Ram looked at a man and woman walking along the sidewalk toward them.

Tran added, "Everything's under control."

"The Drummonds will know I'd be behind the wiretaps."

"We don't even know if they've found them."

"We have to assume they have."

"Okay, so they find them. So what? They can't be traced to us."

"How can you be sure?"

Tran shook his head and said, "Just calm down, will you. Nothin' is going to happen."

"This is it! You and I are finished! Understand!"

Tran grinned and said, "We have learned one thing: Ol' D.L Drummond is dying of cancer. One of them, I think it was the Rosenberg guy, said that Drummond was supposed to provide medical reports to the board every six months as part of some employment agreement, or something. But what the old man did was falsify the reports."

Ram paused and screamed, "I'm serious! We're finished! Get the hell out of town!"

Tran opened the door, got out, bent down, and said, "I'm tired of doing Nugent's dirty work. Its time for me to cash in."

"What's that supposed to mean?"

Tran paused, looked into Ram's eyes, and replied, "We'll be in touch, *partner*," and slammed the door.

Ram heard the phone ring as he walked in the front door of his mansion later that night. He threw his keys on the glass table top and decided to let the recorder take the message. He was definitely not in the mood to speak with anyone.

As he drove back from Chinatown, he couldn't help asking himself what would be worse, being somehow implicated in the wiretapping or being blackmailed by Tran. He should never have listened to Nugent in the first place. Damn him!

On the fifth ring the recorder clicked on and a computerized voice came on: "At the sound of the tone, please leave a message."

"Ram, this is Kate."

Croft was taken aback.

Kate said, "If you're there, please pick-up. I really need to speak with you. Its important.

Ram hesitated for a moment. What does she want? he thought to himself.

"Ram, please."

He picked up the phone.

―――

Kate was planning her strategy on the way to Croft's home. Although Mike Sidowski told Clay there was no way to link Croft to the wiretaps, she managed to convince herself Ram would back down on his assault on the company if she said they were going to the police. But the closer she got to River Oaks, the less confident she became that her ploy would work.

Memories resurfaced of the time she and Ram spent together at his Aspen home. They skied all day. His chef prepared a fabulous meal every night and they would make love in front of the large flagstone fireplace.

She had always wondered if she had been the only woman to ever truly see Ram's gentle side. Beneath that hard, seemingly all-powerful image was a lonely man who desperately wanted to be in love.

His dream was to buy a villa in Tuscany or southern France and for them to travel the world and visit all the great historical sites she had always wanted to see, a passion she had inherited from her mother.

It sounded so tempting, but Kate realized she couldn't go through with it. She couldn't turn her back on her family and run off with a man who they despised.

―――

Ram had to regain his composure from his meeting with Tran. He didn't want Kate to sense he was shaken. But once he saw her standing in his doorway, he knew he had nothing to worry about.

Kate was visibly agitated. The quiver in her voice when she thanked him for seeing her on such short notice was more like an apology than a thank-you. She was extremely vulnerable. And he planned to use it to his advantage.

Ram kissed her on the cheek.

Kate flinched slightly.

He said, "It's good to see you," and directed her to the living room.

He noticed her look around the foyer. He had renovated the downstairs soon after she broke off their affair and said, "As you can see, I've done quite a bit of remodeling."

"It's nice."

"I may have gone a little overboard, but I suppose I was just trying to keep my mind off certain things."

Kate looked at him. She was about to say something, but then turned and continued walking toward the living room.

Ram asked, "Can I get you something to drink?"

"No, thank you."

"Sure?"

"I can't stay long."

Ram extended his hand toward the couch and said, "Please."

Kate sat down. Ram sat in a chair across from her and thought to himself how stunning she was. Her auburn hair. Her high cheek bones. Her thick, sensuous lips. Her large breasts. He said, "I wish things could have turned out differently for us, Kate."

Kate gulped and replied, "That's all behind us."

"Maybe for you."

Kate avoided eye contact.

Ram asked, "But you didn't come here to discuss old times, did you?"

Kate leaned forward and said, "We know you wiretapped our offices."

"What!?"

In a strained voice she said, "We have proof you wiretapped our building."

Ram chuckled and asked, "Is this some kind of joke?"

"I'm afraid not."

"I don't know what the hell you're trying to pull, but it won't work."

"We...we know it was you."

He shook his head and said, "Clay put you up to this, didn't he?"

Kate didn't respond.

He added, "He's using you, don't you see that?"

"We're going to the police."

Ram grinned and said, "Be my guest. Then expect one more lawsuit!"

Kate blushed. Her shoulders slumped, and she asked, "May I use your bathroom, please?"

Ram frowned and pointed toward the hallway.

Kate got up from the couch and walked to the powder room to the right of the stairs.

Ram knew he had Kate on the defensive. But he also knew neither Clay nor D.L. would send her to see him. That's not their style, he thought. She must be doing this on her own. But why?

He paced the room for a few minutes and then walked into the hallway.

The bathroom door was closed. Despite the water running in the sink, he could hear Kate throwing up and smiled.

Kate flushed the toilet and rinsed her mouth with water. She looked at herself in the mirror and thought how stupid she had been to come. She fixed her hair and opened the door.

Ram was standing in the den. He asked, "Everything all right?"

Kate nodded, walked to the couch, and sat down.

Ram remained standing and said, "You know who may have done this? Mercer."

Kate tried to hide her astonishment and asked, "What makes you think that?"

"They wiretapped the offices of a major shareholder when I was trying to gain control of their company."

"How do you know that?"

"It doesn't matter, I just do."

Kate was speechless.

Ram said, "I never understood why D.L. has old man Mercer on the board."

"What do you mean by that?"

"You'll see," grinned Croft.

"The Mercers aren't going to back you," she said defensively.

Ram grinned and replied, "Really."

Kate became flustered. She got up and said, "I should never have come. I thought I was doing you a favor."

Ram laughed and said, "I'm touched. I truly am."

Kate's face reddened and she said, "You're such a bastard!"

"You haven't seen anything yet, my dear."

Kate stormed out of the room and headed for the front door.

"I am going to destroy your family's precious reputation, Kate. And then I'm going to break up the company and sell it off in pieces. And there's nothing you can do about it."

———

Croft was not a drinker, but sipping the warm cognac and relaxing on the couch seemed to calm his nerves enough to start getting things back into perspective.

Why was Kate so desperate to meet him? he asked himself. Well, it's not important at this stage. Tran said there would be no way to trace the wiretapping back to them. Even though the bastard was caught, he probably knows what he's doing. At least I sure hope so. But what am I going to do with him? Kill him?

The information about D.L. falsifying his medical reports can come in handy. I'll leak it to that reporter from *Business Week* I saw in New York. That ought to throw the Drummonds for a spin, especially before the shareholder meeting. But I need more.

Schultz. I need Manhattan Commerce to apply more pressure. Threatening letters and meetings won't do it. The company won't file for bankruptcy protection, not while the old man is alive. But even if they did, that would make the stock plunge. I'll get the bank to petition the court to appoint a Receiver. That'll be a good ploy at this point. But a Receiver could work to my disadvantage since it would try to protect the bank's interests over the shareholders. How about if the Bank threatens to install a Receiver but not go through with it? It's a given that the stock would plunge because of the bad publicity.

But how am I going to get Schultz to do it? I might have to threaten to reveal all his little side deals he's made on my mergers and acquisitions over the years. I've distanced myself enough from each of the deals that I couldn't be implicated. I could also threaten to let his wife know about his bimbo in New York. And how many times have I loaned him money because of his stupid stock trades? Hell, I've got him by the balls. Now it's time to squeeze.

Then there are the Mercers. I need their support to sway more shareholders. Their price of forty-two dollars a share a week ago is too much. I might be able to swing twenty-five. If they don't agree, I'll threaten to reveal the kickbacks they got on the sale of their company. No, that won't work. I'll have to probably pay them their price. I don't have a choice.

Mercer and Schultz. They're the keys to all this. I've got to act quickly. And luckily, Schultz is in town.

Ram picked up the phone and dialed the banker's number.

CHAPTER 16

Clay and Rosenberg walked into D.L.'s bedroom the next morning to give him the bad news.

Clay said, "We've just been served with a lawsuit from Manhattan Commerce. They want the Court to appoint a Receiver."

D.L. sat up in bed, his brow furrowed. He looked at Al, cleared his throat and asked, "What the hell is a Receiver?"

Al replied, "Given the right circumstances, the Court can appoint someone to act in the capacity of a chief executive officer."

D.L. scoffed and said, "I've never heard of such a goddamn thing."

Al said, "I have to admit, it's a very unusual move, especially with a company our size."

Clay interjected, "This doesn't help Croft."

"Why?" asked D.L.

Al said, "Because a Receiver's first priority is to protect creditor interests, not shareholders. If the Court grants this, Croft basically loses control. And, in some cases, the Receiver has the authority to sell assets in order to make creditors whole."

Clay said, "Schultz and Croft may not be working together like we thought."

"I doubt that," said D.L. He cleared his throat again and asked, "When's the hearing?"

Al replied, "Two o'clock today."

D.L.'s eyes widened. He asked, "Can you delay it?"

"I don't know. The bank has every right to do this since we're in technical default of the loans."

"Who's the Judge?"

Clay looked at Al and then back to D.L. and replied, "Burnhouse."

D.L. chuckled.

Clay didn't understand why D.L. wasn't shocked. He recalled the incident in eighty-six when Judge Gale Burnhouse presided over the case where the Crofts alleged that D.L. had broken his agreement to buy back their shares. D.L. became so irate at the hearing that he called her a 'bitch' and was held in contempt of court.

Al said, "We can ask for another Judge to preside over the case."

"No," said D.L. still grinning. "I've patched things up with the old bag."

Clay and Rosenberg looked at one another.

"I went to her husband's funeral a few years ago and saw her a few times. You know, she's not such a bad sort once you get to know her. But I just couldn't get used to a woman smokin' a cigar."

The three of them laughed.

D.L. looked at Al and said, "There has to be a way to stop this."

Al paused and said, "File bankruptcy. I know that's not what..."

D.L. said, "That's exactly what Croft wants us to do. The stock price drops, and he'll start buying every share he can get his hands on."

Clay said, "We need to buy more time."

Al said, "Croft will probably instigate a class action suit against us alleging mismanagement and negligence and then try to have you kicked off the board. And once it's out about the cancer, he'll allege stock fraud."

D.L. replied, "Unless we start buying up shares."

Clay said, "Kate has been trying."

"Then let's pay double the price, for Christ's sake!"

Al said, "Even if we were able to, we're still in the same boat. The court could appoint a Receiver and then our hands are tied. The entire operation of the company would be out of our hands."

D.L. exhaled a deep breath.

Al added, "I'll try to get an extension, but we can't count on it. All the bank has to do is demonstrate that their collateral had been seriously impaired. And frankly, that shouldn't be too hard."

D.L. looked at Clay.

Clay knew the old man was thinking of Seahorse Canyon. He hoped he wouldn't bring up the subject in front of Rosenberg. Al had enough to worry about.

D.L. looked at Al and said, "Try to buy some more time. A month or so."

Al said, "I'll do my best."

D.L. looked at Clay and said, "I want to talk to you."

Al got the hint. He walked toward the door, turned and said, "I still think filing bankruptcy is our only option," and closed the door behind him.

D.L. turned to Clay and asked, "What do you think?"

"If Al can't stall this, it's all over."

D.L. coughed and drank some water.

Clay said, "I'm going to meet with Croft."

"Al already tried to set-up a meeting and he refused. What good will it do anyway?"

"I want to look at that sonofabitch's face when I accuse him of the bugging."

"You can't prove it though."

"We need to put him on the defensive."

"Christ, son, we're the ones on the defensive here."

Clay refrained from saying that the old man was the one who got the company in its current situation.

D.L. asked, "What about Seahorse Canyon?"

"Brock told me the whole story."

"And?"

Clay sighed, "It's a real long shot."

"What do we have to lose?"

"Only the company."

D.L. grinned.

Clay added, "We may not even get a chance to drill it if the Judge appoints this Receiver."

"Let's say Al buys us more time. How long will it take to drill it?"

"Well, I suppose they could be on location by tomorrow. And assuming there's no major drilling problems, or Mineral Management doesn't shut us down because of the falsified report, I'd say four weeks at the best."

Suddenly, D.L. cringed. He closed his eyes slightly and then re-opened them.

Clay came closer to the bed and asked, "You okay?"

D.L. nodded and said, "Let's see what happens this afternoon and then we'll go from there."

———

Clay sat in the conference room and was relieved when Rosenberg told him Judge Burnhouse gave them thirty days to respond to the bank's petition to appoint a Receiver. However, she made it clear that the company was not in compliance with its loan agreements and said that a very compelling argument must be made for her not to grant the bank's request.

Clay asked, "In other words, she's going to grant it in a month."

Rosenberg nodded and said, "Assuming the bank doesn't withdraw their motion."

Clay's brow furrowed. He asked, "Why would they do that?"

"Their attorney didn't put up too much of a fight. I think the petition was just a ploy to make us look bad at the shareholder's meeting."

Clay rose from his chair and began to pace back and forth.

Al added, "We've got five days to come up with a damage control plan."

"Is there any way..."

"Excuse me, Mr. Rosenberg," said Al's secretary standing in the doorway. "You just received this fax." She handed it to him and left.

Al began reading it.

Clay stopped pacing.

Al exhaled a deep breath, placed the fax on the table, and said, "It's from a reporter at *Business Week*. He's asking if D.L. has terminal cancer." He stared blankly at the table and added, "I'll have to talk this over with Kate."

Clay began pacing again and asked, "Is there any possible way we can delay the shareholder meeting?"

"Only if ten percent of the shareholders, excluding officers and board members, petition the board."

"That doesn't help us," replied Clay as he continued pacing.

Al's eyes lit up and he said, "Unless Kate transfers ten percent of the family's shares to you?"

Clay stopped pacing and asked, "Would that work?"

"I don't see why not. Croft would throw a fit, but technically we could do it. You're neither an officer, nor a board member."

Rosenberg paused and added, "But aren't we just delaying the inevitable?"

"Maybe, but the more time we can buy, the better chance we'll have to find a way out of this shit."

Rosenberg sat back in his chair, exhaled, and said, "We better come up with something damn quick."

CHAPTER 17

The next morning, Croft was anxious to hear what the two men seated across from him in his office had to say, especially after hearing the news that Drummond Offshore was able to delay the shareholders meeting.

Croft nodded to the geologist.

The man in his late fifties handed Croft a report and said, "It's quite clear Drummond's primary focus in the Gulf has shifted from gas plays in water ranging from fifteen hundred to twenty-five hundred feet to deepwater oil projects in the three thousand to six thousand foot range. And based upon their track record, it has not been a wise move."

Croft asked, "Would you consider what they have done to be negligent?"

The geologist blushed and replied, "Well, I don't know if I could go so far as to say that."

"Why not?"

The geologist squirmed in his seat and said, "I just don't agree with their strategy."

Croft leaned back in his chair and asked, "Have they replaced the same amount of reserves they've produced for the past three years?"

"No."

"Could they if they had stuck with drilling shallower deals?"

"It's conceivable."

"So basically they have abandoned a strategy which would otherwise have made the exploration division profitable?"

"I suppose that could be said."

"If that's the case then, why wouldn't they be negligent?"

"I'm not an attorney, Mr. Croft."

Croft leaned forward. He stared into the man's eyes and said, "You need to use the word 'negligent'. Understood?"

The geologist nodded.

Croft stood and walked to the window. With his back turned he asked, "Is there a deepwater prospect they have drilled, or plan to drill, which really stands out as poor judgment?"

Without hesitation, the geologist answered, "Seahorse Canyon. They're moving one of their drillships out to it now." The man reached into his briefcase and pulled out a thick stack of papers and said, "I went through logs and seismic and can find very little justification to drill it. Three other geologists agree with me."

Croft grinned and asked, "How deep is the water?"

"A little over six thousand. And they're going alone - no partners."

Croft turned and looked at the other man, a drilling engineer, and said, "How much will it cost to drill?"

"About forty million. But the *Global Explorer* isn't really up to it. Don't get me wrong, she's one of the best drillships in the world, but she needs a major overhaul."

"I thought that's what they were doing."

"It was in dry dock in Brownsville, but they took it out."

"Is it unsafe?"

The engineer paused and replied, "I don't think I could go that far. But I could say they're taking a big risk since the location they're going to is one of the roughest in the Gulf."

The geologist added, "Shell and others have abandoned drilling some of their wells in the area because of heavy loop currents and mudslides."

Croft smiled and then asked the engineer, "What have you come up with on deferred maintenance?"

The man handed Croft a report and said, "The company has drastically cut back on maintenance on most of their rigs. And in this business, it'll catch up to you real quick."

"Could the lack of maintenance be characterized as neglect?"

"Yes."

"Does this 'neglect' equate to a reduction in the value of the rigs?"

"Probably by ten to fifteen percent."

"You've seen the Bank's audit?"

The engineer nodded.

Croft asked, "Do you think the company purposely under-reported the costs?"

"Definitely."

"Good. Be prepared to back it up in Court tomorrow."

The geologist and engineer looked at one another.

The geologist asked, "I thought we were going to make a presentation at the shareholder meeting."

"It's been delayed for a month. So, I'm filing an injunction to stop the company from drilling more deep wells." Croft leaned forward and looked into the geologist's eyes and asked, "Are you absolutely sure this Seahorse Canyon is a dud?"

The man gulped and said, "I have the most recent seismic done on the area and..."

"What are the odds?" Croft asked firmly.

The geologist paused and answered, "A thousand to one."

Croft grinned.

Croft sat in his office and pondered his next move. Prior to withdrawing his suit to have the court appoint a Receiver, the best way to make Drummond scramble would be to file an injunction to stop all exploration, especially the deepwater program. This would serve two purposes: to slow the losses the company has been incurring and to get shareholders to join him in a class action suit against the company. He could use the testimony his geologist and drilling engineer gave at the Receiver hearing. Perfect.

As he was about to reach for the phone to call his attorney, the intercom on his desk beeped.

His secretary said, "Mr. Croft. Mr. Nugent is here to see you, sir. He insists on seeing you immediately."

Because Ram had not spoken to Nugent since New York, he knew he was going to want an update on the Drummond deal. And, more than likely, he would ask Ram if he had any contact with Tran.

Ram said, " Show him in, please."

As soon as he saw the angry expression on the bald attorney's face, Ram sensed that his father-in-law had sent his delivery boy to issue one of his veiled threats. Ram played it cool and asked, "So what brings you to town?"

Nugent didn't offer a handshake. He sat down in front of the desk and asked, "Have you heard from Tran?"

"Frankly, I was going to ask you the same thing."

"I know you two have met and made a deal."

Ram simply nodded.

Nugent said, "I haven't been able to get a hold of him."

"Me neither."

"This isn't like him at all."

"Then things must be pretty quiet at Drummond."

Nugent leaned forward in the chair, stared straight into Ram's eyes and said, "I find that hard to believe."

Ram felt intimidated. In an attempt to act unconcerned, he shrugged his shoulders.

Nugent paused, grinned slightly, and then asked, "How's the First Nation financing coming along?"

Ram was caught off guard by the comment. He had been confident the financing deal he had been working on with the bank to buy out his father-in-law was being done in secret. He tried to maintain his composure and said casually, "I see you've been doing your homework."

"That's what your *partner* pays me to do."

Ram felt a queasiness in his stomach. He figured this was as good a time as ever to send a message back to Truesdale. He straightened his back, folded his hands, and said, "Tell my 'partner,' from now on the Drummond deal is mine. I'm exercising my option to buy his shares."

Nugent chuckled and shook his head.

Ram added, "Everything is lined up."

"Really. Well that's good to know. But there's only one small problem: Jonas doesn't want to be bought out."

"Well, then he shouldn't have signed the agreement."

"Ah, c'mon, Ramsey ol' boy, you ought to know that doesn't mean shit."

Ram's face turned red. He said, "My attorneys tell me it'll stand up in court."

Nugent grinned and replied, "But if you can't get the buyout financed, what good will that do?"

"I'll get the money."

"Not from First Nation you won't."

"I have a commitment!"

"Not anymore."

Ram's shoulders slumped. Truesdale didn't have any connection with the bank, he thought to himself.

Nugent added, "Maybe you're not aware of it, but your father-in-law has been talking to the bank about financing the acquisition of some shipping line in Spain."

Ram was speechless.

Nugent said, "And it just so happens that First Nation really wants his business. More so, by the way, than they want yours."

Ram pounded his fist on the desk and said, "I've got a deal!"

Nugent grinned and replied, "Not any more, you don't."

"I'll get the financing! With or without First Nation!"

"You just don't get it, do you? You're not going to finance squat without him."

"We'll see."

Nugent chuckled and said, "Well, let's just say, for argument's sake, that you find somebody to look at the deal. But once they find out you're going to jail for wiretapping the Drummond offices, they won't touch it with a ten-foot pole!"

Ram was stunned and said, "I thought you hadn't talked to Tran." Nugent smiled and replied, "I have other sources."

"You set the whole thing up!"

"Do you have proof of that?" Nugent asked calmly.

Ram's mind was racing. This was all a set-up, he thought.

Nugent added, "And by the way, I wouldn't count on Tran hanging around to spill his guts. He'll just vanish into thin air and you'll have to face the music all by yourself."

"Go to hell, Nugent!"

Nugent mused, "You see, Ramsey ol' boy, there's the big fish and the little fish. Jonas, well, he's a whale. And you, you're just a little fish. Unfortunately, that's all you'll ever be."

For the first time in his life, Ram felt that he was capable of murder.

Nugent chuckled and then added, "But you know, your father-in-law isn't such a bad guy. In return for transferring all the Drummonds' shares to him, he'll pay you a nice little advisory fee for your time and trouble. Now that's not such a bad deal, is it?"

Ram didn't reply.

Nugent stood up to leave and added, "And, you *will* stay married to Monique. Jonas says you can still live separately and all that. But there'll be no divorce."

CHAPTER 18

Clay walked out into the hallway after closing his father's bedroom door. The old man was growing paler and there was a slight yellowness of his skin indicating that jaundice was setting in. He was going downhill fast.

It was the first time, since he had come back to Houston, that Clay truly felt sympathy for his father. Yes, there were still many things he could never forgive him for, but this was not the time to harbor resentment. It was a time to make amends.

As he leaned against the railing and looked aimlessly at the marble floor in the foyer below, Clay came to the realization that he had fully accepted the responsibility to get the family through the current crisis. It was indeed a heavy burden. Not only the family's livelihood and pride was at stake, but employees who had been with the company for years would lose their jobs if Croft succeeded. Sure, he thought to himself, I could fail. But if there's a chance I can beat him at his own game, the company would be mine to run. I could make a fresh start.

Clay walked toward his old room. He was anxious to see it, especially after he heard the ranch hands had carried boxes marked 'Clay' from the storage barn.

He opened the door. He was surprised at how much trouble Ramona had gone through to fix up his room as it was during his high school and college days. The twelve-point trophy Whitetail Deer hung above his bed. Football, basketball, and baseball trophies were on the shelves. Neatly folded on his bed was the green and white blanket his grandmother had made. And on top of the dresser were several photographs of him and Dirk.

He picked up a picture and remembered it was taken by his father while on a hunting trip in South Texas when Clay had shot the buck. Both Clay and Dirk knelt in front of the deer. Clay held the head upright by its antlers and Dirk held a rifle.

They were sophomores at UT. The reason he recalled the year was because he remembered getting a lecture from his father and mother about being put on probation for poor grades. Mom, of course, was the one doing most of the lecturing while the old man tried to appear concerned. But what Mom didn't know was that the bad grades were the least of it. The old man had had to wire money to bail him out of jail the previous semester for fighting in a bar.

Dirk always seemed to keep out of trouble, he thought to himself. And he always somehow managed to get good grades without really having to study. Dirk inherited Mom's study habits. And I inherited the old man's.

Clay sat down on the bed and wondered how things would have been if Dirk were still alive. Aside from all the competition and occasional jealousy between them, how would they be dealing with the current situation?

Dirk never backed away from a confrontation, but he always seemed to have a better sense of when, and when not to, lock horns with someone. There were times, however, when Dirk would over-think a problem and hesitate to take action until he had all the facts. Clay, on the other hand, was more impulsive. But as the old man used to say, 'A bad decision is sometimes better than no decision.'

Clay's thoughts drifted to Kate. He put the picture on the end table and couldn't help think about them embracing in his office.

There was a genuineness when she was in his arms. And his instincts told him she felt the same way.

———

A few hours later, Clay was sitting in his father's study gazing at the map of Seahorse Canyon and drinking his fourth vodka-tonic when Kate arrived home from the office. She looked tired.

He rose from the couch. When they embraced, he immediately knew something was wrong and asked, "What's goin' on?"

She didn't reply.

When Clay looked into her eyes, there was fear. He said, "I'll get you a drink."

She nodded and sat down on the couch.

He walked to the wet bar, poured her a scotch, and returned.

Kate said, "I've been wanting to tell you something...something I did."

Clay handed her the drink and remained standing.

Kate drew a deep breath and said, "You're not gonna like what I have to tell you."

"Well, then let's get it over with," said Clay, sitting next to her.

Kate looked into his eyes and said, "It was stupid what I did." She began to tremble and added, "I went to see Croft last night...at his house."

"What the hell for?"

"I thought I could threaten him, you know, about the wiretapping."

Clay didn't want to upset her more than she already was and asked, "What did he say?"

"He said the Mercers were probably behind it. He said they wiretapped somebody's office when they were trying to sell their company."

Clay exhaled a deep breath.

"I'm sorry, Clay. I was just trying to help. That's all."

"I told you I wanted to meet with him!"

"I know. I'm sorry."

He finished his drink and said, "Now he's going to be able to cover his tracks!"

"I know, Clay, it was a stupid thing for me to do."

Clay got up, walked toward the desk, and said, "I was trying to get some leverage. We could have even leaked the wiretapping to the media to make him sweat."

"But you said there was no way to prove it."

Clay's brow furrowed and he said, "Since when do you have to prove anything for the press?" He shook his head and scoffed, "I still can't believe the old man gave you his proxy!"

Kate felt as if she had been slapped.

Clay knew he shouldn't have said anything about the proxy. He walked toward her. He placed his hand on her shoulder and said calmly, "I didn't mean that."

Kate shoved his hand off her, looked into his eyes with a determined look and said, "How did I ever think that a drunk like you could ever help us?" She stood.

Clay grabbed her by the arm and said, "I didn't ask for any of this."

"Get your hands off me!"

Clay quickly released his grip and said apologetically, "I'm sorry. I'm just upset."

Kate wiped a tear from her eye and said, "Go back to the Bahamas where you belong!" and stormed out of the room.

Clay walked to the bar and poured himself another drink. The hell with her, he thought to himself.

CHAPTER 19

The next morning, Kate picked up *The Wall Street Journal* from the dining room table.

Her worst fears had been realized. The headline read:

Allegations of stock fraud surface at Drummond;
founder misrepresents health problems.

What a time for this to happen, she thought. She knew the stock would drop on the news, but that was immaterial at this point.

Kate heard Al Rosenberg greet Ramona in the hallway.

He walked into the dining room and said jokingly, "Nothing like waking up to good news, huh?"

Kate frowned.

Al tried to act reassuring and added, "D.L. and I talked about this a few days ago. He's going to issue a statement regretting that he mis-informed the board and shareholders."

"This is really going to hurt our credibility."

Al put his briefcase on the table, opened it, and said, "I know. But we've got another problem that's more immediate." He withdrew a one-inch-thick document and slid it across the table and added, "Croft has filed for an injunction to stop the deepwater drilling program. He is contending that..."

Clay walked into the room. He looked badly hung-over and said, "Good morning," unenthusiastically. He sat down, glanced at the paper, and said to Kate, "By the look on your face, I take it we didn't get good press this morning."

Kate shoved the paper to him.

Clay glanced at it.

Al pointed to the document and said, "And Croft has just filed an injunction to halt all deepwater drilling."

Kate noticed Clay's eyes widen.

Al said, "It says that the company has acted negligently by continuing a drilling program that keeps losing money."

Kate looked at Clay's expressionless face and figured he was too hung-over to grasp everything.

Clay asked Al, "So what's Croft's setting us up for? A class action suit?"

Al nodded.

"When's the hearing?" asked Clay.

"Two o'clock this afternoon."

Kate felt her neck stiffening, but tried to show Clay that she was not panicking.

Al said, "We'll argue that it's over-reaching and..."

Clay interrupted, "What are the chances of it being granted right away?"

"Minimal," replied Rosenberg. "A lot of fact-finding has to be done to substantiate their claims."

"Then this is just a ploy to make us look bad?"

"Exactly."

Clay exhaled a deep breath. He looked at Kate and said, "I think the both of us should go to the hearing. I think it's time I have a little chat with Croft."

Al's face reddened and he said, "I don't think that's such a good idea."

Clay paused, looked at Kate and then said to Al, "Ask his attorney to have him there."

———

Kate's mind was racing while she, Clay and Rosenberg sat in the back seat of D.L.'s limo on the way to the Federal Courthouse. Al kept reading a stack of papers and jotting down notes in preparation for the hearing. Strangely, Clay seemed at ease and simply stared aimlessly out the window.

The only time she and Clay had spoken to one another since breakfast was when she asked him why he wanted her to attend the hearing. In a flippant manner Clay answered, "You have a vested interest, don't you?"

Kate's intuition told her that Clay had some sort of plan in mind. She knew he had met with D.L. around noon. What little scheme had they come up with?

Kate, Clay, and Al walked down the hallway outside the courtroom where the hearing was to be held and joined their attorneys. Croft was huddling with his lawyers at the far end of the hall.

Kate glanced at Clay. Then, without saying anything, Clay began walking down the hall toward Croft.

One of the attorneys in Croft's group looked at Clay walking toward them. He tapped Ram on the shoulder and whispered something. All the lawyers looked in Clay's direction.

As Clay approached, Kate saw Croft separate from the group. He and Clay shook hands. Croft said something to the attorneys and they walked away.

Clay began talking and kept his poise. Croft seemed to be more the listener, but appeared to interrupt Clay during the discussion. Around five minutes later, they shook hands and Clay made his way back.

He joined the group and said, "There won't be a hearing."

Kate was stunned.

Al asked nervously, "What did you..."

Clay raised his hand and said, "I'll tell you in the car."

———

Clay was the last one to climb into the back of the limo. He looked at Kate's and Al's anxious faces and knew he had to be direct and to the point.

He said, "Croft has agreed to stop the injunction and any other legal actions. In return, we're going to drill a deep well in Seahorse Canyon. If the well is productive, based upon certain criteria, Croft will tender all the shares he controls to the family at twenty-seven dollars per share."

Kate and Al looked at one another. Their mouths gaped open.

Clay continued, "If the well doesn't meet the criteria then the family has to tender its shares at the same price."

Al's face grew red and he threw a stack of papers to the floor.

Clay put his hand up as if to call a truce and said, "Everything is subject to being ironed out between us and Croft. We still have to come up with an agreement that will be administered by the Judge."

Al shouted, "Did you and D.L. cook this up?"

Clay looked at Kate. Her shoulders were slumped and her mouth was slightly open. She was in a state of shock.

Al continued, "Do you honestly think Croft will agree to such a thing if he knows he's not sure he'll come out on top?"

"I admit it's a gamble, but..."

"Gamble my ass!"

Clay's nostrils flared. He said calmly, "Well, I don't see you coming up with any bright ideas."

Al kicked the papers on the floor.

Clay added, "There's a meeting at our offices tomorrow morning with Croft and his people to negotiate the agreement."

Al said, "I won't have any part of this!"

"That's fine with me," Clay said. He turned to Kate and said, "If we reach an agreement, we're going to need you to sign it."

Kate looked at him.

With a slight grin on his face, he said, "You've got the authority to stop it."

———

Kate walked into Brock's office later that afternoon. He was standing with his back to her and gazing out the window.

She asked, "Has Al spoken to you?"

Brock turned around and nodded.

Kate asked, "What are the chances of this well being productive?"

"Slim to none," he frowned. *"If* they can even drill it."

"If?"

"The area they're drilling has some of the worst conditions in the Gulf." Brock lowered his head and said, "It's all my fault. I should have never said anything to Pops."

Kate's eyes widened. She asked, "What are you talking about?"

"This well...the area...was a project I had been working on for a few years. I told Pops about it and Clay mentioned it about a week ago."

Kate felt pissed she hadn't been told.

The vein in Brock's neck bulged and his face turned red. He shouted, "Can't you see what he's doing? All he cares about is selling his stock and then leaving! He doesn't give a rat's ass about us or the company!"

"You're wrong!"

Brock chuckled and said, "He's put on a pretty good act. And you've bought it!"

Kate felt faint and sat down in the chair across his desk.

"You've got to stop this deal!" shouted Brock.

Kate shook her head and said, "How am I supposed to do that?"

"You've got the stock proxy, don't you?"

"Dad could take the authority away from me anytime he wants."

Brock walked around his desk, looked her in the eyes and said, "Not if he's found to be incompetent."

Kate looked at him in amazement and asked, "You can't be serious?"

"Damn right I'm serious." He leaned over, put his hands on the arm of the chair and asked, "What other choice do you have?"

"I...I could never do that to him."

"If you don't, Croft is going to end up owning this company. Is that what you want?"

———

Clay was walking down the hall toward his office when he saw Brock get off the elevator.

Clay picked up some phone message slips off Kitty's desk and told her to hold his calls.

Brock was walking briskly toward him and shouted, "I want to talk to you!"

Clay waved his arm in the direction of his office. Brock entered the room and Clay closed the door behind them.

Brock turned around and yelled, "You sonofabitch! You're never going to get away with this! I know what you're up to!"

"Oh, and what's that?"

"You just want to dump your stock for a higher price than you can get in the market!"

"Back off, Brock! You don't know what you're talking about!"

"I know about the loan from Pops. You're probably hoping he dies so you don't have to pay him back! And I know you're just trying to use Mom! I've seen how you look at her! Do you honestly think she'd fall for some drunk like you!?"

Clay's face tensed. He stepped toward Brock.

Suddenly, Rosenberg opened the door and said, "That's enough of this!" and stood between them.

Brock yelled, "First you kill my father and now..."

The three of them stood silently for a moment.

Clay looked into Brock's eyes. In a low tone of voice, he replied, "You don't know how many times I've wished I had been the one to die," and walked out of the room.

CHAPTER 20

Clay sat at the bar of some redneck joint east of downtown. Except for an African-American woman with long, stringy hair braids sitting in a booth, the place was full of construction and refinery workers. He had left his office nearly two hours earlier and had no idea what town he was in, but it was somewhere on the way to Baytown.

The vodka-tonics were having the usual numbing effect. But he was becoming increasingly irritated by a husky, bearded man wearing oil-stained blue overalls sitting a few stools down from him. The man kept staring at Clay and then would turn to his beer-drinking buddies, say something, and they would all laugh.

Clay gulped his drink. With the help of leaning against the bar, he stood and walked toward the man.

The redneck said, "I like that blue, silky tie you've got on there, pal. Come on over here and I'll wipe my ass with it."

The men laughed.

Clay smiled, walked up to the man, lifted the tie off his shirt and said, "Be my guest."

Faces turned serious.

The bartender shouted something, but Clay couldn't hear over the loud country and western song playing on the juke box.

Two men walked into the front door to Clay's left. He waved to them as a ploy to get the man to look over. It worked.

Clay wound up and hit the man in the jaw with his right fist. His knuckles cracked from the blow.

The man turned slightly — as if he had been slapped.

Clay followed with a left. The man blocked it with his right forearm and then followed with a left that landed above Clay's temple.

Clay rocked backwards. He regained his balance and then countered with a flurry of punches to the man's face and stomach. The man fell to the floor.

Suddenly, Clay felt a kick on the back of his left leg. He turned. He blocked a punch from one of the man's friends with his left arm and landed a right to his face.

In the corner of his eye, Clay saw the bartender rushing from behind the bar with something in his hand.

Three other men pounced on Clay. He kept flailing and managed to land some blows.

He noticed the bearded man he had knocked to the floor was on his knees. Clay kicked him in the chest. The man crashed to the floor again.

Suddenly, Clay felt a sharp blow to the back of his neck. His knees buckled. He managed to turn. The bartender was holding a sawed-off baseball bat.

Clay tried to regain his balance. He stumbled backward and then fell to the floor. The last thing he heard was a gun shot.

———

Clay leaned against a black sedan with his hands cuffed behind his back and looked at the African-American woman. There was a police badge attached to her belt.

The overweight, middle-aged woman smiled and said, "You know, I always wanted to fire my gun off in a bar. Just like the cowboy movies."

Clay was not amused. His neck was throbbing.

"My name is Elsa Tiller. I'm a homicide detective with Houston P.D. What's your name?"

"Clay Drummond," he slurred.

"What do you do, Clay Drummond?"

"I'm...my family owns Drummond Offshore, a drilling company."

Tiller's eyebrows raised, and she said, "You're slummin' a bit, aren't you?"

Clay didn't respond.

Tiller continued, "Well, it's your lucky day. The bartender isn't goin' to press any kind of charges, but he doesn't want to see your face around here again. And I've got the sneaky suspicion you won't be." She handed him a bag of ice and added, "And the good ol' boy you leveled. Well, he don't want his parole officer to know he was in a bar. So, Clay Drummond, I'm just going to haul you back to Houston and we'll get someone to pick your drunken ass up. Sound okay with you?"

Clay nodded. He put the ice on his neck and grimaced.

Tiller said, "If you promise not to give me any trouble, I'll take those handcuffs off."

"Yeah...I mean, no. I won't give you any trouble."

She unlocked the handcuffs and said, "I have to say this: I ain't seen anyone do an ass-whippin' like that for awhile."

She opened the back door and Clay got in.

She walked around the front of the car and climbed behind the wheel.

Clay asked, "What about my car?"

Tiller looked in the rearview mirror and replied, "You need to get somebody to pick it up. Is that a problem?"

He felt faint and replied, "I guess not."

Tiller said, "Now, don't go pukin' in my car, you hear?"

Clay lost consciousness, slid across the back seat, and hit his head on the window.

———

Clay sipped a cup of lukewarm black coffee outside Elsa Tiller's office at police headquarters and considered himself fortunate. The detective had brought him to police headquarters on the twelve hundred block of Travis in downtown as opposed to the old police station on the other side of town where he would have probably sat in a jail cell.

Tiller told him he had to have someone pick him up. Clay had said he could call a cab, but Tiller was insistent.

He had called Rosenberg, but he was on his way to Dallas on the company jet. And he didn't have Kitty's home phone number. Unfortunately, he had to call Kate. He felt humiliated.

———

Kate walked down the hallway toward Tiller's office and saw Clay sitting in a chair. He was leaning forward with his elbows on his knees and looking down at the floor.

As she approached, his head rose and he frowned.

She didn't want to make the situation any more awkward than it already was and simply said, "Let's get you out of here."

Elsa Tiller entered the hallway, introduced herself, and asked, "Can I see you in my office, Mrs. Drummond?"

Kate nodded and followed Tiller into her office.

The office was unkempt. A number of files were piled high on her desk. Styrofoam coffee cups and fast food paper wrappers were strewn across the top of filing cabinets.

To Kate's left, there were several plaques and photographs on the wall. She noticed one of the pictures was of Tiller and the Mayor at what appeared to be a police awards ceremony.

Kate said, "Thank you for bringing him in."

Tiller replied, "No problem," and motioned for Kate to be seated before sitting down. "Did he tell you where I found him?"

"No."

"In some rat-hole bar near Baytown."

"Baytown?"

"Luckily, I was interviewing a witness in a case I'm working on. Frankly, if I hadn't have been there, he'd probably be in real bad shape."

Kate shook her head and asked, "Is he under arrest?"

"No." Tiller leaned forward, folded her hands together, and added, "He passed out in the back of my car and then woke up and started mumbling something about wiretapping. Do you know anything about that?"

Kate felt herself stiffen.

Tiller continued, "I asked him what he was talkin' about and he kinda spaced out on me."

Kate was doing the best she could to hide her astonishment and replied, "I don't know anything about a wiretapping."

Tiller's brow furrowed slightly. She paused and said, "I didn't say 'a wiretapping' just wiretapping in general."

Kate changed the subject and asked, "Can I take him with me now?"

Tiller leaned back, smiled and said, "You know, my brother Sam worked for your company one summer. On some rig out in the Gulf."

Kate was becoming irritated and said, "That's nice."

"I saw that article in, I think it was, Texas Monthly, about you and how you're the highest ranking woman executive in the offshore drilling business." Tiller paused and added, "I've also read about this Kraft, or whatever his name is, who's trying to buy you guys."

"Croft. His name is Croft."

"Yeah. This is kinda like a family feud, isn't it?"

Kate felt very uneasy with the line of questioning, but answered, "I suppose you could say that."

Tiller stood up and said, "Why don't you take your brother-in-law home now and let him sleep it off."

"Thank you."

———

Kate pulled out of the police station's underground parking lot, made a right on Travis and took the next right on Polk. Neither she nor Clay had said a word since they left Tiller's office, but Kate figured it was time to break the ice.

She wanted to ask him why he said something to Tiller about the wiretapping, but she knew he would get upset. Instead she asked, "Why were you in Baytown?"

Without looking at her, he said, "Does it really matter?"

Kate paused and said, "You said on the phone that you were in a scuffle. What happened?"

Clay glared at her and said, "Listen, I'd rather not talk about it, okay?"

"I just want to help."

Clay didn't respond and looked out the passenger side window.

Kate kept quiet for a moment and then finally mustered enough courage to say, "Clay, I think you need counseling. You're a functional alcoholic."

Clay glanced at her and asked, "A what?"

She gulped and said, "At least go see someone I know and just talk to him."

"Stop the car!"

"What?"

Clay pounded his fist on the dashboard and yelled, "Stop the goddamn car!"

"Don't be ridiculous!"

Clay reached for the car door handle.

Kate slowed down and began to pull into the right lane. Before she reached the curb, Clay opened the door and began to climb out.

She panicked and brought the car to an abrupt stop. A car behind her beeped its horn.

Clay said, "Thanks for the lift," and got out.

Kate put the car into park and began to climb out.

Suddenly, she was blinded by headlights. A pick-up truck slammed on its brakes. It came to a stop within a few feet of her. The male driver began yelling obscenities.

Kate saw Clay standing on the sidewalk with his mouth gaping open. Once he saw that she was unharmed, he walked away.

———

Kate was still a little shaken by the time she arrived at Four Oaks, but she was determined to find out how much involvement D.L. had in the deal with Croft.

She knocked on his bedroom door and entered.

D.L. was switching television channels, smiled at her, and said, "You know, I'm beginning to understand why they call it the boob tube. The only thing that's worth watchin' is *CNN* or that country and western music video station." He switched off the TV.

Kate walked around the side of the bed. She leaned down, kissed his forehead and for the next minute or so told him about what had happened to Clay. She concluded by saying, "I really think he needs to go into rehab."

D.L. folded his arms and said, "He's just lettin' off some steam." He smiled and added, "Well, at least we know he's still got a lot of piss and vinegar left in 'em."

Kate frowned and said, "I'm serious. He needs help."

"C'mon, Kate. Hell, half of them shrinks are just as screwed up as their patients. He's just trying to figure things out right. He'll be fine. You'll see."

Kate knew she wasn't going to get anywhere and asked, "Were you aware of the deal he made with Croft at the courthouse?"

D.L. paused and answered, "I knew about his plan. But it's far from any kinda deal."

"Did you put him up to this?"

"No."

"But Brock said you've been asking him about this Seahorse Canyon area."

"Brock came up with the idea to drill the block, not me," D.L. said defensively.

"But he never thought you wanted to drill it."

"Clay sees something to it."

"So you agree with him?"

D.L. raised his hand and said, "I never said that."

"You know what Clay is trying to do, don't you? He just wants to sell his stock."

"What makes you think that?"

"Because the only reason he came back was because he's broke."

D.L. didn't respond.

Kate asked, "You loaned him money, didn't you?"

D.L.'s face turned red. He glared at Kate and replied harshly, "That's none of your business."

Kate realized nothing would be accomplished by getting into a shouting match. She put her hand on D.L.'s arm and said, "I'm sorry, Dad. I didn't mean to upset you."

"Clay will do what's best for the family, Kate. I know it."

"Will you at least talk to him before he meets with Croft tomorrow."

D.L. nodded and said, "Chances are they won't come to terms anyway. This whole thing may just buy us more time."

Kate wanted to believe him, but her instincts told her that he and Clay were hiding something.

———

Kate lay in bed trying to fall asleep when she heard a car pull up to the front of the house. She got up, walked to the window, and saw Clay climbing out of a taxi.

She put on her robe with the intent of going downstairs and apologizing for what she had said in the car. But why, she thought to herself. She didn't do anything wrong.

She walked toward the door and overheard Ramona in the foyer telling Clay that D.L. wanted to talk to him. She then heard him climbing the stairs.

Once he reached the top, instead of walking in the direction of D.L.'s room, she heard him approach her room. She quickly climbed back into bed.

There was a light knock on the door. He whispered, "Kate. Are you awake?"

She didn't reply.

He added, "I need to talk to you."

Kate pulled the covers up further. She then heard him exhale a deep breath and walk away.

CHAPTER **21**

By noon the next day, Kate couldn't keep her mind off the meeting down the hall between Clay, Rosenberg, Croft, and a battery of attornys. What made her even more curious was when Kitty told her that Clay and Al had taken breaks from the negotiations to call D.L. She finally realized the best thing for her to do was to go back to Four Oaks.

She gathered her purse and briefcase and walked out of her office. She noticed Al standing in front of the elevators. He had a disgusted look on his face.

She walked toward him and asked, "How's everything going?"

Al shrugged his shoulders and said, "I don't know. I've been told to butt out."

"By Clay?"

"And D.L." He pushed the elevator button three times and added, "I guess my opinion doesn't matter anymore."

Kate's worst fears were being realized.

Al said, "The major terms of the agreement have already been made. They're drawing everything up as we speak."

"What's been agreed to?"

"They're betting the company on one well that probably doesn't have a chance in hell of coming in." Al was close to tears and added, "I don't want any part of this. This is absolutely insane." He stared into her eyes and said, "It's over...unless you can do something to stop it." Al looked around to make sure he wouldn't be overheard. In a low tone of voice, he said, "You have the proxy powers, Kate. You can stop it."

"Dad could take it away just as easily as he gave it."

Al paused and said, "Most of the shares are held in Trusts, right?"

Kate nodded.

Al continued, "The terms of Trust state that D.L. can't exercise any control over how the Trust is managed. In other words, he can't legally force you to give up your powers." Al adjusted his glasses and whispered, "You're in the catbird seat, Kate. Whether you like it or not."

———

That evening, Kate was sitting in the dark at D.L.'s desk sipping her scotch when she heard the helicopter carrying Clay land at Four Oaks. She knew Clay would have to have a drink. Maybe the alcohol would loosen him up and he'd tell her the details of the deal he had struck with Croft.

Clay walked through the front door. As expected, he made his way into the study. He flipped on the wall light switch and was surprised to see Kate.

"Hi," she said.

Clay tried to act casual and replied, "Mind if I join you."

"Please."

Clay walked to the bar and poured himself a drink and asked, "Have you talked to Rosenberg."

Kate nodded and answered, "He wasn't a very happy camper."

Clay grinned.

Kate asked, "Is it a done deal?"

"Yup."

Kate knew she had to exercise restraint if she was going to learn much and asked, "Care to fill me in?"

Clay nodded and said, "First of all, the agreement will be administered by the Judge."

"Burnhouse?"

"Yeah."

"Who's idea was that?"

"It was kinda a mutual thing." Clay sipped his drink and continued, "This is the deal: "We're going to drill a well in the southern Gulf, a block that's referred to as Seahorse Canyon. If it's productive and meets certain criteria, we have the option to buy all the shares Croft controls at twenty-seven dollars per share. If the well doesn't meet the criteria, he buys us out under the same terms."

"The Trusts and the shares Dad holds?"

"Yeah."

"You must be pretty sure the well is going to be good."

Clay grinned and replied, "Nothing is a sure thing, especially when you're drilling in ten thousand feet of water."

"Is there any production in the area?"

"Not within seventy-miles."

"So it's a wildcat?"

Clay nodded.

Kate sat back in her chair, took a sip of her drink, and asked, "So, when is all this supposed to happen?"

"We'll go to court in a couple of days and have the Judge reaffirm it and then start drilling immediately."

Kate paused and asked, "Just like that?"

"Yup. And we've got twenty-one days to reach total depth and run the logs."

"What if there's a storm?"

"We're gambling that there won't be one."

"In August?" Kate realized her voice was getting louder and higher pitched.

"We just have to keep our fingers crossed and hope Mother Nature cooperates."

Kate shook her head and asked, "These criteria. What are they?"

"Basically, the well must show the potential that there can be a field of roughly five hundred million barrels."

"But you're drilling only one well. How can you determine a field from that?"

"By calculating what we call the pay-zone or thickness of the productive zone. This shows up on the electric log data which will then be transmitted by satellite from the ship to the courtroom where there will be a panel of three experts to interpret it for the Judge. And then the well has to be tested...flowed for a few days."

"That's it?" she asked sharply.

Clay sipped his drink and said, "Pretty much."

Kate asked, "Does Dad agree with all this?"

Clay nodded. And then with a slight grin, he said, "But the agreement has to be signed by you. No signature, no deal."

Kate shouted, "I'll be damned if I'm going to agree to this!"

Clay chugged his drink, put it on the desk, and replied, "Then we'll just sit back and watch Croft pick away at us like a vulture."

"You sonofabitch!"

Clay placed his hands on the desk, leaned over, and said, "Listen, Kate. Unless you can come up with something better, you don't have much of a choice but to agree to this. It's all in your hands now, my dear."

———

Croft gazed across the night skyline from his fifty-fifth floor office and thought the deal with the Drummonds was too good to be true. Did they have something up their sleeve? Were they simply trying to buy more time? The fact that D.L. and his sons had broken their commitment to buy his and his father's shares in eighty-six was never far from his mind.

Why would the Drummonds risk their shares on one well that has a thousand to one chance of being a producer? And why would they agree to a buyout on terms? Twenty-five percent down and paid out over three years. This gave Ram the opportunity to arrange junk bond financing rather than having to go through First Nation. Now, there was no way Truesdale could stop him.

Finally, the Drummond deal was his. And rather than get in a prolonged legal battle, which could take several months, if not years, he figured he would be in control of the company within three to four weeks.

But throughout the negotiations, while the attorneys and technical experts bickered over the details, he kept thinking about how he could make sure the well would never get drilled in the first place.

First, he figured he needed to get Minerals Management to stop, or at the very least, delay the drilling so that the company could not meet its twenty-one day deadline. Arlen Mercer could pull that off, especially if he was paid a premium for his shares. Perfect!

Secondly, he had been reading about how several environmental groups, like Greenpeace, had been lobbying Congress to restrict deep-water exploration. Their rationale was that the deeper the drilling, the more the risk of blowouts and oil spills. In fact, conservationists had threatened to file injunctions to stop drilling in waters deeper than five thousand feet. And what better deal for them to jump on than one being drilled in over ten thousand feet of water - a new world record.

Not only could an injunction delay drilling, but maybe some of those eco-terrorists could disrupt operations. If those whackos trying to protect an owl in Oregon put nails in trees so that loggers would injure themselves, they sure as hell could come up with a way to disrupt drilling operations. And the easiest way to get around any kind of tortuous interference issue in the agreement would be to simply make an anonymous phone call. That'll rile them up.

Lastly, Croft knew the controversy with the Mexican government over oil rights in the southern Gulf of Mexico could be re-ignited. If there was even the slightest chance the Mexican government believed that the Seahorse Canyon well would drain oil reserves in their territorial waters, drilling would, at the very least, be delayed. Simply having his geologist write a report implying that should do the trick.

All of this can be done, he thought, to make it absolutely airtight. I'll be in control of the company. I can sell it off in pieces and make a fortune.

But what about Kate. I shouldn't have talked so harshly to her the other night. Maybe there is a chance we can get back together. Since I'll control the company, maybe I don't have to sell everything off right away. Maybe she and her kids could continue to work there. There has to be a way I could get her to love me again. I know she still cares for me. I know it.

CHAPTER 22

"Have you seen the agreement with Croft?" Kate asked Brock the next morning as she walked into his office.

Brock nodded and said, "I can't believe Pops went along with this."

Kate sat down across from the desk and asked, "Is there any possible way this could work out?"

Brock frowned. He picked up a copy of the agreement that he had placed several yellow post-it tabs on to mark pages and replied, "Well, the first thing is to drill the well in twenty-one days. Based on the water depth and depth they plan to drill, I calculated it would take at least five weeks. And that's if nothing goes wrong."

"Clay said even if there's a storm, the well still has to be drilled."

Brock nodded, pointed to a large map on the wall, and said, "There's a tropical depression forming around Jamaica as we speak."

Kate exhaled a deep breath. She asked, "What about these tests and stuff on the well."

Brock leafed through the document, found the page he was looking for and replied, "There are three technical criteria that must be met when the electric logs are run." He pointed to the wall at the long sheets of graphs with squiggly lines on them and continued, "Oil and gas rock formations look like sponges with pores. One of the things logs do is to measure the number of these pores, or porosity. They also give us an indication of what we call permeability, which basically is how many channels there are in a formation. Oil and gas migrates. The more migration, the larger the field."

"The agreement says that certain...percentages have to be met."

"Once, or should I say, *if* they reach total depth, they run the logs and the porosity must be in the range of twenty-six to thirty-six percent, which is damn high. Very few wells we've drilled over the past few years have even come close to that. And as far as permeability, it's measured in what we call milli-darcies. The agreement says the well has to exceed five hundred."

"And that's going to be hard to do?"

"Extremely."

Kate slumped in her seat. She looked into Brock's eyes and said, "You came up with this...this theory about the well? Is there any chance..."

"There isn't a chance in hell the well can be drilled in twenty-one days."

"But let's, for argument's sake, say it can be drilled in time."

Brock paused and said, "The only chance we'll have is if we hit a very large submarine fan. It's a sand formation that *can* be highly productive."

"So it is possible."

"I suppose," he replied. "But it's highly unlikely."

"Why?"

"Because there's no geological data anywhere on that block to support it. This is just a theory, Mom. These fans were formed from underwater volcanic activity millions of years ago and are more likely to be found in water depths of twenty or thirty thousand feet."

"Then how could Clay think that any of this is possible?"

"He's just doing this to unload his shares. It's as simple as that."

In a quivering voice, Kate replied, "I just can't believe he'd do that. I really can't."

Brock paused and said, "I think Clay has convinced Pops to go out in a blaze of glory."

———

Kate sipped on her Merlot after ordering the Pecan Smoked Pork Tenderloin at one of her favorite restaurants in town, the Rainbow Lodge. The cozy, three-story renovated house that overlooked Buffalo Bayou was an ideal place to relax and collect her thoughts over lunch.

She gazed at the Bayou gliding slowly past the gardens and thought about her conversation with Rosenberg. Legally, she could put a halt to the deal with Croft, but should she? After all, Dad had built the company from scratch. He should be able to choose its fate. What about Clay? She remembered D.L. saying that he would never turn his back on his family. Despite what Brock said, something inside told her that Clay genuinely wanted to help. It was, she supposed, going to be his way to redeem himself. But can he pull it off? He had to stop drinking if he was to have a chance.

Suddenly, she noticed Ramsey Croft walking down a stairway toward her table. Kate did the best she could to maintain her composure.

With a slight grin on his face, he walked up to her table and said calmly, "How are you?"

Kate nodded and replied, "Just fine."

"Mind if I have a seat?"

Kate looked around at the surrounding tables. Luckily, the restaurant was having a slow day and most of the customers were elderly women. She replied, "I suppose."

Ram sat down and said casually, "I recommend the Rainbow Trout. It was excellent."

Kate felt herself tense. She tried to make small talk and replied, "I've had it before. It's good."

Ram said, "I really don't care for the decor, but the food is always good." He paused and then said, "You must be pretty disappointed."

"About what?"

Ram grinned and replied, "About the deal Clay negotiated."

With a slight smile, she said, "Oh, that."

"Seriously, you have to feel let down."

Kate wanted to put on an act and say that the deal was in the family's favor, but she knew Ram would see through it. She realized this could be an opportunity to learn what might be on his mind and replied, "I'm a bit disappointed."

"Your father-in-law has also made a lot of unfortunate mistakes."

Kate sipped her wine and asked, "What do you plan to do with the company after you gain control?"

Ram was startled by the question and replied, "I'm not sure at this point."

"I'd hate to see a lot of our people lose their jobs."

Ram leaned back in his chair and asked, "If I keep the company intact, would you consider staying on?"

Kate's first impulse was to say not in a million years, but she was intrigued by where Ram was going with this. She said, "Under the right circumstances."

Ram smiled and said, "I'd like to see Brock and Kendra stay around as well."

How did he know about Kendra working at the company? There hadn't been any announcements. She chose her words carefully and replied, "They want to see the company survive as well."

Ram seemed pleased and asked, "I am curious. Was it D.L.'s idea for Clay to come back?"

Kate frowned and said, "He came back on his own."

"Does he still drink heavily?"

"Like a fish."

Ram chuckled and said, "I thought so."

By Ram's tone of voice and body language, Kate sensed he still had very strong feelings for her. She said, "I hope he goes back to the Bahamas and never comes back."

Ram grinned.

Kate added, "You know, I have to hand it to you, Ram, you really played your cards right in all this. I have to give you a lot of credit." By the look on his face, Kate knew she had managed to stroke his ego.

"Are you serious with this radio station guy? What's his name?"

"Rex Novack."

Ram nodded.

"No, not at all," said Kate. "We're just friends."

"I'm glad."

Kate smiled.

Ram looked into her eyes and asked, "Do you think...maybe...we could start seeing each other again?"

Kate's strategy was working. She said, "Don't you think we should wait until after the well is drilled?"

"I suppose you're right," he said trying to hide his exhilaration. "I still have the Aspen house. There's no reason why we couldn't slip out of town quietly for a few days."

Kate put her hand on his, smiled, and said, "We'll see."

Ram placed his other hand on hers and replied, "I want it to be like it was, Kate."

Kate simply nodded.

Ram looked at his watch and said, "I have to go." He stood and added, "I'm really glad we talked."

———

Kate looked up at him. She did the best she could to look vulnerable and whispered, "Me, too."

Kate walked through the front door of her home in Tanglewood later that night and met Rex. She said, "I'm sorry we haven't been able to see each other," and kissed him on the cheek.

"I've really missed you," he said as he held her in his arms and began kissing her neck just below her left ear.

Kate leaned her head back and was immediately aroused. It had been over a week since they had made love.

Rex continued kissing her lightly from one side of her neck to the other.

She didn't know why, but for a split second, the image of her and Ramsey Croft making love in front of the fireplace in Aspen flashed through her mind. She asked, "How about a drink?"

"No," said Rex. "I want to make passionate love to you on the stairs."

Kate laughed, grabbed his hand, and led him through the dining room and into the kitchen.

She grabbed a Heineken out of the refrigerator and handed it to him and then poured herself a scotch and water.

When she turned around, Rex's demeanor had changed from a boyish anxiousness to more serious. She asked, "What's wrong?" and walked over to him.

Rex paused and seemed to be searching for the words and replied, "If you're having second thoughts...I mean, if you aren't ready to get married, just tell me."

Kate grabbed his hand and said, "This is a really tough time right now, Rex. I really don't know what I want."

Rex looked into her eyes.

Kate added, "Dad doesn't have much longer to live. The whole thing with Croft. Clay. It's all so hard right now."

In a weak tone of voice, he asked, "Why didn't you tell Clay about us?"

"I don't know. I guess I hadn't had a chance to."

Rex frowned.

Kate asked, "Why does it even matter?" I don't need this right now, she thought to herself.

He stroked her cheek with the back of his hand and said, "Listen, I know I can never take the place of Dirk. I can live with that. I can. All I want to do is make you happy."

Kate smiled. She wanted to confide in him about the wiretapping, the meeting with Croft, and the dilemma Clay and D.L. had put her in, but she knew she had to deal with it herself. Besides, it seemed the more she talked about it, the more likely she would fall back into a depression.

Rex added, "We'll get through all this."

Kate nodded and said, "I'll be staying at the ranch for the next three weeks or so to take care of Dad. Brock and Haley and Kendra are coming out, too."

Rex avoided eye contact and replied, "That's probably a good idea."

Kate drew Rex close to her and said, "But I don't have to go back for a few hours."

Rex smiled.

———

Kate arrived at *Four Oaks* at half past midnight and was met at the front door by Ramona, who was clearly upset about something. Kate's first thought was that it had something to do with Dad and she regretted that she had stayed so long in town.

Ramona said, "Clay came home about a half hour ago. He passed out in the study and I had to get some of the hands to carry him to bed."

Kate exhaled a deep breath and shook her head.

CHAPTER 23

Clay's head was throbbing as he made his way down the stairs the next morning. He hoped Kate had left for work. Unfortunately, she was reading the newspaper in the dining room.

Before he could say good morning, she looked up from her paper, and with a scowling look on her face said, "Well, look what the cat drug in. Out doing a little partying last night, were we?"

Clay grumbled and poured himself a cup of coffee.

Kate stayed on the offensive and added, "Did you remember the ranch hands hauling your ass to bed last night?"

Clay sat down and answered, "I could have made it."

"Not according to Ramona."

"Was she up?"

Kate nodded and said, "And for some reason, *I've* been gettin' grief all morning."

"Why you?"

Kate shrugged her shoulders and answered, "All I know is that she's really pissed. You're in *her* house now, you know."

"She's just..."

Ramona walked through the kitchen door, looked at Clay, and said, "You probably can't stomach breakfast this morning, can you?"

Clay was taken back by the harsh tone of voice and answered, "Yeah, I could eat something."

Ramona untied her apron, threw it on a chair and said, "Well, then go ahead and make it yourself," and stormed out of the room.

Clay looked at Kate while she chuckled.

He said, "Jeez-sus!"

"You know she doesn't like anybody drinkin' too much."

Clay shook his head and replied, "You know, when Dirk and I were teenagers, her husband, Carlos, came home drunk as hell one night. She had locked her bedroom door, but ol' Carlos kept pounding away saying he wanted in, and she told him to go out to the barn." He sipped his coffee and continued, "We figured he left. And then, all of a sudden, we hear this crashing sound. We got up, ran into the hallway, and saw that he knocked the door down." Clay smiled and added, "He was getting up off the floor and kept saying, 'You better be glad I want to still crawl in bed with you, old woman!' Then, I'll never forget this: she picked up a porcelain pitcher next to her bed and threw it at him. It hit him right in the head and knocked him out cold."

Kate laughed.

Clay said, "Mom and Ramona had to drag him to the hospital to get something like ten stitches."

"You better be glad she didn't do that to you last night."

"Ah, she'll get over it," he scoffed.

Kate put her paper down and asked, "Where did you go anyway?"

"I was just playing cards with a few of my old buddies."

"You shouldn't be driving when you're drunk like that."

"Okay, Mom," he replied sarcastically.

Kate didn't care for his remark. There was a slight pause in the conversation and then she said, "I talked to Brock about the Seahorse Canyon deal."

"And?"

"He said that there wasn't a chance in hell it could get drilled in twenty-one days."

Clay frowned and said, "He's wrong."

"It looks like you and Dad have made up your mind anyway."

"So you're not going to try to stop it?"

"I'll go along with it on one condition."

"And what's that?"

"If you get some help for your drinking problem."

Clay's eyebrows raised. He replied, "I could stop any time I want."

"That's bull and you know it!"

"I'm going to be spending a lot of time on the rig. And I assure you there isn't any booze out there."

Kate exhaled a deep breath and said, "It's nothing to be ashamed of, Clay."

"Ah, c'mon, Kate. Don't start this."

Kate paused and said, "I needed help once and got it."

Clay's brow furrowed. He asked, "With drinking?"

"No, I overdosed on sleeping pills a few weeks after Dirk's death. Luckily, Dad found me in time."

Clay was speechless.

Kate added, "I never thought I would go to some shrink, but I found a doctor who really helped me through everything. It's not a sign of being weak or anything like that, Clay. Can you please just talk with him? That's all I ask."

Clay felt very uncomfortable and said, "I've just been under a lot of pressure, that's all."

"And you don't think that's going to get worse with this crazy deal of yours?"

Clay had to admit to himself that he was drinking more than usual. He said, "I *do* need to cut back a little."

"His name is Henry Massey. He runs a rehab clinic in Kingwood. The place is really nice...exclusive."

Clay sighed, "*If...if* I talk with this guy, I don't want anybody to know about it."

"I promise."

"Don't tell the old man or Ramona or anyone else."

Kate smiled and replied, "It'll just be between you and me."

Clay paused and said, "Okay. I'll talk with him, but that'll be it."

Kate got up from the table, kissed him on the cheek and said, "I'll call him right now and try to get you an appointment this afternoon."

———

Clay was curious why a rehab clinic would be so far out in the country as Kate drove down a long, dead-end road cut through thick stands of pine trees. He pictured the place would look like a hospital or be in some sort of sterile building. But when they finally reached it, he was surprised to see a large, two-story Victorian home.

He asked, "This is it?"

"I told you it was exclusive. It's really peaceful."

"You stayed out here?"

"For about two weeks."

"What do you do? Just sit around?"

Kate smiled and replied, "I'll let Dr. Massey tell you."

She parked the car.

They walked up a flight of steps and through the front door.

Clay looked around. The foyer had a small seating area, rather than a formal reception area. The staircase was made of thick oak and everywhere he looked there were antique furnishings and even lamps with lampshades with those stringy things hanging down.

A slightly-built, middle-aged man with curly black hair wearing wire-rimmed glasses walked down the hallway toward them. He smiled, hugged Kate, and said in a very calm tone of voice, "It's good to see you, Kate. You look great."

Kate embraced him firmly.

The man looked over Kate's shoulder and said, "And you must be Clay. I'm Henry Massey."

The guy seemed kinda feminine, Clay thought to himself. He extended his hand.

The doctor cupped his hands over Clay's and said, "It's a pleasure meeting you."

Clay managed a smile.

Kate said, "Well, I'm going to run and do some shopping while you gentlemen have a talk."

Massey looked at Clay and added, "I'm looking forward to getting to know you."

Clay felt a bit uneasy and wondered if the guy was a homosexual.

Kate kissed Clay on the cheek and said, "I'll be back in an hour or so, okay?"

Clay nodded.

Massey said, "Please come with me, Clay."

Clay followed the doctor through a living room and into a large library with wood bookshelves extending from the floor to ceiling.

"This is our reading room," said Massey. "Over the years, many of our former residents and friends have been generous contributors to it."

Clay noticed a section in the corner for magazines and newspapers.

Massey must have noticed him looking at the area and commented, "Other than one TV in the dining room, this is our only source of daily news. No radios or computers."

Massey walked into a small office and asked Clay to have a seat in an armchair with blue, velvet-like material.

Clay looked behind the desk and saw several photographs of children and asked, "Is that your family?"

A wide smile appeared on the doctor's face. He replied, "Yes. I have seven children, four boys and three girls and five grandchildren." With a gleam in his eye, he added, "My wife and I have truly been blessed."

Clay had clearly misjudged the man's sexual orientation.

Massey added, "I'm sorry she couldn't be here to meet you. She's at a retreat in Santa Fe with some of our residents." He settled in his chair, crossed his legs and asked, "What has Kate told you about us?"

"Very little, except that she has...stayed here."

Massey smiled and said, "She is a remarkable woman."

Clay nodded.

Massey continued, "I used to be one of your typical practicing neurologists who was part of the Western medical establishment. It was not until I realized that my wife was seriously abusing drugs and alcohol that I found my true calling."

For the next few minutes, the doctor explained how he started the clinic twelve years ago and how he tries to counsel no more than ten 'residents' at a time. He emphasized that his practice requires that he gives each person a great deal of personal attention.

He then explained that the house sits on over fifty acres, has several hiking and horseback trails, and that his four nursing assistants can arrange Yoga, Tai Chi, or any other mind-body relaxation classes.

Clay didn't know what Tai Chi was, but didn't want to show his ignorance.

Finally, after dispensing with the introductory part of the routine, Massey asked, "So, may I ask why you've come to see us?"

Clay's first impulse was to say because Kate wanted him to, but then simply replied, "I drink too much."

"Are you an alcoholic?"

"An alcoholic? No, I don't think so." Clay was beginning to feel slightly uncomfortable. "I could stop."

"What is your definition of an alcoholic, if I may ask?"

"Well, I guess I really don't know."

Massey grinned slightly and said, "That's a good start."

Clay wasn't sure what that meant.

The doctor continued, "Kate and I have discussed your history at length and, if you decide to let us work with you, I certainly want to know more. But the most important question I have for you is this: Do you want help?"

Clay paused and said, "I suppose so."

"If you aren't sure, Clay, I can't help you."

Clay didn't expect the guy to be so blunt.

Doctor Massey repeated calmly, "Do you want help?"

Clay gulped and replied, "Yes."

———

An hour and a half later, Kate was rocking on a chair on the front porch of Massey's home when Clay joined her. When he sat in the chair next to her, she noticed he had a spacey look on his face and she wondered if she had had the same reaction when she first met the doctor.

She asked, "How did it go?"

"Fine."

"He's very perceptive, isn't he?"

Clay nodded, looked at her and replied, "I never talked like that before. You know, opened up."

Kate smiled and asked, "So what would you like to do?"

"He suggested that I stay here for two or three days and see how I like it."

"Are you going to?"

Clay looked at her and seemed to snap out of his trance-like state and said, "I think it would do me a lot of good, but I should be on the rig."

"I'm sure a few days won't hurt. Wouldn't it be good to just get away from everything. Brock will take care of things."

Clay paused and said, "I suppose you're right."

"I'll tell you what. You stay here tonight, and I'll bring you some clothes in the morning."

Clay simply nodded.

———

D.L. had to admit to himself that he liked the chair lift Kate had installed along the stairway as it came to a stop at the bottom of the stairs. What he didn't like, however, was the fact that Brock had to pick him up and put him in a wheelchair. The whole thing made D.L. feel like an invalid. And even though it was a relief to finally get out of his room, he was not in a good mood.

Brock wheeled him into the dining room. Kate, Kendra, Haley and Rosenberg greeted him. As usual, the ladies hugged him.

No matter how everyone tried to be up-beat, D.L. sensed that they were surprised about his appearance. He said, "This is what a dying man looks like."

No one commented, although Kate frowned and shook her head.

D.L. asked, "How 'bout a scotch?"

Kate replied, "I don't think that's such a good idea with all the medication you're taking."

"Ah, the hell with the medication."

Ramona came out of the kitchen carrying a serving dish of T-bone steaks.

D.L. said to her, "Get me a scotch."

Ramona looked at Kate who nodded.

D.L. wheeled himself up to the head of the table, looked around and asked, "Where's Clay?"

Kate paused and replied, "He's out of town."

"Where did he go?"

"I'm not sure," she replied.

D.L. looked at her suspiciously and asked, "You sent him off to that shrink doctor friend of yours, didn't you?"

Everyone at the table looked at Kate.

D.L. scoffed, "Work is the best medicine."

"Not always," Kate replied.

D.L. thought to himself, what the hell does she know? She tried to kill herself once.

Ramona brought him his drink, served him steak, a twice-baked potato, and broccoli.

Everyone passed around serving dishes in silence.

D.L. sipped his drink, looked at his steak, but didn't eat. He then looked down at the other end of the table at Rosenberg and said, "This deal with Croft. Call it off."

Al's eyes widened. He asked, "What are you talking about?"

"You heard me. Cancel it."

Al looked at Kate and then back to D.L. and replied, "We've already agreed to it. The agreement has been signed."

"Well, find a way to get out of it. I don't like the smell of this whole thing."

"You...you agreed to the 'whole thing!'"

"The hell I did. It was Clay and Brock's idea."

Brock was about to say something, but Kate put her hand up as a signal for him to be quiet.

D.L. continued, "The only reason that bastard agreed to it was because he probably couldn't get a bank to give him the money."

Al's face reddened, and he said, "I told you that before."

"When? You never said that!"

Al exhaled a deep breath.

D.L. added, "He's got something up his sleeve. I don't know what it is. Just get out of it!"

"It's too late!" shouted Rosenberg.

D.L. said, "Well, then I'll have to do it." He turned to Kate and said, "I want you to give me back your stock proxy."

Kate blushed and began to tremble slightly.

Al asked, "What do you mean give it back to you?"

"Don't you understand English, for Christ's sake?" He looked around the table and said, "You're all just waitin' for me to die, aren't you? None of you gives a damn about what happens to the company!" He took a long swig of his drink and added, "I'm going to the office tomorrow. I'll straighten this goddamn thing out!" He threw his napkin on the table. It knocked over a glass of water. And then he wheeled himself toward his study.

———

Kate looked around the table. Everyone was stunned.

She had seen D.L. angry several times throughout the years, but never had he been so mean-spirited. She asked Ramona, "What kind of pills is he taking?"

"Darvon...painkillers for his knee."

"That's it?"

"I think so."

Al said, "This must be some kind of, I don't know, stage he's going through. Cancer does that sort of thing."

Kate made a mental note to call Dr. Shahir, D.L.'s oncologist, and said, "We can't let him go to the office. He'll reveal the terms of the Seahorse Canyon deal."

Al nodded and replied, "I agree, but the confidentiality clause isn't very realistic in the first place. Once Minerals Management finds the plan of exploration was falsified, word will get out anyway."

Kate asked, "What are you talking about?"

Brock looked at Al and back to Kate and answered, "The rig was originally permitted to drill in six thousand five hundred feet of water.

But the location was changed, and we'll be drilling into a trench that bottoms-out at a little over ten thousand feet."

Al asked Ramona, "Could you get us another bottle of wine?"

Ramona nodded and walked into the kitchen.

Al leaned forward and whispered, "D.L. got Tito to issue a false drilling report."

"Jee-zuz!" said Kate as she shook her head.

Brock said, "Minerals Management could stop the drilling *and* fine the hell out of us."

"Knowing Tito," added Al, "he'll take all the blame and probably be banned from working in the Gulf."

Kate exhaled a deep breath and said, "I don't like this whole deal with Croft either. But, whatever we do, we have to try to stop Dad from stirrin' things up."

Al said, "Good luck."

———

D.L. sat in his wheelchair among the boxes of files in his study and realized that he had never felt so exhausted in his whole life. It seemed as if the cancer was sapping his energy more and more everyday. But he wasn't going to give into it. He'd be damned if he was going to let it take him before *he* was ready.

He also felt alone. He felt as if no one could ever understand what the company, and the many employees who had been so loyal to him over the years, meant to him. He had started with nothing and built something that was special, something enduring. Not too many people in this world could say that. Yes, it had been a struggle every step of the way, but it had all been worth it. And I'm not going to let this damn cancer or Croft or anyone destroy it.

CHAPTER 24

Ramsey Croft smiled after he ended the phone call with a junk bond dealer who had agreed to finance the Drummond deal. Despite having to pay fourteen percent interest, he knew he could pay off the acquisition loan with the sale of the company's oil and gas reserves. He figured he would only make one, possibly two, interest payments.

The next step would be to refinance the company's debt with traditional bank financing. It shouldn't be a problem. He had run the projections himself. And once Wall Street knew the details of how he would restructure the drilling division, the value of his shares would soar. He figured that within six months every major offshore drilling company in the world would want to acquire Drummond.

Conservatively, he stood to make around one hundred and twenty to one hundred and sixty million dollars. And the whole process was going to take about eighteen months, two years at the most.

Suddenly, the receptionist buzzed him. In a quivering voice, she said, "Mr. Croft, Mr. Truesdale insisted on seeing you."

"He's here?"

"He's on his way to your office. I'm sorry."

Ram hadn't counted on confronting his father-in-law with his plan to exercise his option so soon. He would have preferred to wait until the junk bond deal was funded and then he could simply send Truesdale a check.

Truesdale opened the door to his office and said, "We need to talk." He placed a thick black binder on Ram's desk and remained standing.

Ram remained seated.

Truesdale was an imposing figure. He stood at around six foot four and weighed over two hundred and fifty pounds. But the most striking part of his physical features was his enormous head and protruding, dimpled chin.

Ram wanted to go on the offensive and said, "I don't appreciate you barging in like this! I'm busy!"

Truesdale smiled and replied, "Trying to get financing for the Drummond deal, I take it."

"Not *trying*. I have. And I'll be buying you out."

"Just like that, huh?"

Ram nodded.

"Not if I don't want to be."

"You don't have a choice. We have an agreement. I'm going alone on this one! And there isn't a damn thing you can do about it!"

Truesdale grinned and replied, "Really. Well, I wonder what would happen if word gets out that you were behind the wiretapping of Drummond's offices?"

Ram was stunned, but managed to say, "Nugent...he set it all up."

"Do you honestly think I care if he goes to jail, too?" Truesdale pointed to the binder he had placed on Ram's desk and said, "Here's also a little bedtime reading for you. It's a chronology of just about every dirty side deal you and that buffoon, Schultz, did over the years. My guess is that you two have committed securities, bank fraud, tax evasion, embezzlement, and even money laundering." Truesdale leaned over Ram's desk and added, "The Justice Department could find this very interesting reading."

Ram picked up the binder, opened it, and skimmed the first few pages. It was a summary of the various transactions he and Schultz did as far back as nineteen ninety-two. How did Truesdale find all this out? Schultz must have spilled his guts.

Truesdale said, "I've done my homework, haven't I? With a little help, of course, from your old buddy Schultz."

Ram was speechless.

Truesdale said, "Don't force me to do this." He chuckled, "I wouldn't want my daughter to have to visit you in prison."

"You sonofabitch!"

Truesdale laughed and said, "I have to get to Chicago, but Nugent and I will be back tomorrow night. I want you to have the papers drawn up assigning me all the shares *we* control. Stick in an advisory fee of two million for you, and then we'll call it a day. Sound good?"

Ram didn't respond.

Truesdale began walking out and added, "Be at Brennans tomorrow night at eight." He grinned and said, "We'll celebrate."

———

D.L. wheeled himself down the hallway and entered Rosenberg's office. Al was on the phone and told the caller he had to call him back.

D.L. said, "I've called a meeting with all the exploration people."

Al got up from his chair.

D.L. said, "I want to find out what the chances are that Seahorse Canyon is going to work out."

Al shook his head. He tried to remain calm and explained, "None of them, except Brock, knows that we're going to drill in ten thousand feet of water."

"Why not?"

"We have a confidentiality clause in the agreement, remember? We have to break it to them right before we tell Minerals Management that the plan of exploration we filed was wrong."

"Ah, the hell with that!"

"Don't do this D.L.! We've got enough to deal with!"

D.L. wheeled himself around and headed for the door.

Al moved in front of him.

D.L. shouted, "Get out of my way!"

"Let me handle everything, please."

D.L. looked into Al's eyes and said, "This is still my company!"

Al gritted his teeth and stepped aside.

———

Croft needed to blow off some steam at a shooting range after his meeting with Truesdale. He adjusted his eye glasses, flipped the safety off his new Berretta Elite nine millimeter handgun, and with both hands steadying it, took aim at the target fifty yards away.

He had read the documents his father-in-law left and was astonished at how much backup information there was: copies of checks; wire transfer receipts to several different offshore bank accounts; and locations of safety deposit boxes where Ram kept cash. It was clear that Schultz had provided some of the information, but there were several transactions that didn't even involve him.

How could Truesdale dig all this up, he wondered? Was Nugent behind it? He must have been. Who else may have been involved? Could Monique have known about any of this?

Ram exhaled a breath, squeezed the trigger, and fired the first shot. He couldn't see where the bullet hit, but knew it would either be in the bulls-eye or within an inch or two of it.

Despite who was involved or how the information was obtained, Ram was boxed in. There was no way out. Truesdale had won again.

He exhaled another breath, gritted his teeth, and began firing until he emptied the remaining nine shots in the clip.

He hated Truesdale, now more than ever, and would do whatever he had to do to get rid of him. At this point, he would even consider having both Truesdale and Nugent killed. But how? Who could do it? Tran?

He placed the warm gun on a table and pushed a button to retrieve the target. As the target began moving toward him on a wire, he wondered whether Tran was capable of murder. He has dumped a body in the ship channel. But murder! That was different. Even if Tran wouldn't do it, maybe he knew someone who would.

The target stopped within a few feet of him. As expected, the grouping was dead center and had completely torn out the bulls-eye.

———

Kate was dining alone at the ranch when Rosenberg arrived.

He walked into the dining room and said, "All of the geologists have quit."

Kate was stunned and asked, "All because of the meeting with Dad?"

Al nodded and said, "By tomorrow, I'm sure the press will get wind of Seahorse Canyon and then the board and shareholders will come out of their shoes." Al took off his glasses, rubbed his eyes and asked, "Shouldn't we issue a press release?"

Kate nodded. She put her fork down, pushed her plate aside, and said, "Face it, Al, the directors and stockholders can bitch all they want about us agreeing to the deal with Croft, but it's our shares that are involved, not theirs."

"They're going to think we've sold them out."

Kate frowned and said, "They can think whatever they damn well choose!"

Al blushed and seemed surprised by her strong tone of voice. He replied, "I suppose this whole thing was going to be found out sooner or later."

"Is it possible any of the directors or shareholders could take legal action to stop us from drilling the well?"

Al pondered the idea and said, "I'm not sure. I don't see how they could. Of course, if the well is a dud, they could make a very strong claim we were using corporate assets in an attempt to enrich ourselves." Al paused and then said, "But the family could always reimburse the company the amount it lost."

"Which would be how much?"

"About seven million, according to Clay. But that doesn't mean things won't get real ugly for awhile."

"Can things get any uglier than they are now?"

Al grimaced and said, "We've got to find a way to control D.L. He'll make things worse."

Kate paused. She knew what she was about to suggest would shock Al and said, "We need to sedate him."

Al's eyes widened and his jaw dropped. He replied, "You can't be serious?"

"You have a better way?"

"Well," he said defensively, "it just seems a little drastic, that's all."

"I have an appointment with Dr. Shahir tomorrow afternoon to see if he can prescribe some sort of sedative."

"D.L. won't take anything like that."

Kate leaned forward and said, "Well, we'll just have to make sure he doesn't know what he's taking, won't we?"

Croft had second thoughts about meeting with Tran as he walked into the smoke-filled Vietnamese restaurant. Could he trust him? How could he be sure Tran wasn't still working for Nugent?

Tran was seated at the same corner table where they had originally met.

Ram sat down.

Tran seemed irritated and asked, "So what's the big rush to meet?"

Ram looked around to make sure no one would overhear their conversation and said, "My father-in-law..."

"Jonas Truesdale."

"How do you know that."

Tran took a drag on his cigarette and replied, "Go on."

"He's blackmailing me."

"With what?"

"That's not important, is it?"

"Is it serious enough to put you in prison?"

Reluctantly, Ram nodded.

Tran asked, "So what do you want me to do about it?"

"I wanted to know if you knew someone...someone who could take care of this for me."

Tran grinned and said, "You mean kill him."

Ram nodded and replied, "Nugent, too."

"You know what they say," quipped Tran, "the only good lawyer is a dead one."

Ram was not amused and asked, "Do you know someone or not?"

Tran took another drag on his cigarette and asked, "How much are you willing to pay?"

"I don't know. What does this sort of thing cost?"

"Two hundred thousand, if you want it done right."

"That's not a problem."

"You'll need to pay half now and half after it's done."

"Pay you?"

Tran nodded.

"How do I know you won't run off with it?"

Tran smiled and answered, "You don't."

Ram didn't respond.

Tran stood to leave and asked, "Let me know what you want to do?"

"Sit down," Ram said harshly.

Tran sat.

Ram added, "He and Nugent are coming back into town tomorrow. I'm having dinner with them at Brennans. It's a restaurant downtown."

"What time?"

"Eight."

Tran stroked his chin and asked, "Where will they be staying?"

"Truesdale always stays at the Ritz."

"The one near the Galleria?"

Ram nodded.

Tran asked, "How will they get to the restaurant?"

"Huh?"

"Taxi? Limo?"

"Oh, Truesdale always hires a limo when he's in town."

"Do you know what service he uses?"

"I don't know, why?"

Tran pulled a pen from his shirt pocket. He wrote something on a napkin, shoved it across the table, and said, "Wire transfer the money to this account by noon tomorrow."

"So, whoever you'll get to do this...they're good?"

Tran grinned and replied, "Don't worry about it. The less you know, the better."

CHAPTER 25

Clay was jogging along one of the hiking trails behind the clinic at ten o'clock the next morning. It was already ninety-seven degrees; the humidity was suffocating. But it felt good to work up a sweat.

He had met with Dr. Massey at eight o'clock. It was more or less a get-acquainted session. Massey asked him some basic questions about where he was born and some of his childhood experiences in West Texas. Surprisingly, Clay had done most of the talking.

At the end of the hour session, the doctor told Clay he wanted to talk about his adolescence and college years tomorrow and asked Clay to start thinking about what were the most painful times in his life and when he started drinking heavily.

Clay had pondered the question after he left Massey's office. The first thing that came to mind was Heather's first miscarriage. From that point, Clay began his drinking and gambling sprees and having affairs. And it was not long after that the friction between him, the old man, and Dirk also began to build.

He couldn't blame every stupid thing he had done in his life on his failed marriage, but it certainly contributed to his reckless behavior. And the more he thought about it, the more he realized that the only way to make a fresh start was to have someone to share his life with. Was that someone Kate?

Clay quickened his pace. He thought, I have to stop drinking and running away from my past. It's time to start over. I'll prove to Kate that I can clean up my act. It's not too late. I can do it. I know it.

———

Kate knocked on the door of Clay's room at around noon, but there was no answer. She knocked again, entered carrying a suitcase of his clothes, and heard the shower running.

She put the suitcase on the bed.

The bathroom door was open and steam was floating into the room. She could see the silhouette of Clay's body through the white shower curtain. She admitted to herself that it was more sensual not seeing him completely naked.

For a brief moment, she recalled how she and Dirk would take showers together. How they would lather each other with soap, their playfulness and their love-making afterwards.

Clay turned off the shower.

Kate walked to the window and looked out over the pool and toward the walking trails beyond.

She remembered her walks, wondering what she would do for the rest of her life. Dirk was dead. The kids were in college. And she was growing restless with the housewife routine of tennis, lunches at the club with her girlfriends, and charity activities. Her life needed meaning.

It was during her recovery that D.L. suggested she come to work at the company. He told her that Carl Warren, the Director of Investor Relations, had announced he was going to retire in six months and that she would be perfect for the job.

At the time, she had never imagined herself working at the company. She had no training for such a position and knew very little about business. She recalled telling Carl that she couldn't even balance her checkbook. D.L.'s reply was that they had accountants for that sort of thing.

She declined D.L.'s offer at first, but then he convinced her to at least work as Carl's assistant for a few months to get a feel for the job. She loved it. And, according to Carl, who treated her like a daughter, she was perfect for the position.

Kate heard the cabinet door in the bathroom open and said, "Clay, I've brought your clothes."

Clay walked into the room with a towel draped around his waist. He and Dirk had the same build except Clay was slightly taller and his waist was thinner. Despite the years of abusing his body with alcohol, he still looked in pretty good shape.

He smiled and replied, "Thanks, I was beginning to wonder what I was going to wear today."

He had not yet shaven and looked a little rugged, but she liked that. She asked, "So, what have you been doing?"

"I met with Massey this morning."

"How did it go?"

"Good," he said cheerfully. "He's pretty easy to talk to."

Kate was surprised by the answer. She figured it would take Clay at least a few days for him to feel comfortable.

He added, "And then I went jogging in the woods."

Kate smiled and said, "It's a great place, isn't it? Peaceful."

Clay nodded. He opened the suitcase, pulled out some boxer shorts, placed them on the bed, and replied, "I think it'll be good for me to stay here a few days, maybe a week. There isn't much I can do on the rig right now anyway.

"Brock says everything is on schedule." She lied. The crew had been having some problems.

Clay sat down on the bed. He grabbed her hand and gently drew her closer.

She sat next to him.

Clay avoided eye contact and said, "I've been thinking about you ... us."

Kate tensed slightly.

He looked into her eyes and added, "I guess I was just wondering if...if we could just put everything that happened behind us and, you know...start over again."

Kate didn't want to give Clay false hope that they had a future together, but on the other hand, she felt she had to somehow boost his spirits. She had to be careful how she responded and replied, "It's certainly been rough, hasn't it?"

By the look on his face, he was disappointed by her comment. He asked, "Can you...will you forgive me for what I've done? What I've been like?"

Kate didn't know how to answer.

Clay continued, "I've put you, and everyone else, through a hell of a lot lately."

She smiled and said, "Everything is going to work out."

Clay paused and asked, "Will everything work out with us?"

He seemed so vulnerable, Kate thought to herself. She replied, "I don't know, Clay. I'm confused right now, confused about a lot of things."

"I guess I need to know if we at least have a chance together."

Kate began to quiver. She looked into his eyes and nodded.

Clay's face brightened. He kissed her lightly on the lips and then her neck.

Kate felt herself becoming aroused.

She felt the wetness of his lips. She stroked his beard. They kissed deeply.

Clay began to gently lean her back onto the bed.

Kate said, "Clay, we can't do this."

He looked into her eyes.

"This isn't right," she said and got up and walked out the door.

———

Kate was in tears by the time she reached her car. She fumbled in her purse to find her keys and hoped she didn't leave them in Clay's room. She didn't want to face him again. How could she have been so weak, she thought to herself? I *have* to exert more control over this crazy situation!

She finally found her keys. She unlocked the door with the button on the key and climbed behind the wheel. She quickly turned on the engine, lowered the windows, and blasted the air conditioning. She was perspiring heavily.

She put her hands on the steering wheel, leaned forward, and rested her head on it. What was she getting herself into now?

She thought of Rex and felt that she had betrayed him. He was a good, kind man. But did she really love him?

They had been good friends over the years. And even though she knew early on that his intentions were much more than just friendship, she allowed herself to get involved. And now, she was doing the same thing with Clay.

But her feelings for Clay were different from the feelings she had for Rex and for Croft, who had been the first man she had been with since Dirk. Rex was just a friend. Ram was a result of deep loneliness. But what about Clay? What drew her to him so strongly? Was it because she felt sorry for him? She didn't know. All she knew was that it seemed so right. And so wrong.

She looked at her watch. Two-fifteen. She was running late for her appointment with Dr. Shahir. She didn't feel like talking about D.L.'s state of mind and was having second thoughts about asking Shahir to prescribe a sedative. But she knew she had to go through with it. That was a priority now. This thing with Clay, well, she would just have to deal with that the best way she could.

———

I'm sorry to bother you with all this, but I didn't know where to turn," Kate said to Dr. Shahir, who was sitting behind his desk. "He's really acting...erratically."

Shahir smiled in such a way that Kate knew he had had this type of discussion many times before. He replied, "This is all to be expected. But you have to realize, someone like your father-in-law, who has been in control all of his life, is now faced with something that is much stronger than him." The doctor paused and added, "A terminal patient who is going through a lot of pain wants, on one hand, to die...get it all over with. But, on the other hand, his survival instincts kick in. It's quite a conflict."

"But it doesn't seem like he's in a lot of pain."

"I assure you, he is. Frankly, I'm surprised he can do what he's doing. Most patients wouldn't have the energy."

"But what about the paranoia? I've never seen him like this."

"That's all a part of it. The only thing I can tell you is that you and the rest of the family have to be patient."

Kate fidgeted in her seat. She was trying to muster up enough courage to ask him to prescribe a sedative.

Dr. Shahir asked, "Do you want me to give him something to calm him down?"

Kate nodded and said, "But if he knows it's a sedative or anything like that, he may not take it."

"Then we'll give him something in liquid form, but you have to be careful not to give him too much."

"I'll give it to him myself."

Dr. Shahir reached for a prescription pad. He wrote something on it, handed it to her and said, "This should help, but what he needs now more than anything is patience and love."

In a strained voice she replied, "I'm going to be by his side to the end."

———

D.L. sat in his wheelchair as Ramona instructed a ranch hand to put the last of Victoria's files next to his bed. He was getting bored watching TV, he had read enough oil industry magazines, and didn't have the energy to read any more Louis L'Amour paperbacks.

Ramona had that scowling, disapproving look on her face he had come to know over the years. At first, he figured she didn't want him to clutter his room with the old, dusty boxes. But when he started pulling photographs out of one of the boxes, he remembered overhearing a conversation she had had with Kate. Ramona had said going through Victoria's files would only make him more unhappy.

D.L. had to admit he became depressed the first few times he looked at the files. But for some strange reason, he felt a strong urge to retrace his life no matter how painful it would be.

CHAPTER 26

Croft sat alone at a corner table at Brennans and wondered if his father-in-law and Nugent were dead. He checked his watch: eight fifty-five. They were almost an hour late.

Suddenly, he was startled by the maitre d' appearing at his side.

The man said, "Mr. Croft." He leaned down and whispered, "There is a phone call for you. It appears Mr. Truesdale has been in some sort of accident."

———

Croft's heart started to pound harder when he saw a group of police cars, ambulances, fire trucks, and news vans on the Southwest Freeway across from Greenway Plaza. Even though the woman detective told him to come directly to the scene, she didn't give him any details.

Eastbound traffic was being diverted to a feeder road and he wasn't sure how he was going to get to the scene. He pulled up to a policeman directing traffic, rolled his window down, and said, "I'm supposed to see a Detective Tiller."

A news helicopter flew overhead and the policeman couldn't hear what Ram said, but motioned him to move on.

Croft waved his hand for the man to come closer and yelled, "I'm here to see Detective Tiller."

"What's your name?"

"Ramsey Croft."

The man pulled a walkie talkie from his belt and began speaking into it. Ram couldn't hear what he was saying over all the noise.

Amid the chaos in front of him, Croft was able to see smoke coming from what was left of a limousine that Truesdale and Nugent must have been in. He remembered Tran asking how his father-in-law got around town when he was in Houston and figured he may have tampered with the brakes or something.

Curiously, there didn't seem to be any other cars involved with the accident. He assumed if the brakes failed, the limo would have at least run into other cars.

But what baffled Croft even more was how the police knew to call him at the restaurant. Truesdale or Nugent must still be alive, he thought to himself.

The policeman walked up to his car. He directed him to pull up and park on the left side of the road against a concrete barrier and told him Detective Tiller would be right with him.

Croft parked the car and got out to get a better view of the crash scene.

Within a few minutes, a short, stocky African-American woman with hair braids walked up to him and said, "Mr. Croft, I'm Detective Elsa Tiller."

They shook hands.

Ram asked, "What happened?"

"It seems as if a bomb was planted underneath the car Mr. Truesdale was traveling in."

"A bomb? How did you know to call me?"

Tiller's brow furrowed as if she were puzzled by his question, and replied, "We found his date book. Your dinner appointment with him was written down in it."

At that instant, Ram realized he should have asked if Truesdale was alive.

Tiller added, "I'm afraid Mr. Truesdale is dead," and looked at Ram for a reaction.

Ram's mouth gaped open. He did the best he could to appear grieved by covering his face with his hands and then said, "He was my father-in-law."

Tiller paused and said, "I'm sorry."

"Was there another man?"

Tiller nodded and asked, "Do you know who he might be?"

"Probably his attorney, Marty Nugent. The three of us were supposed to have dinner."

"I know this must be hard, Mr. Croft, but we need someone to identify the bodies."

The thought of the idea made Ram shiver.

She continued, "The bodies are being taken to the morgue. If it's okay with you, I'll have someone take you there and then have you brought to my office downtown."

Ram nodded.

"Again," said Tiller, "I'm truly sorry."

"Thank-you."

———

Croft walked down the hallway to Tiller's office with the policewoman escort who had taken him to the morgue. He could not keep the image of Truesdale's and Nugent's charred faces out of his mind. The stench from their burned hair and skin was also something he would never forget.

He had called Monique from his cell phone after leaving the morgue. After telling her what had happened, there was a surprisingly long pause. She then said that she would fly to Houston later tonight and then suddenly started to break down.

One of her butlers came on the line and Ram suggested that her doctor be called. She would definitely need her shrink to get through this, Ram had thought.

Tiller came out of her office, thanked the policewoman, and motioned for Croft to come in.

Ram sat in a chair across from her desk.

Tiller must have noticed Croft looking at the mess on the filing cabinets because she picked up a trash can and pushed the styrafoam cups and fast food paper wrappers into it. She said, "Please excuse the mess. It's been pretty hectic around here lately. Long hours, you know."

Ram grinned slightly.

Tiller sat down and asked, "Can I get you anything?"

"No...no, thank you."

Tiller continued, "Have you called your wife?"

"Yes."

"Is she in town?"

"No, she lives in New York. But she said she's coming in later tonight."

"Are you separated?"

Ram was irritated by the question and asked, "Does it matter?"

Tiller paused and answered, "I suppose not."

"How long is this going to take?" he asked impatiently.

Tiller leaned forward and replied, "I know this must be very unpleasant, Mr. Croft. There's just some paperwork that has to be taken care of." Tiller picked up a pen, checked her watch, and wrote something on a legal pad. She then asked, "What's your wife's name?"

"Monique."

"Okay, you had planned to meet with your father-in-law and his attorney at Brennans. Was this for business or pleasure?"

"Business."

"So you and your father-in-law were business associates?"

"Yes."

"And Mr. Nugent?"

"He was his...our attorney working on a business transaction."

"May I ask what this transaction is?"

Ram was becoming increasingly annoyed, but realized that he should cooperate. He answered, "A stock deal."

"Through Croft and Company?"

Ram was surprised by the question. She must have done some research about him. He replied, "Yes."

"Does it involve a local company?"

Ram was not in the mood to answer and asked "What does that have to do with all this?"

"I'm just doing my job, Mr. Croft."

"Shouldn't you be trying to find who did this, for Christ's sake?"

Tiller maintained her composure and answered, "This is just routine stuff, Mr. Croft. I can assure you, I'm not going to do any sort of insider trading or anything like that."

Ram sensed that he needed to lighten up. He did the best he could to grin and answered, "Drummond Offshore." He noticed Tiller's eyes widen.

She asked, "So you know the Drummond family?"

"Yes."

"Is this some sort of a takeover attempt or something?"

"No, not really."

Tiller jotted something on the pad and then asked, "Does your father-in-law or Nugent have any enemies that would be capable of doing anything like this?"

A lot of people hated the pricks, Ram thought to himself. He replied, "Nobody I know of."

"Is your father-in-law worth a lot of money?"

"Yes."

"A few million? More?"

"Forbes had him down for five hundred."

"Five hundred million?"

Ram nodded.

"Whew! So what happens to all that? Who inherits it?"

Ram fidgeted in his chair and answered, "Most of his assets are in a foundation, but the remaining estate goes to my wife."

"He wasn't married?"

"His wife died several years ago."

"No other children?"

Ram shook his head and realized he was perspiring.

Tiller paused and then said, "We traced the plate on the limousine to a service who told us your father-in-law was staying at the Ritz. You've probably heard that the Prime Minister of Israel is in town."

"I've read about it."

"Well, he and his entourage are also staying at the Ritz. We suspect someone was trying to assassinate the Prime Minister, but planted the bomb underneath the wrong limo."

What a lucky coincidence! Ram thought to himself.

Tiller added, "So what that means is that the FBI is going to be turning over every rock and will probably want to talk to you and your wife."

"I don't have a problem with that."

"Are you planning to go out of town?"

"Probably to New York for the funeral."

"Other than that?"

"I was planning to go to my home in Aspen in a few weeks," he lied.

"But your office can get in touch with you?"

"Of course."

"Would it be possible to have your wife come in tomorrow morning, say around ten."

"I'll ask her."

Tiller handed him a business card and said, "Let me know if that's a problem."

"Okay."

She stood, offered her hand, and said, "I appreciate your cooperation, Mr. Croft. Again, my condolences."

———

At ten minutes past midnight, Croft waited in his car outside a hangar at the airport for the Gulfstream jet carrying Monique to come to a stop. She was probably a mess, he thought. More than likely, she had been hitting the sauce or popping Prozac to calm her nerves. He was certain, in any event, that her father's death was going to screw her up more than she already was.

Ram climbed out of the car.

The jet parked and a hostess Ram had not seen before opened the doorway.

He walked up the steps, smiled at the young woman, and made his way to the back of the plane.

Lily, a middle-aged woman who always traveled with Monique, was packing a carry-on bag. Ram had always suspected that they were lovers.

Monique come out of the restroom. She looked like a wreck.

Despite a heavy coat of make-up, she couldn't hide the puffiness and dark circles under her eyes. She also had her signature wide-eyed, crazed look on her face.

As he approached her, Monique began to shake slightly and then held out her arms.

They embraced, but did not exchange a kiss.

She reeked of alcohol and cigarette smoke.

In a consoling tone of voice, Ram said, "I'm really sorry, Monique."

She was having a hard time standing. Ram took her by the hand and they sat down. He looked at Monique's escort who immediately got the message to leave them alone.

Monique sniffled and said, "Do the police know anything yet?"

"They think someone was trying to kill the Prime Minister of Israel. He was staying at the Ritz, too."

Monique began to weep and then said, "Who would do such a thing? Why?"

Ram put his hand on hers and replied, "I don't know, Monique. I don't know." For a brief instant, he genuinely felt sorry for her. Yes, there had been a time when he loved her, but he could never forget the endless badgering and the times she would run to Daddy every time they had even a mild argument. The hell with her. He refused to feel any remorse. He was glad the bastard was dead.

Monique wiped her eyes and said, "Will you come back to New York with us? The funeral..."

Ram nodded and said, "We've got to see the police in the morning and then we can go."

Monique paused and said, "Spend some time with me, Ram. Please. I've missed you."

Ram smiled, rubbed her hand, and said, "Let's take one thing at a time right now, okay?"

CHAPTER 27

The next morning Kate poured herself a cup of coffee in the dining room, opened the folded newspaper, and was shocked to see the main headline with a picture of Jonas Truesdale:

Suspected Car Bomb Assassination Attempt on Israeli Prime Minister Kills New York Industrialist

Wealthy Industrialist, Jonas Truesdale, and his attorney, Martin Nugent, and a driver whose identity has not yet been disclosed, were killed in a car bombing that police believe may have been intended for the Prime Minister of Israel. The limousine, rented through the Ritz Carlton where Truesdale and Nugent and the Prime Minister's entourage were staying, exploded at approximately seven-fifty yesterday evening across from the Greenway Plaza on the Southwest Freeway. According to a reliable source, the FBI has taken over the investigation. The local FBI office declined to comment.

Jonas Truesdale is the father-in-law of Houston oil financier Ramsey Croft. It has been reported he and Nugent were en route to a dinner meeting with Croft when the car exploded. Martin Nugent...

Kate's mind was racing. She recalled how much Croft hated his overbearing father-in-law. He once told her that he couldn't wait for the day when he would rid himself of Truesdale.

Ramona entered the room through the kitchen door with a worried look on her face. She said, "There is a Detective Tiller calling for you."

Kate's mind was elsewhere. She replied, "Who?"

"Detective Tiller. With the Houston Police Department."

————

Kate walked down the stairwell from the helipad atop the Drummond Building for her meeting with Tiller. The detective had told her it was urgent they meet. When Kate had asked why, Tiller simply said it was 'very important police business.'

Kate opened the door to the fifteenth floor and walked into the reception area. The receptionist told her that her nine o'clock appointment was waiting in her office.

She walked anxiously down the hallway. Did this have anything to do with Truesdale? she thought to herself. If so, why would she want to speak to me?

Kitty Carver rose from the chair behind her desk as Kate approached and asked, "Is everything all right? What's going on?"

Kate tried to act calm. She shrugged her shoulders, said she had no idea, and made her way toward her office.

She asked her secretary, "Is Al Rosenberg in?"

"No. Should I try to get a hold of him?"

Kate paused and replied, "No, that's okay," and entered her office.

Tiller held a coffee cup and was looking at several photographs of offshore drilling rigs that had been tacked to a cork board on the wall. Kate was considering them for next year's annual report.

Kate said, "Good morning."

Tiller turned around, smiled, and said, "It's always amazed me how all that stuff is done. You know, drilling for oil in the ocean and all that."

Kate put her purse and briefcase on the couch. In an attempt to make casual conversation, she replied, "We now have the capability of drilling in water depths of nearly two miles."

Tiller's eyes widened and she said, "It's amazing what technology has done, isn't it?"

Kate nodded.

Tiller said, "You know, my brother roughnecked for your company once."

"You mentioned that before."

"I did? Boy, my memory is getting bad."

Kate managed a grin. She motioned for Tiller to be seated on the couch, sat down across from her, and asked, "How can I help you this morning?"

Tiller sat down and asked, "I've assumed you've heard about the car bombing last night?"

Kate gulped and nodded.

Tiller said, "The FBI has taken over the case, but I was just following up on a few things to satisfy my curiosity." She sipped her coffee and continued, "I interviewed Ramsey Croft last night regarding the bombing. His father-in-law was apparently going to meet him for dinner."

"I read that."

"Anyway, Mr. Croft told me that they were working on some 'transaction' involving your company. Can you tell me a little bit about that?"

Kate didn't know how to respond and wished that Al were around. She said, "Well, I wouldn't know. It could be a number of things. Mr. Croft and an investment company that he's a partner with Mr. Truesdale in, is the second largest shareholder of our company."

"I see. And the largest?"

"Our family."

Tiller nodded and asked, "I read somewhere that the relationship between your family and the Croft family isn't exactly, shall I say, cordial."

Kate chose her words carefully and replied, "We've had our differences over the years."

Tiller grinned and asked, "Is Croft trying to gain control of the company?"

Kate was surprised by the question. She felt like asking what that had to do with Truesdale, but decided to just keep her mouth shut.

Tiller asked, "I take it you don't want to answer that?"

Kate was getting agitated. She asked, "Is that all you wanted to ask me?"

Tiller smiled. She put her coffee cup on the table, stood and asked, "Is Clay around?"

Kate suddenly remembered Tiller's questions about a wiretapping. She felt herself blush and replied, "He's out of town? Why?"

"Oh, nothing really. Just wanted to make sure he was staying out of trouble, that's all." She reached in her pocket for a business card and asked, "Could you have him give me a call?"

"Sure."

Tiller walked toward the door and said, "Thank you for taking the time to see me this morning, Mrs. Drummond." She turned around and asked, "By the way, have you ever met Monique Croft?"

Kate stiffened and answered, "No...I haven't. Why?"

"No reason, really. I'm just going to have a talk with her this morning, that's all."

———

Kate's hands were trembling after Tiller left. It was clear the detective was somehow trying to link Croft with Truesdale's death.

She recalled a conversation she had had with Croft on a ski lift in Aspen. He was confiding in her that he was not happy with his marriage and, in particular, his business relationship with Monique's father. Even though he didn't elaborate, she could see in his face an intense hatred for Truesdale.

Could Ram be behind the car bombing? she wondered. Would he be capable of such a thing?

———

Later that morning, Croft waited outside Tiller's office while Monique was being questioned. His first inclination was to have an attorney present, but then realized Tiller might become suspicious. After all, there was nothing to worry about. The police and FBI were after someone who was trying to kill the Prime Minister. Tran had planned it perfectly.

Ram was relieved to see Monique and Tiller walking out of the office. The interview had taken less than ten minutes.

Tiller said to both of them, "Again, I apologize for the inconvenience of dragging you down here. I will relay my report to the FBI and hopefully they won't have to bother you."

Ram managed a grin and replied, "Thank you." He looked at Monique and added, "We've been through enough already."

"What did you talk about?" asked Ram as he opened the car door for Monique in the underground parking lot.

She sat in the passenger seat, looked up at him and replied nervously, "About Daddy's recent travel schedule and how long he had known Marty."

"That's it?"

"Well, she did tell me that the FBI had some leads."

Perfect, Ram thought to himself as he closed the door. Now, how do I rid myself of Tran?

———

Ram opened the door to his refrigerator later that evening to get a glass of milk for Monique while she was upstairs packing for their trip to New York in the morning.

Suddenly, he noticed a movement to his left. He turned and was startled to see Tran sitting on a stool. He said, "How the hell did you get in here?"

"It wasn't very hard, really. You should buy yourself a better security system."

Ram closed the refrigerator door and whispered, "What are you doing here?"

Tran frowned and asked, "How did ol' Truesdale and Nugent look at the morgue?"

The images of their charred bodies resurfaced in Ram's mind.

Tran chuckled, "Was there much left of them?"

"How did you know I was there?"

Tran didn't respond.

"You shouldn't be here!" whispered Ram.

"Don't worry about it, old sport. Nobody saw me come in, I assure you."

Ram exhaled a deep breath.

Tran asked, "What was the Detective's name who questioned you?"

"Tiller."

"What did she ask you?"

"Why I was going to meet Truesdale and Nugent at Brennans."

"What did you say?"

"Business."

"Did you mention Drummond Offshore?"

Ram paused and said, "I had to."

Tran's eyes widened and he asked, "You *had* to?"

"What difference does it make?"

Tran's face tensed and he replied, "What happens if the Drummonds went to the police about the wiretapping? Remember? They could put two and two together."

"What do you mean?"

"A car bombing and wiretapping, you dumb ass! What happens if the Drummonds reported the wiretapping?"

"You said there was no way anyone could trace..."

Tran shook his head and said, "We could definitely have a problem if this detective starts snooping around."

"She said the FBI is looking for someone who was trying to kill the Prime Minister."

"Yeah, that's what she told you."

Ram replied defensively, "Tiller would have found out that we were trying to take over Drummond anyway."

Tran frowned, and he asked, "What else did she ask you?"

"If I knew of anyone who would want to see either of them killed."

"And?"

Ram gulped and said, "I told her I didn't know of anyone. And she also asked about how much he was worth and who inherits the money."

A serious expression came over Tran's face, and he asked, "Who does?"

"I told her most of his assets are in a foundation, but Monique...my wife...gets a large part of the estate."

"You don't stand to gain anything?"

"Not a penny."

"What else?"

"She said the FBI might want to question me. That was about it."

"So the investigation has been turned over to the FBI?"

"That's what she said."

Tran picked up an apple from a bowl, rubbed it on his shirt and said, "We're going to have to assume the police were told about the wiretapping. And the only way they can link me...us...to it would be through Clay Drummond. He can identify me." He bit into the apple, chewed a few times, and added, "He's going to have to be taken care of."

"What do you mean by that?"

"What do you think?"

"No!"

"What choice do we have?"

"No, don't do anything. I'll be back from New York in five or six days."

Tran climbed off the stool and walked up to Ram. He looked into his eyes and said, "Call me when you get back."

———

Kate sat down on Clay's bed because she wasn't sure if he was paying attention to what she was saying. He seemed distracted and edgy, probably because he hadn't had a drink in a few days.

Clay finally looked up and said, "Croft is a ruthless bastard, but I can't believe he'd have anyone killed."

Obviously, Kate couldn't tell him about conversations she had had with Croft about Truesdale. She replied, "I agree, but this detective really seemed like she was trying to find a way to implicate him." She paused and added, "And I think she wants to question you about the wiretapping comment you made."

"I'll tell her everything."

"Including the shooting?"

"Why not?" Clay rubbed her hand and said, "I don't know what to make about all this, Kate. I'd better come back to the ranch. I'm worried about you and the kids. This is getting pretty crazy."

Kate had to admit to herself that she was scared, but she knew that it was more important for Clay to stay sober. Doctor Massey told her he would have some anxiety attacks. She replied, "I think you should give it another week or so. Then you'll be able to make a fresh start. Isn't that what you want?"

"But I feel good now."

"Even Doctor Massey said you needed at least a week to work things out for yourself."

"I should be out there...on the rig."

"Brock was out there yesterday and said everything is going fine."

"Does he still think we don't have a chance in hell?"

"I don't know, Clay. I suppose, like all of us, we're just hoping it works out." She smiled and added, "I suppose we'll all find out pretty soon, huh?"

Clay nodded. He looked into her eyes and asked, "Can you stay here tonight?"

"I don't think I should. I have a busy day tomorrow."

Clay put his arms around her.

Kate felt him shivering slightly and wondered if it was a part of the withdrawal symptoms. She said, "We have plenty of time to be together."

He embraced her more firmly.

She kissed his cheek and added, "I'm proud of you, Clay. Just hang in there. We'll get through this."

———

That evening, Clay walked onto the front porch to meet Elsa Tiller. He shook her hand and said, "Thanks for coming out this far from town."

The detective looked at the surroundings and replied, "This doesn't look like any rehab clinic I've ever seen."

Clay smiled and said, "It's pretty peaceful."

"I'll say."

"Mind if we sit out here?" He pointed to the overhead fans and added, "They'll keep us pretty cool."

"Sure."

They sat in the rocking chairs.

Tiller said, "It takes a lot of guts to face your drinking problem."

Clay wanted to downplay his 'problem' and replied, "Kate thought it would be a good idea if I got away from things for awhile."

Tiller grinned and said, "I wish I'd come to a place like this when I was trying to...get my life together."

Clay was not in the mood to talk about his or her drinking. In addition to his exhausting talks with Dr. Massey, he had been cornered by a few of the residents who wanted to share with him their stories. Drunks, it seemed to him, loved misery for company. In an effort to change the subject, he asked, "What did Kate tell you about the wiretapping?"

"Just that some electronics guy who was putting in your phone system found the bugs." She began rocking her chair and asked, "Why didn't you report it?"

"I thought we could use it against Croft."

Tiller paused and asked, "How do you know he was behind it? This sort of industrial espionage goes on more than you think."

"It just seems like something he'd do."

"But you don't have any proof."

Clay shook his head.

Tiller asked, "So your plan was going to be to say: 'You better back off on trying to take over the company, or I'll go to the police'?"

Clay remembered the old man thought it was a stupid idea. He replied, "Something like that. But Kate went to see him before I could."

"Why'd she do that?"

"I don't know."

Tiller's brow furrowed.

Clay asked, "Kate didn't say anything about the shooting?"

Tiller's eyes widened. She asked, "Shooting?"

"The guy who found the bugs and I chased a man in a Southwestern Bell uniform down to the garage. And then some oriental guy jumped out of a van and started shooting at us."

Tiller stopped rocking her chair and asked, "Did you get the license plate number?"

"Everything happened too fast."

"Would you be able to identify either man?"

Clay knew he probably could. He got close enough to notice the scar on the oriental man's face and probably recognize a photo of the other man, but he didn't want to be bothered with helping the investigation. After all, he had more important things to worry about after he got out of rehab, "No. They were both too far away and everything happened too fast."

Tiller paused. She didn't appear to be satisfied with Clay's response and began rocking again and asked, "So, what's going on with this... takeover?"

"It's been called off, for now. We struck a deal with Croft that if we drill a well in the Gulf that's a producer, we'll be able to buy his shares at a certain price. If the well doesn't come in, then he'd buy our shares under the same terms."

Tiller stroked her chin.

Clay asked, "Do you think Croft could have been behind the car bombing?"

"I don't know."

"Is he at least a suspect?"

Tiller grinned and said, "Let's just say what you've just told me kinda makes me think we should be looking at Mr. Ramsey Croft a little closer."

CHAPTER 28

Croft was not happy to see the pile of unopened mail and stacks of paperwork on his desk when he returned from New York. It had been a miserable week.

Helping Monique make arrangements for the funeral was agonizing, but he knew he had to put on a good act. He had been by her side at the elaborate church service, burial ceremony, and the dinner afterwards with New York's high society. He even attended meetings with the family's attorneys to wind up all the estate matters. As expected, he didn't get a dime. But despite having to go through all the motions, he managed to work on his plan to make sure the Seahorse Canyon well would never get drilled.

He slipped out of town and went to Washington for a day to meet with a bureaucrat with Pemex, Mexico's state-owned oil company, who was planning to run for Governor of Monterrey. The official agreed to file an injunction against Drummond and the U.S. Government to stop the drilling of the well. The premise was that the well would drain oil and gas reserves from Mexico's territorial waters. In return, Ram agreed to contribute one hundred thousand dollars to the man's upcoming campaign. Even though there was no proof that the well would drain the reserves, the filing of the injunction should delay the drilling.

In return for a ten percent premium for the Mercer family's shares, Ram was able to persuade Arlen Mercer to apply pressure through Minerals Management. The fact that Drummond falsified the drilling location reports more than justified that drilling operations be temporarily shut down. And if that didn't work, Mercer could stop the drilling based upon the safety report written by the engineer Ram had hired.

Then there were the environmental groups. This one was the easiest of all. According to Mercer, the anonymous call he made to Greenpeace about the Seahorse Canyon would rile the environmentalists immediately, especially since it was going to be at a world record water depth.

The backup plans were in place, Ram thought to himself. There is absolutely no way the Drummonds are going to beat me this time around. The image of his father slumped over his desk in the study flashed through his mind.

———

Kate drove east on Westheimer Road. She was still a little unnerved about Tiller's phone call earlier that morning. The detective had been abrupt and practically demanded that they meet at a small coffee shop near the intersection of Westheimer and Hillcroft.

———

Kate joined Elsa Tiller, who seemed very agitated, at a corner booth. After the detective ordered coffee, she looked around to make sure no one could overhear their conversation, and said, "Your Mr. Croft has now become a prime suspect in the car bombing."

Kate was stunned. Her mouth gaped open, and she asked, "What have you found out?"

"The FBI says that the Prime Minister of Israel's limousines and the cars used by the bodyguards were parked in a secured area behind the

Ritz. The area was cordoned off with police and no vehicles, including Truesdale's limousine, could even come near it. In other words, anyone attempting to assassinate the Prime Minister would have known by all the security precautions that Truesdale's limo wasn't the right one."

"I don't understand how that makes Croft a suspect, though."

"I did a little background research on him since I talked to Clay. He's had quite a few run-ins with the Securities and Exchange Commission over insider trading. But no one has been able to nail him."

"He's pretty smart."

Tiller nodded and said, "But if it wasn't for him marrying Monique Truesdale and being partners with his father-in-law, he wouldn't be where he is today."

"The stock market crash in eighty-six wiped him and his father out."

"With a little help from the Drummond family, I might add."

She's really done her homework, Kate thought to herself.

Tiller continued, "I've even looked at some of his past TV interviews. And every time Truesdale's name came up as his partner, Croft cringes. He doesn't...didn't like his father-in-law too much, did he?"

Kate felt herself tense. She replied, "How would I know?"

Tiller paused while the waitress returned with her coffee and then said in a low tone of voice, "I know about you and Croft. His wife told me about it when I interviewed her."

Kate was speechless.

Tiller said, "I'm sorry I had to bring it up."

"What did she tell you?"

"That you and he had an affair."

Kate felt herself blush and replied, "It's been over for more than three years."

I know. But he didn't want it to be over, did he?"

"What do you mean?"

"I looked up a police report where you said he was stalking you."

"I...I have to admit that I was a little paranoid,"

Tiller nodded and said, "Clay told me you went to see Croft to accuse him of being behind the wiretapping. Why?"

Kate squirmed in her seat and answered, "I thought I could help, you know, put pressure on him to stop the takeover."

Tiller seemed slightly irritated by the answer. She sipped her coffee and replied, "You didn't want Clay to confront him, did you? You were afraid Croft might say something about the affair."

"No...that's not true. I just..."

"Clay doesn't know about it, does he?"

Kate paused and replied, "No."

"And he doesn't have to."

Kate nodded and then realized her hands were sweating.

"None of that matters to me." Tiller sipped her coffee and asked, "You only met with him once since the wiretapping?"

"No, I ran into him at lunch about two weeks ago."

"What did you talk about?"

"The deal...Seahorse Canyon."

"The well in the Gulf. Clay told me about it."

"He was trying to find out how I felt about it."

"And?"

"I told him I was... disappointed, especially with Clay.

"Why'd you say that?

"I wanted to find out what he was thinking."

Tiller grinned and asked, "Did you?"

"Not much."

"He's a cocky sonofabitch, isn't he?"

Kate was surprised by Tiller's bitter tone of voice.

Tiller leaned back in her seat and asked, "I need your help. I want you to tell Croft that he's become a suspect in Truesdale's murder."

"Why?"

"Because he may do something stupid like meet with the people who may have done his dirty work, or he'll try to skip town."

"So, you'll have him followed or something?"

Tiller nodded and replied, "But I'm going to keep the FBI out of this. I'll take him down myself."

Kate's first impression of Tiller being ambitious was right. She rubbed her hands together and replied, "I don't know," with a quiver in her voice.

Tiller said, "I assume he wouldn't be able to take over your company if he's behind bars. Get my drift?"

"What makes you think he'd believe me?"

"He's probably still got a thing for you, that's why. Let's use that against him."

Kate didn't know how to respond.

Tiller grinned and added, "Why don't you think it over."

Kate nodded.

"And don't worry about anyone finding out about the affair. We'll keep that just between us," she said with a grin.

———

Clay's normal morning routine was to grab a cup of coffee in the library and a newspaper and to go back to his room. But since he was unusually hungry, he decided to eat the buffet breakfast in the main dining room with the other residents.

As he walked into the room, about a half a dozen people were getting up from their tables and joining others in the TV room.

One woman, whose name Clay had forgotten, noticed him and said, "I think you'll want to see this."

Clay followed her.

He looked at the TV screen. An aerial view of the *Global Explorer* with several boats circling it changed to a shot of a reporter aboard one of them.

An enthusiastic, young male reporter holding a microphone began, "We are here...approximately eighty miles southeast of Brownsville in the middle of the Gulf of Mexico aboard a Greenpeace boat. A drillship, owned by Drummond Offshore of Houston, is in the process of drilling a well which, we have been informed, will be at a world record water depth of *over ten thousand feet*. A spokesman for Greenpeace told us that because of this depth, there is a risk that a blowout would cause *massive* environmental damage." The reporter looked to his left at another boat passing and then added, "As a side note, we have also been informed that Drummond Offshore has struck some sort of deal with Ramsey Croft, a wealthy financier and the second largest shareholder of Drummond. In an unconfirmed report, we were told that the Drummond family, the company's largest shareholder, and Croft have agreed to a buyout based upon whether or not the well is productive, but we do not yet have..."

An hour later, Clay entered Kate's office. She was seated at her desk. Brock was standing by the window looking out. Al sat on the couch, and all three of them had an air of gloom about them.

Clay said, "This whole thing was bound to come out in the open sooner or later."

The room was quiet for a moment.

Al broke the silence and said, "You look pretty good."

Clay turned to Brock and asked, "How's the drilling comin'?"

Brock looked down at the floor before answering and said, "We're about two-and-a-half days behind schedule."

Clay glanced at Kate who avoided eye contact and said, "You told me we were on schedule!"

"I didn't want you to worry. I...figured you needed to rest."

Brock said, "We had a mudslide about five days ago that set us back. There's also been some loop currents to contend with."

Clay shook his head.

Brock asked sarcastically, "And what would you have done about it?"

"I would have been out there making sure we were making up time instead of sittin' on my ass just reading drilling reports!"

The vein in Brock's neck bulged. He replied, "I've been out on the rig three times...while you've been drying out!"

Clay stepped toward Brock.

Al jumped from the couch to get between them.

Kate shouted, "Stop this, goddamn it! Stop it!"

The three men were stunned and stood silently.

"Going for each other's throats is not going to help us right now!" she added. "So sit the hell down!"

Clay, Al and Brock looked at one another. They sat down.

Kate asked Al, "Do we have any recourse if we can prove Croft violated the confidentiality clause?"

"Well, I suppose we could..."

Clay asked Brock, "Has Minerals Management found out about the falsified plan of exploration yet?"

Brock nodded.

Clay turned to Kate and said, "Croft will hide behind the fact Minerals Management disclosed it." The thought of Mercer being behind all this entered his mind.

Kate must have noticed the expression on Clay's face and asked him, "What is it?"

Clay replied, "Mercer."

Kate, Al and Brock looked at one another.

Clay said, "He'd do it if Croft paid him enough under the table. And there's several things he could come up with to shut down the rig."

In a strained voice, Kate asked, "So what do we do?"

Clay got up from his chair and said, "Unfortunately, nothing." He then looked at Brock and said, "How 'bout we get out to the rig?"

———

Two hours later, Clay looked out the window of the helicopter as it approached the Global Explorer. Two news helicopters hovered above the ship and four boats that Clay guessed were owned by Greenpeace circled her.

The helicopter began to bank left.

Through the headphone mouthpiece, Brock said, "Look at the starboard bow."

Clay peered through the window and saw a boat being moored alongside the ship.

Brock added, "It's Minerals Management."

———

Clay put his hand on the lever to the door. As soon as the helicopter touched down on the ship's helipad, he jumped out and headed toward the aft control room.

Brock followed.

Clay entered the control room. Tito Martinez, Captain Ricci, and Auburn Puckett were speaking with a man who more than likely was with the agency.

When Clay approached them, the tall, mustached man holding a clipboard looked at Clay as if he recognized him.

Sal Ricci said, "Mr. Dodson, this is Clay and Brock Drummond."

Dodson nodded and said to the three of them, "This is an order to stop drilling at once. We must..."

Clay interrupted, "On what grounds?"

Dodson turned to him and said, "For starters, Mr. Martinez here filed a false plan of exploration."

Tito looked down at the floor to avoid eye contact.

Dodson added, "And from what we can see, you have a dozen or more safety violations."

Ricci's face grew red. He asked, "How the hell do you know?" in his heavy Italian accent. "You haven't even inspected her."

Dodson didn't respond. He removed a document and handed it to Ricci and said, "You must cease and desist all drilling operations immediately."

Clay shouted, "Who put you up to this?"

Dodson's face reddened. He asked, "What are you talking about?"

"Who at the agency gave you these orders?"

Dodson frowned. He looked at Ricci and said, "Give the order to halt drilling, Captain."

Clay grabbed the man by the arm and said, "Answer my question!"

Dodson began to shake slightly and said, "I don't have to answer a goddamn thing!"

Ricci said to Clay, "We need to..."

Clay yanked Dodson's clipboard from his hand.

"Those are official documents!" yelled Dodson.

"Official documents my ass!" replied Clay as he leafed through the pages. The last sheet of paper was a copy of a fax from Arlen Mercer directing Dodson to halt drilling operations.

Dodson snatched the clipboard from Clay's hand and said, "I'm going to make sure this ship doesn't get out of port for months!"

Clay asked, "Do you want to know *why* Mercer wants to stop us?"

Dodson stormed out of the control room.

For a moment, everyone was silent.

Finally, Ricci said to Clay, "I'm afraid we have to comply. I don't have a choice.

Clay looked at him, nodded, and then, out of frustration, kicked over a chair.

————

When Clay arrived at the ranch that evening, he was met at the front door by Kate. Brock had phoned her about what happened on the drillship.

Kate attempted to give him a hug, but Clay was in no mood for affection. He needed a drink.

He walked into the study and headed for the wet bar. As he began to make himself a vodka tonic, he heard Kate enter the room.

"Clay, I don't think that's going to help."

He paused before pouring vodka from the crystal decanter, turned around and replied, "I just need to come down. Only one."

Kate walked toward him. She hugged him and said, "You don't need it, Clay. Please. It's not going to help."

Clay knew that once he felt the soothing effects of the first drink that he'd have to have another. He put down the decanter and replied, "Okay, you win."

Kate smiled and kissed him on the cheek.

Clay said, "That damn Mercer! I knew he'd sell us out!"

Kate asked calmly, "It's over then?"

"I'm at least going to pay that sonofabitch a visit."

Kate's eyes widened. She asked, "And do what?"

Clay didn't respond.

"No, Clay! It's just going to make things worse."

"How much worse can they get?"

"Stay here with me, Clay. Please."

Clay gently took her hand off his arm and said, "Everything is going to be all right," and left the room.

———

Thirty minutes later, Clay pulled up to Arlen Mercer's house in Memorial. Luckily, Mercer's Jaguar was parked out front. Since it was a Friday, he figured Arlen had come home from work to freshen up before going out on the town.

He got out of his truck, walked to the door, and rang the doorbell. No answer.

Maybe he was in the shower, he thought. He tried opening the door. It was locked.

Clay went to the picture window. The curtains had been drawn, but he was able to see movement. He yelled, "Arlen! I need to talk to you!"

There was no answer.

"I know you're in there!"

Arlen opened the door. He was frightened and asked, "What the hell are you doing?" He looked over Clay's shoulder to see if any of the neighbors were around.

Clay pushed Arlen into the house and said, "I know what you did!"

"What are you talking about?"

"You had *Explorer* shut down!"

Arlen paused and said, "You're crazy!"

"I saw the fax you sent Dodson! You gave him the order!"

Mercer's face was expressionless.

Clay asked, "How much was the payoff from Croft this time?"

Mercer's face reddened. He replied, "You filed a false plan of exploration...and the rig is a safety hazard."

Clay grabbed Mercer's shirt and yelled, "How much did he pay you?"

Mercer knocked Clay's arm away with his forehand and said, "I'm just doing my job."

"Just like you did when Croft bought your company, huh?"

Mercer became incensed. He swung at Clay.

Clay blocked Mercer's punch with his left forearm. He landed a right to his jaw. Mercer wobbled slightly and then lunged toward Clay. Clay managed to land another right to the side of his head. Mercer tackled him. They crashed to the hardwood floor and rolled.

Mercer managed to gain the advantage and began punching Clay in the face. Blood poured out of Clay's nose. His head banged against the floor every time Mercer landed a blow.

Somehow, Clay mustered enough energy to roll to his left. Mercer fell to the floor.

Mercer got to his feet first. He attempted to kick Clay in the chest. Clay turned. Mercer's foot barely landed on his shoulder. Clay quickly got to his feet.

Mercer raised his hands and clenched his fists. Clay did the same.

They stepped toward one another. Mercer swung a wild right. Clay ducked and immediately followed with a right uppercut to Mercer's jaw and then punched him in the stomach.

Mercer keeled over. Clay landed two blows to his face and one to the back of his head. Mercer fell to the floor.

Clay wiped blood from his nose and said, "We know all about you and Croft!"

Mercer got up on all fours and looked at Clay. Clay kicked him in the ribs. Arlen fell back to the floor again.

Clay yelled, "We've got proof you and your father got kick-backs when you sold your company!"

Mercer scoffed and asked, "What proof?" as he got to all fours again.

"Let *Explorer* resume drilling or we'll go to the Texas Attorney General — who happens to owe a few favors to the old man."

Mercer looked into Clay's eyes to gauge whether or not he was bluffing.

Clay added, "You're going to jail, Arlen! You, your father, and that sonofabitch, Croft!"

"You're lying." Mercer coughed and added, "You don't have a damn thing."

Clay kicked him in the ribs again. Mercer fell face-down on the floor and moaned.

Half out of breath, Clay asked, "Are you stupid enough to take that chance?"

Mercer looked up at him.

Clay sensed Arlen was taking the bait and added, "I'll give you one last chance! Either take back the order or else!"

Mercer didn't respond.

Clay turned and headed for the door. Once he reached the porch, he heard Mercer mumble something. Clay turned around.

Mercer was on his knees. He put his hand up, nodded, and said, "Okay...okay. I'll take care of it."

———

Kate heard Clay's truck pull up to the house. She rushed out of the dining room and met him at the front door in her blue silk robe. She immediately knew he had been in a fight.

His shirt was torn and bloodied. The corner of his left eye was dripping blood. And he limped slightly as he climbed the steps.

She gasped, "Are you all right?"

Clay looked up at her. With a grin, he replied, "Never been better." He handed her a sheet of paper and said, "I made Mercer send this fax off. We can start drilling immediately."

Kate's eyes widened. She asked, "What did you tell him?"

"Let's just say he didn't call my bluff." He cringed and added, "He's always been a bad poker player."

Kate grabbed him by the arm and led him toward the door.

Clay hesitated before entering the house and said, "I don't want Ramona to see me like this. She'll get all bent out of shape."

"She's spending the night with her sister in town."

Kate led him to the kitchen.

Clay sat at the breakfast table while Kate grabbed some wash cloths from the pantry.

Clay attempted to take off his jean shirt.

She wet the cloths under the faucet and said, "I'll do that. You just relax." She unbuttoned the shirt, pulled it off slowly, and then began gently dabbing a wash cloth on his eye.

He asked, "Is it swollen?"

Kate nodded and said, "You'll probably need some stitches."

Clay winced slightly and said, "I've got to get back to the rig."

"Not right now," she replied. She lifted the cloth off his face and sat down next to him. She grabbed a clean one and began to rub down his chest and shoulders.

Clay ran his fingers through her wet hair and said, "Just get out of the shower?"

Kate nodded and kept rubbing him down.

He leaned toward her, smelled her hair, and said, "You certainly smell better than I do."

Kate smiled.

He put his hand on her face and gently stroked it. He then kissed her on the neck and then her ear.

Kate quivered slightly.

She felt his hand on her waist. He untied the sash, slipped his hand inside her robe and gently rubbed her stomach and then her breasts.

She became aroused and said, "Not here, Clay."

———

At four a.m., Kate was awakened by the sound of a helicopter landing. She looked to her left and noticed Clay had left her bed.

Their lovemaking had been wonderfully passionate and she felt content and warm.

She got out of bed, put on her robe, and looked out the window.

Clay started to board the chopper but then looked up at her window and waved.

Kate smiled and blew him a kiss.

CHAPTER 29

Later that morning, Clay was having coffee in the ship's galley with Ricci, Puckett, and Tito. He looked across the table at Tito and asked, "We're about what, two days behind schedule?"

Tito nodded.

Auburn Puckett adjusted his wire rim glasses and added, "Twenty-seven hours to be exact."

Tito said, "And we're going to lose a little more time because we've got to come out of the hole." He glanced at Clay and added, "The drill bit is about shot."

"We're at about eighty-two hundred feet," replied Clay. "If Brock is right, we'll be drillin' into softer formation in about...," he calculated the feet per hour and said, "four hours or so."

Tito's face reddened. He replied, "The bit could break off any time now."

Clay didn't want to usurp Tito's authority in front of Ricci and Puckett, but needed to set the tone that he was in charge. He said, "We'll keep drilling."

Ricci and Puckett glanced across the table at one another.

Tito frowned slightly.

Clay asked Puckett, "Are the backup power systems operating?"

Puckett's face reddened. He replied, "Not yet."

The four of them sipped their coffee in silence for a moment.

Ricci asked Clay, "Is the news right...about this thing with Croft?"

"You mean the deal we have about the well?"

Ricci nodded.

"Yeah, pretty much," said Clay. "Bottom line: if we don't get this well drilled and prove we've got a big field by next Sunday at five o'clock, Croft will end up with control of the company."

Ricci asked, "Can the deadline be extended in the case of a storm?"

"Nope."

Ricci paused and then said, "There's a tropical depression forming near the Yucatan Peninsula. They've named it 'Darwin'."

Clay's eyes widened.

Ricci added, "It could continue on a northwesterly track toward us, but it's too soon to tell."

———

Croft arrived at his office at nine-thirty and noticed two packages on his desk.

The first was the divorce papers to serve Monique. He had thought about it a great deal last night. And even though he was anxious to get this charade of a marriage over with, the timing wasn't right.

The other eight-and-a-half by eleven manila envelope he knew was from Tran. He opened it and pulled out a photograph with a small yellow post-it stuck to it. The photo was of Kate and Detective Tiller in a coffee shop. The note said:

Restaurant eleven o'clock tonight.

———

"Kate," said her secretary over the speaker in the phone, "Detective Tiller is here to see you."

Kate stopped scrolling through her telephone call management program.

The secretary asked, "Are you available?"

With everything that had been going on, Kate had forgotten to call Tiller and tell her she wouldn't have any part of setting up Croft.

She pressed the button on the phone and said, "Show her in," and got up from her desk.

Tiller walked into the room and appeared tense.

Kate said, "Good morning. A cup of coffee?"

Tiller waved her hand and answered, "No, thanks."

Kate was a bit intimidated and said, "I really haven't had much time to..."

"I need your answer," Tiller said bluntly. "Now!"

"I...don't want to get involved. I've got too many other things to worry about right now."

Tiller closed the door, stared into Kate's eyes, and said, "Then I'm going to have to make you a suspect in the Truesdale murder. And I can assure you, your little fling with Croft will come out and tarnish your pristine reputation."

"What? How dare you..."

"I don't have time to screw around here."

Kate was shaking with anger and asked, "Why are you doing this? I haven't done anything wrong!"

"I don't know that, do I?"

"How...why would I..."

"I'm not asking you to commit a crime here! I'm asking you to cooperate in an investigation! If you don't then I can only reach the conclusion you had something to do with it. It's as simple as that!"

"I really don't think I can be of any help!"

"He's still got the hots for you, doesn't he? Like all men, their brains are between their legs."

"This...is blackmail!"

Tiller grinned and replied, "I'd say it's just playing hardball."

Kate shook her head, walked toward the window, and looked out aimlessly.

Tiller said, "If I walk out this door, my dear, I will do everything I can to make your life miserable."

Kate turned, gripped the back of her chair, and said, "You have no right to do this!"

"Maybe not. But, I'm doing it." Tiller stepped closer and added, "This is what I want you to tell him."

———

Croft slammed the phone down after his engineer told him Mercer had allowed the *Global Explorer* to continue drilling. He got up from his chair, picked up a pile of magazines and newspapers, and threw them against the wall. That goddamn Mercer! he thought to himself. I'm going to make him pay for this! He kicked some magazines and then sat down to regain his composure.

He realized the drilling could still be stopped. Greenpeace's emergency injunction to halt operations should be filed in the next day or two. There were no assurances that they would be successful, but the Mexican government will be filing their own injunction. That'll be a real killer. But the Drummonds have strong ties in Washington. This, however, is a legal issue, not a political one. They won't be able to stop the courts. But what happens if both suits fail? Could the geologist be wrong about the prospects of the well? Maybe the Drummonds have more geological information than we do? Why else would they agree to such a risky proposition?

He got up from his chair again. He stepped on an opened oil industry magazine on the floor and caught sight of an advertisement about transmitting data from offshore rigs by satellite.

He bent over and picked it up. That was how the information on the Seahorse Canyon well will be relayed back to the courtroom, he remembered. Could the transmission somehow be altered to change the data? Tran might be able to pull this off.

———

After he watched three roughnecks make a pipe connection on the drilling deck that evening, Clay walked to the railing and watched the sun slowly sink into the sea.

Seagulls circled the ship. They were either looking for table scraps that were often thrown overboard from the galley or waiting for crew members who were fishing to throw back their catches.

There were also migrating songbirds perched on the railings around the ship. No one had ever given Clay a reasonable explanation about how or why they showed up on rigs. There were no bugs for them to feed on and they didn't eat fish. Nonetheless, they never went hungry. The kitchen crew would always find spots around the ship, away from the watchful eyes of the gulls, and feed them breadcrumbs.

Clay put his foot on the railing. Oblivious to the sounds of the machinery and the roar of the diesel engines, his mind began to wander.

He wondered how his life would be different had he gone back to West Texas after college and worked the two rigs his father still owned. It would have been a much simpler life. He probably would have married a local girl and settled down and had a bunch of kids. But the allure of the offshore industry and his father's desire that the twins follow in his footsteps was all too strong.

The business had been interesting and had taken him all over the world. But eventually the long hours and the pressures took their toll on him. His personal life suffered. And, as he explained to Dr. Massey, his tumultuous marriage to Heather was the start of his downward spiral.

But it wasn't all her fault, he recognized. They both thought they were falling in love with one another, but in reality, they had fallen in love with what they thought was an ideal — the ideal of being part of one of the wealthiest families in Texas and being considered the best in a very competitive and risky business.

But he had to admit to himself, despite the ups and downs, it felt good to be back in the thick of things again. And it especially felt good to be sober. Yes, he still had the urge to drink. But as long as he stayed consumed by the tasks at hand, he knew, with Kate's support, he could defeat his demons.

But, he asked himself, what if the Seahorse Canyon well isn't successful? What will happen with Kate and me? Maybe it won't be so bad if I fail. The family will be paid a handsome sum for its stock. And then maybe Kate and I could leave Houston and spend our days somewhere where we can just be together, away from all the pressures. We could just lead a simple life. Somewhere, where no one knew, or cared, about the Drummond name.

But I *am* a Drummond. And no matter how much I have tried to escape the family obligations, I always seem to come back to the fact that I have a duty to see that the company will flourish and that the old man's legacy will live on. In a way, things seem to have been pre-destined — for better or for worse.

———

"Why do you have to insist on meeting in this place?" Croft asked Tran as he sat down at a table in the smoke-filled Vietnamese restaurant and rubbed his eyes.

Tran took a drag of his cigarette, exhaled in Croft's direction, and said, "That photo of Kate Drummond and Tiller proves they're working together."

Ram looked around to make sure no one overhead their conversation and replied, "What makes you think that?"

Tran leaned forward in his chair and replied, "What else could it be?"

"What the hell does Kate know anyway?"

"She knows about the wiretap."

For the first time, Ram sensed Tran was genuinely worried. He remembered Nugent telling him that Tran would 'vanish into thin air' if things got tough. Ram said, "But there's no way to trace the wiretaps to us."

Tran shook his head and said, "Don't you see?"

Ram whispered, "Keep your voice down."

Tran added, "Tiller has somehow either made a connection between you and the bombing or thinks she will."

"But what about the Israeli Prime Minister?"

"She may have just said that so you would go on thinking you're not a suspect."

That had never entered Ram's mind. He thought about his talk with Kate at the Rainbow Lodge and wondered if it was all some sort of set-up. He asked, "When was this photo taken?"

"A couple of days ago. Why?"

Ram was about to tell Tran he spoke with Kate, but realized it might make him more paranoid than he already was. He needed Tran for one last job and asked, "Have you read about the Seahorse Canyon deal?"

Tran's eyes widened as if he were surprised Croft had changed the subject so quickly and nodded.

Croft continued, "The results of the well will be sent by satellite from the drillship to monitors in the courtroom." Ram leaned forward in case someone was eavesdropping and asked, "Is there some way the transmission or signal, or whatever it is, can be altered?"

Tran paused and answered, "I'm familiar with the system that's used, but the data is encrypted. And from what I've heard, it's a pretty sophisticated code."

Ram exhaled a deep breath.

Tran added, "But...there could be a way to intercept the signal and then falsify the data."

"How?"

"These monitors — you said they'll be in the courtroom?"

Croft nodded.

Tran spoke out loud to himself, "I'd need to get access to them. That shouldn't be a problem, but I'll need to know what type of information the transmission should be." He looked at Croft and asked, "Isn't it some kind of graph or log or something?"

Croft nodded, "An electric log."

"Then I'd need to get one of these logs that shows the well isn't any good."

Croft didn't know a damn thing about logs, then thought about the geologist he had hired and said, "I've got a geologist you could meet with."

"Isn't that going to be a little suspicious?"

Croft rubbed his chin. He asked, "What if you were a reporter? You know, someone doing a story on Seahorse Canyon and you wanted to know what these logs looked like or something."

Tran nodded and then said, "That might work. I could replace a phony log, or one from another well, with the real one."

"I'll set up a meeting," Ram said enthusiastically.

"Tell him I'm a free-lance reporter. Use the name Lee ...Wong Lee."

"I'll call you tomorrow morning at nine o'clock."

Tran nodded and then asked, "When will all this happen?"

"Next Sunday. The deadline is at five o'clock."

"Now...what's in this for me?"

Ram paused and then asked, "What do you want?"

"Another five hundred thousand. Two fifty now and two fifty after it's done."

Ram knew he was just using this as a backup plan. He was still confident that the environmentalist's injunction and suit from the Mexicans would stop the drilling. But five hundred thousand was a small price to pay for peace of mind, he figured. He replied, "Okay. You've got a deal."

Tran grinned and said, "But this thing with Kate Drummond and the detective. I think we've got a problem. You better be on your guard if she approaches you."

CHAPTER 30

The next morning, Brock's prediction that they would encounter softer formation came true. Whether they had encountered a geological structure holding vast oil reserves remained to be seen. Nevertheless, they were slowly making headway to get back on schedule. But it was not enough for Clay.

He turned to Tito, Ricci and Puckett in the aft control room and said, "We need to put more weight on the bit."

Tito's eyes widened.

Clay said, "We've got to make up for lost time.

Puckett picked up a clipboard lying on top of a control console, cleared his throat and said, "I've done some calculations." He kept looking at the clipboard to avoid eye contact and added, "I took how much hole we've drilled and at what speed and compared it with the bit manufacturer's maximum allowable drilling rate table. The bit is already thirty to thirty-five percent beyond the threshold."

Tito shook his head. He was about to say something, but Clay put his hand up to stop him from responding.

Clay asked, "Did you take into account the type of formation we're drillin' in?"

Puckett blushed. He leafed through some papers and replied, "The manufacturer doesn't say anything about that. It's simply based on a mathematical calculation."

Clay looked at Tito, grinned slightly, and then asked Puckett, "So what's your recommendation?"

Puckett gulped and replied, "To stop drilling immediately and replace the bit, of course."

Clay crossed his arms and said, "I see. And how long have you been a drilling engineer?"

Captain Ricci chuckled.

Puckett replied, "Well...I'm not one. I'm just doing the math, that's all."

Tito's nostrils flared. He said, "I'll tell you what, when you get around thirty years under your belt of drilling everywhere from West Texas to the North Sea, come on back and tell him what he ought to do."

Clay was surprised by Tito's defence of him.

Ricci grinned, turned to Puckett and said, "There are just some things in this world that don't always fit in some mathematical equation."

Puckett looked at Clay and said weakly, "I...I was just tryin' to help, that's all."

Clay grinned and replied, "I know." He put his hand on Puckett's shoulder and added, "They're just bustin' your chops."

Everyone smiled.

———

Clay and Tito stood along the railing outside the aft control room drinking coffee and looking aimlessly out at the calm sea.

Clay finished a sip and asked, "What's the latest on the storm?."

"It seems to be developing just off the Yucatan and there's another depression to the east of it that might push it further toward us."

Clay paused and said, "Let's keep our fingers crossed."

Tito nodded.

Clay finally broke the pause in the conversation and asked, "Remember when me and Dirk had that contest using the old man's rigs to see who could reach TD first?"

"Yeah, south of Odessa."

"The South Cowden Field."

Tito nodded and said, "You two just about burned up the draw-works."

Clay chuckled, "The old man almost killed us."

"I remember him hollerin' that college was making both of you even more stupid than you already were."

Clay smiled and said, "At least I beat Dirk."

Tito grinned. Then in a more serious tone of voice, he said, "You know, I still think about him a lot."

Clay didn't respond. Instead, he looked out to sea and recalled how Tito and Dirk had been so close.

Dirk had always had a soft spot for Tito and considered him family, unlike Clay who, in his younger days, tended to see Tito more like the hired help.

Tito said, "About the hearing, Clay. It was a freak accident. No one could have known how bad the storm was going to get."

Clay looked at him.

Tito added, "I want you to know, I...was just upset, you know."

"I know."

Tito turned to Clay and extended his hand and asked, "No hard feelings?"

"No hard feelings."

They shook.

Tito said, "You know you can count on me to do whatever it takes to meet this deadline."

With their hands still clasped, Clay replied, "What do you say we do this for the old man...and for Dirk?"

Tito nodded and his eyes watered.

————

Kate felt nervous enough without people staring at her while she walked down the hallway toward Croft's office suite. She would never be doing this if it had not been for Tiller's strong-arm tactics and only hoped that the humiliation she was about to put herself through would somehow pay off. How? She had no idea. This was crazy.

An attractive, impeccably-dressed secretary rose from her chair. She said, "Mr. Croft will see you now," and pressed a button on top of the desk.

Large mahogany doors, bordered by shiny brass, slowly swung open.

Kate figured that Croft wanted to give visitors the impression that they were entering some sort of sacred shrine of high finance or something. What an arrogant bastard! she thought.

She entered the room and was struck by the coldness of it. The furniture was black leather and ultra-modern. The only bright color in the room was from several post-modern paintings.

Ram looked up from his desk, rose, and walked toward the center of the room to meet her.

He had probably choreographed this ritual, she thought to herself, and heard the doors automatically close behind her.

With a slight grin, Ram asked, "I just had these doors installed. What do you think?"

"It's...a nice sense of entry," she answered and reminded herself not to show any nervousness.

Ram approached.

Kate remembered not to flinch if he greeted her with a kiss like she did at his house.

Ram kissed her on the cheek. Kate did the same.

Croft said, "This is a surprise, considering what you said at the restaurant about taking it slow."

"I know. I'm sorry. But, I have something to tell you that can't wait."

The grin vanished from Ram's face. He motioned for her to be seated on the black leather couch. He sat across from her.

Kate recalled Tiller telling her 'Come right out with it and watch closely for his reaction.' She put a concerned look on her face and said, "Detective Tiller has made you a prime suspect in Truesdale's murder."

Ram's eyes widened slightly. He gulped and said, "That's ludicrous!" He looked down at the floor to avoid eye contact, leaned forward in his chair and asked, "She told you that?"

"Yes."

"When?"

Kate sensed she hit a nerve. She kept straight-faced and replied, "A few days ago."

Ram chuckled and asked, "Is this some kind of...?"

"I didn't tell her what you said about Truesdale –- that you couldn't wait to get him and Monique out of your life."

"That doesn't mean I wanted him dead."

"I told her pretty much the same thing."

"And how on earth did she come up with all this?"

Kate shrugged her shoulders and answered, "I'm not sure. She did say that she knew he was threatening you with something, but didn't elaborate."

Ram began to rub his hands together. He snickered and then replied, "This...is incredible!" He paused and asked suspiciously, "Why did she come to you about this?"

Kate tried to look embarrassed and replied, "She said she dug up a...police report. When I was afraid...

Ram's nostrils flared slightly. He said, "I never understood why you did that."

"I was scared and confused. It was stupid."

Ram shook his head, sat back in his chair, and asked, "Why are you telling me all this?"

Kate knew this was the most important question of all and answered, "Despite what's going on with Seahorse Canyon and the company, Ram, I don't think you'd be capable of doing something like that." Kate sensed Ram was buying it. She continued, "What we had was special. And even though it didn't work out, I think about what it could have been like."

The doubting expression on Ram's face melted. He said, "We can still have all that, you know."

Kate nodded. She looked at her watch and replied, "I'm sorry. I have to go," and stood up.

Ram rose from his chair.

Kate walked toward him.

They embraced and stood silently for a moment.

Kate then looked into his eyes and said, "I can't wait until all this is over. I'm tired. I just want to get away from all this."

Ram's face lightened up. He replied, "We can go anywhere you want, Kate. Anywhere."

She smiled.

———

Kate was emotionally drained by the time she drove into a Seven-Eleven parking lot on the outskirts of downtown to meet Tiller. She spotted the detective's black sedan parked in the far corner of the lot and pulled up next to it.

Tiller got out of the car. She walked around the front of the Mercedes and looked at Kate trying to gauge how the meeting had gone with Croft.

Tiller climbed in the passenger side, shut the door, and asked, "How did it go?"

"I told him what you wanted me to."

"And he bought it?"

"Yes. He *'bought'* it," she replied with disdain.

Tiller grinned and said, "He'll go to the people who did his dirty work now."

Kate asked, "How do you know he even did it?"

"I know."

Kate smirked and said, "Well, good luck, anyway. I did my part."

"Oh, not so fast, my dear. You have one more thing you've got to do."

"I did what you told me! That's it!"

Tiller chuckled. Her face turned serious, and she said, "You're going to go pay Monique a little visit and then your job is done."

"Monique?"

"You need to gain her confidence and get her to open up."

"That's ridiculous! I had an affair with her husband!"

"Ah, c'mon. I wouldn't worry about it. She told me their marriage was on the rocks for years. Besides, she looks like the type that was screwin' around on him anyway."

Kate was stunned.

Tiller continued, "All you have to do is ask her if her father was blackmailing Croft."

"That's all, huh?" asked Kate in a sarcastic tone.

"Yeah, what's so hard about that?"

"You don't think Ram will find out?"

"That's the whole point." Tiller paused and added, "Like I said before: If he's behind bars, he's sure as hell not going to be able to take over your company, right?"

Kate thought, no matter how much she hated Tiller forcing her to do it, she *does* have a point. Even Brock said it's a long shot that the Seahorse Canyon well will be productive. Maybe this is the best chance we have to stop him. Kate looked at Tiller and asked, "Can I sleep on this?"

Tiller grinned and replied, "Sure. But I wouldn't wait too long. That court deadline you have to meet is only six days away."

CHAPTER 31

The next morning, D.L. watched from a chair in the corner of his bedroom as workers from the Hospice service set up a bed. He felt his depression deepening once he realized it was the same kind of bed Victoria was in during the last months of her life.

Kate and Haley walked into the room.

D.L.'s spirits immediately improved. He cleared his throat and said to Haley, "You're waddling more like a duck every day."

The girls laughed, walked toward him, and took turns kissing him on the forehead.

Haley felt for a spot on her bulging belly and said to him, "Touch here."

D.L. carefully placed his hand on the spot and felt a kick. He said, "Damn, this boy wants to come out!"

Haley giggled and replied, "He's due in a week and a half."

"I think he's going to want to pop out sooner than that."

Kate said, "Ramona thinks so, too."

There was a pause in the conversation as one of the male workers barked to another man to test the reclining feature on the bed.

D.L. wanted to lighten the moment and said, "While you're at it, why don't you boys find me a cute nurse instead of that old hag they want to send me."

The men didn't know how to respond and looked at one another.

Kate said, "I made sure that'll never happen."

Everyone laughed.

On a more serious note, D.L. asked Kate, "How's the drillin' coming?"

"Clay said they're almost back on schedule, despite Mercer's little ploy."

"I'm sure Croft will try to pull something else."

Neither Kate nor Haley responded.

D.L. asked, "So Clay and Tito are overseeing everything out there?" He wished he could be out there with them.

Kate nodded and replied, "Clay's coming back this afternoon and said he'll be out here tonight."

"How's ol' Rosenberg holdin' up?"

"He's fine," replied Kate. "In fact, he just got a short-term loan to cover expenses for the next few months."

D.L. was pleased. He slapped his hand on the arm of the chair and said, "I'll tell you this, girls, we're gonna get that well drilled in time, and we're gonna have a hell of a field. Mark my words."

They smiled.

D.L. cleared his throat again, looked at Haley and added weakly, "And I'll be around to hold my great-grandson."

Kate and Haley did the best they could to hold back their tears. Then both hugged him.

————

As soon as Clay arrived at the Drummond Building, he was summoned to Rosenberg's office to meet with Al, Kate, and Brock.

He asked, "What's up?"

Al was seated at his desk. He adjusted his wire-rim glasses and re-plied, "We just got served with an injunction to stop the drilling...from Greenpeace and several other environmental groups."

Clay paused momentarily and asked, "On what grounds?"

"They have several," answered Rosenberg. "The main one being that the well poses a serious threat to the environment due to its water depth."

Brock said, "They're saying that the technology to contain a blow-out at those depths is not proven."

Al leafed through the thick document and added, "They use the term 'environmental disaster' probably a dozen times."

Clay noticed Kate was looking at him hoping he would say some-thing to refute the assertion. Unfortunately, he couldn't. He asked, "What else are they saying?"

Al replied, "That the *Explorer* should have been overhauled before moving onto the location and that it's a safety hazard. And they also throw in the fact that we falsified the plan of exploration."

Clay crossed his arms and said, "The report shouldn't be an issue. We'll simply pay the fine."

"I agree, but it sure as hell makes us look bad."

"As far as the safety issue, Minerals Management has given us the go-ahead to keep drilling."

Kate tried to lighten the conversation and said, "Not without a little friendly persuasion on your part, I might add."

Clay smiled.

Al said, "That's all fine, but Mercer can't control what his superiors in Washington might do. They could reimpose the order to stop drilling once they get wind of this."

Clay hadn't thought of that possibility.

Brock said, "It seems to me that this blowout issue is the most damaging."

Clay didn't want to respond for fear of making Kate more on edge than she already was.

Al said, "And to top it all off, the case will more than likely be consolidated with the Croft settlement deal."

"With Judge Burnhouse?" Clay asked.

"Yup," replied Al. "And the hearing is the day after tomorrow."

————

Thirty minutes later, Kate entered Clay's office. He was standing at the window peering out over the city with a sheet of paper in his hand.

She closed the door and asked, "I guess this is what they call a curveball, huh?"

Clay turned around and grinned.

She walked up to him and they embraced.

Kate asked, "This is pretty bad, isn't it?"

Clay answered, "I'm afraid so." He paused and then added, "To make things even worse, a tropical depression that's been developing along the Yucatan Peninsula is likely to develop into a hurricane." He handed her the sheet of paper. It was a fax from the U.S. Weather Service. He said, "The *Explorer* will be right in its path."

Kate felt herself tremble. She asked, "So what does this mean?"

"Based on a hurricane moving at an average of fifteen miles per hour, we'll have no choice but to stop drilling in around forty-eight hours. And it could be sooner depending upon what category it becomes."

Kate looked aimlessly at the report.

Clay added, "But it's probably not going to make a difference anyway. This injunction could stop us dead in our tracks." He turned away from her and looked out the window.

"You did the best you could, Clay. Everyone knows that." She embraced him from behind and said, "Especially me."

"I was so damn stupid to have agreed to that deadline."

"You didn't have a choice. Al even said Croft would've walked out of the room if you hadn't agreed to it."

"I should have called his bluff."

Kate didn't know how to respond and began to gently massage his neck.

Clay added, "But we weren't exactly negotiating from a position of strength, you know."

She kept massaging him and replied, "I know."

"If we could just stop this injunction."

Kate walked in front of him, looked into his eyes, and said, "What do ya' say we get out of here, go back to the house, make love, and I'll fix us a nice lunch."

Clay smiled.

They embraced.

———

A few minutes past midnight, Croft pulled into an unlit warehouse parking lot in Chinatown. He felt uneasy about meeting Tran somewhere alone, but it was he who insisted that they not meet in that disgusting restaurant again.

Ram turned off the engine and got out.

Suddenly, he heard some cats hissing and growling near a dumpster at the side of the building. They fought for a brief moment and then there was silence.

He heard footsteps inside the warehouse.

A door to his left opened. A dim light from within illuminated Tran.

Tran looked around and then motioned for him to come in.

There was a table, desk lamp, and two chairs in the middle of the warehouse floor.

Tran closed the door behind him, walked toward the table, and said, "Kate Drummond paid you a visit, didn't she?"

"How'd you know?"

Tran chuckled, sat down, and replied, "I can tell by the look on your face."

Ram didn't respond.

Tran asked, "What did she tell you?"

"She said Tiller told her I'm a suspect."

Tran paused and said, "I've been doing some checking on this Tiller. She's trying to work her way up the ladder and probably figures that by nailing your ass, she'll earn some Brownie points." Tran pulled a cigarette from his pocket and lit it.

Ram wondered if Tran had bugged the police station.

Tran took a drag, exhaled, and said, "They...she doesn't have any proof. But she's making you sweat, isn't she?"

Ram didn't respond.

Tran leaned back in his chair and said, "I had a very interesting meeting with your geologist friend. He showed me what type of equipment they'll be putting in the courtroom and then took me to some petroleum library."

Ram was still thinking about Tiller.

Tran said, "I got a few examples of what these electric logs look like. I even had him pick ones that were dry holes."

Ram finally shifted his concentration to what Tran was saying and asked, "Did he suspect anything?"

"Not at all," he said proudly.

"So you've got everything you need?"

Tran nodded and replied, "All I do is jam the signal before it reaches the antenna that'll be on the roof of the courthouse. Then I'll transmit the signal that shows the false log."

"How?"

"I'll be right outside the courthouse in a news van with one of those satellite dishes on top of it."

Ram was impressed.

Tran asked, "But what's the likelihood of these environmentals' lawsuit stopping everything?"

"I'm not sure what's going to happen." Ram thought about telling Tran about the suit he expected the Mexican government to file any day, but decided to keep his mouth shut.

Tran said, "The deal is I get paid the other two hundred and fifty no matter what."

Ram nodded. His thoughts drifted back to Tiller, and he asked, "What about..."

"Shhh!" said Tran with his finger up to his mouth. He turned off the lamp.

The warehouse turned pitch black.

"What?" whispered Ram.

Tran didn't respond.

Ram whispered again, "What is it?"

There were footsteps near the front door of the warehouse.

Ram froze. His heart was nearly pounding out of his chest.

Tran whispered, "Stay here."

Ram heard the chair slide along the concrete floor.

Tran made his way toward the back of the building.

The back door slowly opened. A dim light from another building poured in. Tran stood in the doorway. He held a pistol with a silencer at his side and then raised it.

Ram rose from his chair.

Tran looked back. He motioned for Ram to stay put and then he disappeared into the alley.

––––––

Ram felt paralyzed. He had lost track of how long he had stood in the middle of the empty warehouse. He wished he had brought a gun.

Suddenly, there were two spits from a silencer and a groan.

"Croft!" Tran said. "Get out here!"

Ram ran through the back door, around the side of the building, and saw Tran struggling to pull a body behind him. He was shocked.

"Help me with her, for Christ's sake!"

Her? thought Ram. Once Tran came further into the light, he could see the face. Detective Tiller!

Ram froze.

A trail of blood followed the corpse.

Ram screamed, "What have you done?"

Tran was grunting while he continued to pull and replied, "She had a gun!"

"You didn't have to..."

"Shut up and pull her to that dumpster over there. I'm going to check to see if there's anyone else."

Ram yelled, "Let's get out of here!"

Tran said, "Do what I say!" and rushed toward the parking lot in the front of the building.

Ram looked at Tiller's twisted, bloodied face. Her eyes were wide open.

He grabbed her bloody arm and began to pull. It slipped out of his hand. Her limp arm fell to the ground.

Suddenly, he heard a gurgling sound. She's still alive! He stepped back from the body. What should he do if she tried to get up?

The sound stopped. The body didn't move.

Tran ran back from around the corner of the building and joined him.

Croft said, "She's still alive!"

"What?" replied Tran out of breath.

"She made...some kind of sound. I don't know."

Tran knelt over the body, felt her pulse, and said, "She's dead." He got up and added, "She came alone. Her car is parked down the street."

He looked at the dumpster. He added, "Let's dump her in there and get the hell out of here!"

"Wait! Are you sure?"

Tran bent down, grabbed her arms, and said, "Put her legs in first and then come back here and help me push her up."

Ram's stomach was queasy. He felt like he was going to throw up. He reluctantly placed her legs over the lip of the dumpster.

Tran lifted her torso and said, "This bitch is heavy."

Ram helped.

Tran said, "One...two...threeee."

The body landed on the bottom of the dumpster and made a loud thud.

Ram looked at his hands and the front of his shirt. They were covered with blood. His stomach wrenched. He threw up violently.

Tran laughed and said, "Now get out of here! I'll get in touch with you in a few days."

Ram wiped his mouth and ran to his car.

CHAPTER 32

"I've got an idea," said Clay to Al Rosenberg as he joined him in the executive conference room the next morning with a sheet of paper in his hand. "I'm going to contact all these industry trade groups." He handed the list of associations to Al and added, "We'll get them to testify at the hearing that drilling the Seahorse Canyon well is environmentally safe."

Al read the names on the list, looked at Clay and replied, "But *will* it be safe?"

"If we take the right precautions."

Al didn't appear enthusiastic. He frowned and replied, "The hearing is tomorrow morning at eight o'clock, you know."

"I've already made some calls."

"The best way to defend ourselves," said Al as he took off his glasses and wiped them on his tie, "would be to refute their claims with scientific proof. Can that be done?"

"The problem is that no one has ever drilled at this water depth. It'll all be theoretical, but we may be able to spin it to make it sound like it's a proven fact."

Al put his glasses back on and said, "Maybe it's worth a try. But Burnhouse doesn't like a lot of technical stuff thrown at her. If we send three or four credible people who don't ramble on in front of her, she might buy into it. At the very least, she may delay action. But can you get 'em to do it?"

Clay leaned on the desk and said, "Listen, the old man has always given his time and money to these organizations and never asked for anything in return. It's time we call in some chits."

———

Clay walked into Brock's office. Brock was seated with his back to him staring into a color monitor. As Clay walked closer, he saw the U.S. Weather Service web site showing an aerial view of the swirling storm.

Clay asked, "How's it look?"

Brock turned around and replied, "It's slowing, but not enough."

Clay exhaled a deep breath and asked, "Do you have any Rig Locator reports?"

Brock began looking through piles of papers on his desk and asked, "Why?"

"I want to see what the nearest drillship is to Seahorse Canyon."

Brock grabbed a thick report and started leafing through it.

Clay examined the mud logs thumb-tacked on the wall of the well.

Brock said, "This shows that the only ship in the Gulf is Oceanic's *Deepwater One*. It's roughly fifty miles away. She's in Walker Banks."

"Amtex and Oceanic are partners in it, aren't they?"

"Yeah, but it says: 'En route to Nigeria'." Brock looked at the front page and added, "As of three days ago."

"Can you find out exactly where it is?"

"Sure, but why?"

"Isn't C.R. Markham still Chairman."

Brock nodded.

Clay crossed his arms, put his hand on his chin, and said, "If we could get Amtex to have the *Deepwater One* to stand by to drill a relief well, we might be able to convince the Judge that a lot of the risk to the environment will be minimized."

Brock's eyes widened. He asked, "What makes you think they'd help us out?"

"Don't they have blocks north of Seahorse Canyon?"

"Yeah."

"A discovery might help prove up their prospects."

"Maybe."

"And besides, Markham and the old man go way back."

———

That evening, D.L. sat up in bed and listened to Clay explain how industry trade groups had agreed to come to the hearing the next morning and testify on behalf of the company. He was pleased.

Clay pulled his chair closer to the bed and added, "What do you think about this? What if we could get *Deepwater One* to stand by to drill a relief well in the event of a blowout?"

D.L. pondered the question.

"Wouldn't that limit the risk?" asked Clay.

D.L. nodded and said, "How do you plan to pull that off?"

"Maybe you could call C.R. Markham and see what you could do."

D.L.'s brow furrowed. He replied, "I think he's in the Baltics or somewhere like that."

Clay paused and asked, "It wouldn't hurt to give him a call, would it?"

D.L. picked up his black address and phone book. He cleared his throat and in a gravelly voice replied, "I'll call his wife, Sally, to see if I can get hold of him."

———

At two o'clock in the morning, Kate pulled on some sweats, combed her hair, and walked downstairs. She entered the dining room where Clay, Brock, Rosenberg, and five representatives from oil industry trade groups were discussing their strategy for the court hearing. The smell of Ramona's egg burritos filled the air.

The men rose from their chairs.

Kate greeted each man by his first name and thanked them for their support. They were representatives of DeepStar, a joint industry development project focused on advancing technologies in deep water, the International Association of Drilling Contractors, the Society of Petroleum Engineers, the American Association of Petroleum Geologists, the American Petroleum Institute, and the National Ocean Industries Association.

One of the men, who had been a former Vice President of Drummond and was now a CEO of a competitor, said, "I'm sure I speak for all of us, ma'am. D.L. would be doing the same thing for us if we were in this situation. You can count on us."

Another man added in a thick Texas accent, "Hell, we'd go out to *Explorer* and roughneck if we thought that would help."

Everyone laughed.

Clay slapped the man on the back and replied, "We just may take y'all up on that."

Kate got the feeling, as she had so many times in the past, that the close-knit oil business fraternity was alive and well. And she was proud to be part of it. She smiled and said, "Please be seated. May I offer you all some coffee?"

Clay remained standing while the other men sat down. He stretched his arms above his head, rubbed the back of his neck, and asked Kate, "Can I see you for a minute?" and began to walk toward the study.

Kate finished pouring the last cup and then followed him.

Clay closed the door behind them. He then put his hands around her waist, leaned her back, and kissed her on the mouth.

They both laughed.

Kate felt herself blush.

Clay pulled her up.

With a devilish grin on his face, he cocked his head toward the couch.

Kate blushed and then gently slapped him on the chest.

He embraced her firmly and kissed her again.

She whispered, "Later."

Clay growled.

Kate asked, "How's it going?"

"Great! We've been going over a lot and Al is kinda role-playing as if he were the Judge. I think we'll make a good case."

"Tell me again how a relief well would work?"

"In the event of a blowout, or other trouble, a well can be drilled to either contain the blowout or save the well."

"And you're trying to convince Amtex to keep its ship out there while *Explorer* is drilling?"

Clay nodded.

Kate thought this would be as good a time as any to tell him about her conversations with Tiller. She said, "I've met with Tiller a couple of times. She thinks Croft was behind Truesdale's murder."

Clay's eyebrows rose.

Kate continued, "She has a hunch Truesdale was somehow blackmailing or holding something over Croft's head and that's why he had him killed."

Clay leaned back on D.L.'s desk, paused and asked, "Does she have any proof?"

"I don't know. But she wants me to go to New York and ask Croft's wife, Monique, if she knows anything."

"His wife?"

"His *estranged* wife. I guess they've been separated and living apart for years."

Clay crossed his arms and asked, "Why you? And what good would it do?"

Kate knew she had to chose her words carefully and said, "I've met her socially a few times, and she knows some of my girlfriends. And I guess Tiller figures that if she hates Croft's guts, she may tell me something."

Clay had a doubtful look on his face and responded, "Why doesn't Tiller ask her herself?"

Kate had anticipated his question and replied, "Because she thinks Monique would get her attorneys involved and not talk."

Clay pondered for a moment and then said, "And you're supposed to just come out and ask "Was your father blackmailing your husband?"

"Not exactly. I would just say that Tiller told me she suspects that."

Clay paused and replied, "Chances are, she'll tell Croft."

"Tiller says that's the point. She says that'll make him do something stupid."

"Like what?"

"I don't know. She said she's following him and that he may get back in contact with whoever he hired to kill Truesdale. She said if she made the connection he could be arrested and be forced to stop the Seahorse Canyon deal, especially if we could prove he did the wiretap."

Clay shook his head and said forcefully, "Let Tiller do her own goddamn dirty work!"

Kate knew Clay was right, but she feared Tiller would carry out her threat. She said, "I was only trying to help."

"*If* Croft was behind the murder, what makes you think he wouldn't do something to you if you poke your nose into things?"

Kate was horrified. That possibility hadn't entered her mind.

Clay held her and said in a softer tone, "Things are getting pretty crazy, Kate."

CHAPTER **3 3**

Kate was extremely tired when she entered the kitchen at nine-twenty the next morning. She had had less than three hours of sleep and wanted to go to the court hearing, but knew her nerves couldn't handle it.

She poured herself a cup of coffee, sat down at the kitchen table, and unfolded the newspaper Ramona had placed on D.L.'s serving tray. The front page read:

Decorated Detective Murdered in Chinatown

Kate skimmed through the article. Elsa Tiller! She gasped and then began to shake uncontrollably.

———

Amid a circus of reporters and news cameras, Clay and Rosenberg stood outside the courtroom waiting for the hearing to begin. The reporters had been hounding them with questions for the past fifteen minutes, but were beginning to give up after Al had said repeatedly that the company had no comment.

Clay was encouraged to see all the representatives from the various trade organizations there. Many of D.L.'s old friends were also present to lend whatever support they could to the effort. In fact, one of them, a gin rummy pal of D.L.'s from the club, said he would be happy to stand up and "tell that old bitch Burnhouse a thing or two".

Despite the overwhelming feeling of support, Clay was disappointed that they had not heard from C.R. Markham. He knew it was a long shot to get Amtex's help, especially with a potential hurricane brewing in the Gulf. But without *Deepwater One* standing by to drill a relief well, their chances to get the Judge to dismiss the injunction would be close to impossible.

Clay saw Al check his watch and then frown. It was time to go into the courtroom.

Suddenly, there was shouting from the back of the crowd. Clay turned around and saw Brock plowing through the throng of reporters.

Brock finally reached Clay. He whispered into his ear, "Markham came through," and then handed Clay a fax on Amtex stationery.

―――――

Clay, Rosenberg, and Brock walked out of the courtroom two and a half hours later victorious. They hugged one another and were congratulated by all their supporters.

Despite the plaintiff attorneys' vigorous objections, Judge Burn-house was convinced having *Deepwater One* stand by to drill the relief well reduced the risk of environmental damage. However, she imposed the condition that the rig must be present until drilling was completed.

The reporters converged on Rosenberg. He began to read a prepared statement while Clay and Brock headed for the car.

―――――

Clay and Brock got a pat on the back from Bert Glover, D.L.'s chauf-feur, outside the courthouse before climbing into the back of the limo.

Brock's cell phone rang. He answered.

Clay noticed Brock's eyes widen and his face turn red. His smile turned to a frown while he listened intently to the caller.

"What's goin' on?" Clay asked anxiously.

Brock put his hand up for Clay to stop talking.

Brock thanked the caller, ended the call, and said, "Darwin has just been elevated to a hurricane. It's turning north by northwest at about seventeen miles per hour with winds gusting at sixty-five to seventy miles an hour."

Clay exhaled a deep breath.

Brock added, "It's predicted to quickly gain strength. It could be a Category Three or Four."

Clay paused. He leaned forward and said to Bert, "Call the hangar and get them to fuel the jet. I've got to get to Brownsville."

Bert nodded and picked up his phone.

Brock asked, "I'll go out with you."

Clay smiled and said, "I appreciate it, Brock, but you've got a baby on the way." He patted him on the shoulder and added, "Besides, I need you to take care of things here."

———

Clay realized that their court victory was fleeting once he heard the latest weather report a few minutes before the helicopter landed on *Global Explorer.* It was going to be virtually impossible to complete the drilling of the well before they would be forced to move off location.

The chopper touched down on the helipad. He looked at his watch. It was four-twenty. Within forty minutes, he mused, it will be exactly seventy-two hours to the deadline.

He climbed out and looked at the horizon to the south. Dark clouds had formed. The sea was white-capped. The wind had picked up. And he smelled rain.

Clay had been onboard several rigs before the onslaught of a hurricane. Drilling would halt. The crew would button down anything loose on deck. And the ship would start heading for shore to wait it out. That was normal operating procedure. But this situation was different. Everything was on the line. And he knew he would be faced with the dilemma of weighing the risks to the crew and ship with the survival of the company.

———

Clay entered the aft control room and noticed Tito and Auburn Puckett were looking at a long sheet of computer paper. He immediately sensed it was bad news.

Tito looked at Clay and said, "Based on the projected speed and path of the hurricane, we're going to have to move off in twenty-four hours...if not sooner."

Clay replied, "It should slow down if it gains strength."

"This," said Puckett, "takes into account it slowing from eighteen miles per hour to twelve."

Tito added, "It would be unusual for storms on this track to move slower than that."

Clay tried to bolster spirits and asked, "Who wants to bet me a steak dinner that it'll slow down to less than twelve?"

Tito and Puckett managed to smile.

Clay asked Tito, "When will *Deepwater One* be here?"

"Within two or three hours." He paused and added, "You realize ... Minerals Management isn't going to give us one inch of leeway."

"We're back on schedule?" Clay asked.

Tito replied, "Yeah, but we're really pushin' it. The drill bit could twist off any minute."

———

Kate was stunned. She stood up behind her desk, looked at Brock and then back to Al Rosenberg and asked, "Another injunction!?"

"But this time it's Mexico who wants us to stop drilling." He slid a thick document across Kate's desk and continued, "About nine years ago, we leased blocks in the Gulf that includes Seahorse Canyon. The area is the most southerly part of what the U.S. claims to be its territorial waters and Mexico has always disputed where the boundary should be."

Brock said, "Some geologist here in town wrote an opinion that our well would drain Mexico's oil reserves."

Al interjected, "He was probably hired by Croft."

Brock continued, "In my opinion, he fails to make a case."

"But can you make a case that we won't?" asked Kate.

"Since it's a wildcat, the only way to know is to finish drilling and, *if* it's a producer, drill appraisal wells to establish the limits of the field."

Kate's neck was tightening. She rubbed it and then sat down.

Al asked, "Could you come up with *any*...rationale...that the well wouldn't drain from their side?"

"It'll be tough."

Al said, "We have to go to court tomorrow morning. Without that proof, we're screwed. The Judge would have no choice but to grant it."

Kate asked, "Couldn't we somehow make a deal that if we hit oil, we'll give them a percentage of the production?"

Al replied, "Then we'd be cutting into the reserves we have to establish in the agreement with Croft. It would take months to reach a production-sharing agreement anyway."

They were quiet for a moment, considering.

Kate said, "Wait a minute! I just read something about a conference, or something!" She began riffling through some papers. "Here is it is, on U.S./Mexico energy issues. It's today, at the Petroleum Club."

Brock nodded and replied, "It's sponsored by the Departments of Energy and Commerce. I think Secretaries Abraham and Evans will be there."

"What about representatives from Pemex?"

"Yeah. In fact, their senior geologist and chief counsel are suppose to speak."

"Could you get a meeting with them?"

"I suppose...I'll try."

Kate rubbed her chin and asked, "Does Clay know about the injunction?"

"Not yet."

"Let's get him back here ASAP!"

———

Croft noticed Tran's white van parked in a space in The Galleria's underground parking lot that afternoon and pulled into the space next to it. He looked at his hands on the steering wheel. They were shaking.

Tran got out of the van, looked around to make sure no one had followed Croft, and then climbed into the front passenger side. He said, "You look like hell."

Ram had barely slept since Tiller's murder. He asked, "What do you want?"

Tran grinned and replied, "Just to see how you were holdin' up."

He frowned and answered, "Thanks for your concern."

"We're partners, aren't we?"

Ram looked in the side and rearview mirrors and said, "Why haven't you left town?"

"We still have some unfinished business, don't we?"

Ram didn't respond.

Tran added, "You're little ploy to get those environmentalists to stop the drilling didn't work. So what makes you think this Mexican thing is going to do it?"

"It should."

Tran chuckled and replied, "Well, just in case, don't you think we ought to intercept the transmission from the ship?"

Ram hated Tran but knew he needed a backup plan in case the Drummonds were somehow able to get around the injunction.

I've come this far, Ram thought to himself. There's no turning back. This is all going to be over in a few days anyway. He said firmly, "We're done after this! Understand?"

Tran smiled and said, "Sure. Whatever you say."

———

Clay looked at his watch. It was eleven o'clock. The meeting with the Pemex officials in Drummond Offshore's executive conference room had taken over two hours.

He looked across the table at the Pemex Senior Geologist and said, "You know as well as I do, if we hit oil, it could prove up your geology."

"Yes, it could."

"So, we're in this together, aren't we?"

The geologist grinned.

Pemex's Chief Legal Counsel said, "We need assurance that we will be given all the well data, including appraisal wells."

"Okay. Put that in the settlement agreement."

"And we can have our people monitoring all the work?"

"Sure."

"And if your reservoir extends into our waters, you agree to cease and desist all operations until we've reached a mutually acceptable production-sharing agreement."

Clay looked at Brock and Al.

They nodded.

"Agreed," said Clay.

The Pemex attorney looked at the geologist and then back to Clay and said, "Okay, then we'll agree to withdraw our injunction."

Everyone stood, extended their hands across the table, and shook.

CHAPTER 34

Clay rested in his bunk with less than twenty-four hours before the deadline and thought about how lucky they had been. Even though the hurricane had gained strength, it had slowed to nine miles per hour due to a northwesterly high pressure system and had given them more time to 'make hole.' Things were working out better than he had ever expected. And for the first time, he truly felt they had a chance to finish the drilling to the targeted depth.

There was a knock on his door and Tito quickly entered the room. Half out of breath, he said, "The bit...it twisted off!"

———

Clay leapt every third step leading to the drilling deck and Tito followed. Once he reached the top of the stairs, he noticed three crewmen on the drilling floor with disgruntled looks on their faces as the Iron Roughneck, a hydraulic wrench-like mechanism, automatically spun a string of drilling pipe. They were coming out of the hole.

He entered the driller's cabin. Puckett and Ricci were talking to the driller who was seated in front of the console.

Clay asked the driller, "What's our depth?"

The driller, an overweight middle-aged man with a thick, black beard, reddened slightly. He then answered in a deep voice, "Eleven thousand-twenty."

Clay's objective was to reach almost thirteen thousand feet before the deadline and said, "We don't have time to fish it! You've got to go around it. When can you get us back drilling?

The driller replied, "At this depth, around eight hours."

Clay leaned over, looked the man in the eyes and asked, "You know what's on the line here, don't you?"

The driller gulped and then nodded.

Clay remembered Tito telling him that the driller was one of the company's best. He said, "We're all glad that you're the one in that chair," and patted the man on the shoulder.

The man puffed his chest out, straightened his back, and said, "You can count on me, Mr. Drummond." He grabbed a joystick and refocused his attention on the activity on the floor outside.

Tito handed Clay a cup of coffee and they joined Ricci and Puckett.

Clay asked Tito, "Any oil shows yet?"

Tito shook his head.

Clay recalled that the agreement with Croft specified they hit at least seven hundred to eight hundred feet of net pay zone. Based upon the type of formation, and the fact that they'll be using a brand new bit, he figured they could make another one thousand feet before the deadline if they weren't forced to move off the location.

Ricci stepped closer to Clay in order for the driller to not overhear their conversation and said, "We've gotten our fourth warning from Minerals Management to head for shore. The Coast Guard has also issued us several warnings."

Tito said, "And *Deepwater One* said she's leaving in about four hours."

Clay thought about the Judge's order. If the drillship left the location, they were required to halt drilling. But he had no intention of complying.

Clay turned to Tito and said, "We're going to need to move all non-essential drilling personnel to shore immediately."

Tito nodded and said, "I figure we'll have to keep about a crew of thirty. Deepwater One said she'll take about forty or so and two transport ships should be here in about five hours."

"Good."

Ricci frowned and said to Clay, "We are putting the lives of the crewmen who stay behind in danger." His face reddened, and he added, "I'm responsible for them, and I can't permit this."

"The survival of this company is on the line, too."

Ricci's eyes widened. He shouted, "I don't give a damn about the company! Safety comes first! You should know that better than anybody here!"

Tito was about to respond to the Captain's comment, but Clay put up his hand and said, "I know...I know. I agree with you. But we can buy some more time."

Tito interjected and said, "Let's agree that if we start getting winds of, say, seventy miles per hour, and the waves get to fifteen feet, that we'll haul ass out of here. Okay?"

Ricci replied, "That could be a matter of hours."

Tito looked at Clay and asked, "Agreed?"

Clay nodded and extended his hand to the Captain.

Ricci looked into Clay's eyes and then shook.

———

Clay stood in front of a row of monitors in the aft control room and was oblivious to the frenzied activity around him. He looked at a clock above the console. It was twenty past ten — less than nineteen hours before the five p.m. court hearing.

He glanced out the window overlooking the deck. The ship was pointed directly into the oncoming storm and rolled slightly with each successive wave. Due to the heavy rains, visibility was poor. But with the help of flood lights mounted above the deck, he could see the crewmen below performing their tasks to prepare the ship for the worst.

Clay realized he was putting men's lives in jeopardy for the sake of trying to save the company. And what are the chances they are going to find production in the first place? he thought to himself. Is the risk too much? How am I going to live with myself if someone dies?

Clay felt a hand on his shoulder.

Tito handed him a cup of coffee. With a concerned look on his face, he asked, "You okay?"

Clay took the cup. He looked around to make sure no one overhead him and whispered, "Are we doing the right thing?"

Tito didn't reply.

After a moment of silence, Tito finally said, "Your buddy from Minerals Management is on his way out."

"Maybe we should get to shore," said Clay.

"I think we're okay for now."

Clay looked out the window. He noticed some tarps fly off the deck and asked, "What are the winds up to now?"

"Around sixty. And the waves are ten."

Clay looked at the dynamic positioning monitor showing how much thrust the propellers beneath the ship were exerting to keep her stabilized. He knew the ship could withstand waves of twenty feet, but he had never been aboard any rig when it had been in more than fifteen, even in the North Sea.

Tito said, "I just heard from Brock." He looked at his watch and added, "In about an hour, we're gonna be dragged back into court to stop the drilling since Deepwater One headed for shore."

Clay tried to lighten the situation and replied, "Boy, you're just full of good news, aren't you?"

Tito grinned and asked, "What are we going to do when the Judge orders drilling to stop?"

Clay looked at him and said, "Keep drilling."

———

Kate was doing the best she could to appear unaffected by the crowd of shouting protestors and news reporters outside the courthouse as she followed Al, Brock and Bert Glover to the front doors.

Suddenly, she heard Brock yelling at someone. She looked up. The side of his face was black. Someone had thrown a balloon filled with oil.

Two policemen rushed out of the building. They did the best they could to push back the crowd, but to no avail.

People were grabbing at her clothing and a woman a few feet away spit in her face. Kate wiped the corner of her mouth and clutched the back of Bert's jacket and kept moving forward.

Several balloons splashed above the doors and drenched four security guards coming out of the building. Al shouted something and the guards formed a barrier so that the four of them could get through the doors.

Once they were safely inside the building, Kate looked outside and noticed several police cars pulling up to the curb. The crowd began to quickly disperse.

She turned around. Al was trying to straighten out his wire rim glasses and Bert was helping Brock wipe oil off his face with a handkerchief. She then recognized Croft's attorneys, who were waiting for the elevator. They probably helped organize the protest.

———

Clay sat down in front of a color computer monitor in the map room and looked at the picture of the hurricane in relation to the ship's location. The eye had clearly developed and the northernmost counterclockwise swirl of clouds was about to pass over the exact longitude and latitude of the ship. He had never been aboard a rig when a hurricane had been so close.

Captain Ricci rushed into the room. Half out of breath, he said, "We've got a problem!"

Clay turned around and saw fear in the Captain's face.

Ricci added, "We're losing main pump pressure...fast!"

———

Clay and Captain Ricci entered the pump room below deck. Puckett was tapping a pressure gauge on the control panel to check if it was malfunctioning while Tito and two young crewmen anxiously stood by.

Clay asked, "What's up?"

Tito looked at him and said, "We don't know. Something is blocking the water intake vent on the port aft."

Clay looked at the gauges. Main pump pressure was falling rapidly. The image of a tarp blowing off the deck came to mind and he said, "I saw a buncha tarps fly off into the water earlier!"

Tito's eyes widened. He turned to Puckett and said, "Reverse the intake."

"I tried! It's not responding!"

"Try again!"

Puckett nervously turned some dials and then pushed a button with his thumb.

Clay looked at Tito and Ricci and asked, "Was the backup system fixed?"

"No," replied Tito.

Ricci said something in Italian to himself.

Without the backup online, Clay knew it was only a matter of time before the ship's main operating systems, including the dynamic positioning thrusters, would shut down and that they would be hopelessly adrift. Clay asked Puckett, "How long do we have?"

Puckett turned and said, "I don't know! Ten... maybe fifteen minutes! If we're lucky!"

Clay turned to Tito and asked, "How big is the grid?"

"Six by eight feet."

"I need to get lowered down to it."

"One of the thrusters is right under it! You'll be blown out of the water!"

"How far is it above the grid?" asked Clay.

"About thirty feet, I guess."

Ricci said, "You'd have to shut down at least two other thrusters."

Tito put his hand on Clay's shoulder and said, "It won't work! It's suicide!"

"You got a better suggestion?" replied Clay.

———

While he put on a wet suit, heavy weight belt, and a small scuba tank in a storage room on deck, Clay finished explaining to two crane operators over the intercom system his plan to be lowered into the water. Tito, Ricci, and Puckett tried to convince him not to do it, but Clay's mind was made up.

He hooked a flashlight to a harness over his inflatable vest and said to the operator of the stern crane, "Drop me slowly into the water. Once I get a hold of the tarp, I'll cut a hole in it and then attach the line from the bow crane to it. I'll have a microphone on. Okay?"

Both crane operators reluctantly agreed.

Clay turned to Puckett and asked, "How long could you cut the thrusters on that side of the ship before you'd have to turn them back on?"

"I'd guess...less than thirty seconds. But if you're not out of the water by the time they come online, you'll either be sucked in or your line will get tangled up in 'em."

Tito added, "It depends how the ship has drifted. It could be the exact opposite — the thrusters could be blowing out."

Clay paused and replied, "Then I'll release the line and float to the surface using the inflatable vest."

Tito said, "Just in case, I'll be out in a rescue capsule."

Ricci shook his head and said, "This is crazy! There's no way to tell what the computers will do!"

Suddenly, the lights in the room dimmed.

Clay put on his flippers and mask and then opened the door onto the deck. He could barely see a few feet in front of him due to the heavy wind and rain. He looked back at Tito and gave him a thumbs-up.

———

Clay clipped the line from the bow crane to his harness. Through the microphone in his mask, he told the crane operator at the stern to lift him off deck. The slack on the line tightened. He was lifted into the air.

Once he was about thirty feet above the deck, the boom of the crane swiveled and moved him above the water. The strong winds and rain whipped him back and forth. He shouted in the microphone, "Down now! Slowly!"

He saw the rescue capsule being lowered into the water as he began his descent.

———

Once submerged, Clay hoped his voice could be heard over the loud, churning of the thrusters beneath him. He said, "Stop!"

His descent slowed and then stopped. He was relieved.

"Get ready on the thrusters!"

"Ready!" replied Ricci from the aft control room.

Clay turned on his flashlight and shined it on the hull. He figured he was about thirty feet or so from the grid and said, "Okay. Cut 'em." He listened for the roar below him to die down.

He knew there was no way to accurately judge the strength or direction of the thruster's turbulence.

He pulled down on the line from the bow crane to make sure there was enough slack. He unhooked the other from his harness and dove quickly.

The thrusters were winding down.

The heavy weight belt helped his descent. He fought the undercurrent pushing him to his right and away from the water intake grid.

Again, he shined the light on the hull. He wasn't deep enough. He continued his descent.

Suddenly, he saw a large tarp bundled against the hull. He was right!

He fluttered his arms and legs as hard as he could and reached it. He knew he was running out of time. He drew his knife and began cutting a hole in the tarp.

Heavy static came over the microphone. It cleared up for a split second, and he heard Ricci's voice, "Coming online! Coming online!"

Clay heard a whining noise. The thrusters were starting up again.

The tarp was hard to cut through. He felt the wash of the propellers starting to blow him away from the hull. He ripped two holes in the tarp, released the line on his harness, and hooked it through the holes.

He pulled the string on his inflatable vest. It inflated.

Suddenly, the explosive surge of the propellers blew him away from the hull. His mask ripped off his face. He blacked out.

A few minutes later, Clay felt a rocking back and forth. He opened his eyes. Everything was blurry. Within a few seconds, his vision cleared. He was in the rescue capsule.

Tito said, "You're damn lucky!"

Clay turned his head and grimaced from a shot of pain in his neck. He asked, "Is it...the tarp..."

Tito smiled and replied, "You're the man!"

Clay managed a grin despite the pain he felt over his entire body and said, "I think I'm going to need a chiropractor."

Tito and the four other crewmen aboard chuckled.

———

Kate, Al, and Brock looked at one another in the courtroom as Judge Burnhouse began issuing the order for the *Explorer* to cease and desist drilling.

There was a roar of cheers and clapping behind them.

The Judge slammed her gavel several times and called for order.

Kate knew what the outcome was going to be, but was disappointed nonetheless.

Al turned to her and whispered into her ear, "This doesn't really mean much."

Kate's brow furrowed.

Al added, "This has no bearing on the deal with Croft since there was no stipulation that *Deepwater One* had to stay on location."

"But the drilling will have to stop, won't it?"

Al grinned and asked, "How is she going to enforce it?"

She looked at Brock, who appeared to be reading a message on his palm computer.

He said, "Data from the rig...drilling samples...are being transmitted back to the office. We need to get back."

"What is all this?" Kate asked as she and Rosenberg looked over Brock's shoulder while he reviewed data at a computer work station.

Brock paused to scroll down what appeared to be a graph similar to an electric log, but without the squiggly lines and answered, "Mud logging data. We have a technician onboard who takes samples of the formation cuttings made by the drill bit, and we analyze them for shows — strata that have potential to bear oil and gas."

Kate asked, "Is this part of the stuff that has to be met in the agreement?"

Brock shook his head, kept his focus on the computer monitor, and replied, "Only the electric log data counts."

He adjusted the mouse to move the arrow to the upper left-hand corner and clicked **'ENLARGE'**. He continued, "The agreement says that the electric log technicians onboard are not allowed to give the crew any results. This is the next best thing."

"Maybe this is a stupid question," said Kate, "but can any of the electric log data be tampered with or changed?"

Brock replied, "There's no way. It's sent by satellite transmission from the ship and it's encrypted."

"I see."

Rosenberg asked Brock, "Anything?"

"It looks like we've got oil shows starting at ten thousand five hundred feet." He pointed at the screen and added, "And then here at ten thousand eight hundred."

Kate asked, "That's good?"

Brock nodded and replied, "We've only got about three hundred or so feet of pay zone. We need at least seven hundred and fifty." He swiveled around in his chair and added, "We still have another four or five hundred feet of samples coming and should have them in about an hour or so."

Kate was encouraged by the news.

Brock continued, "The only way we're really going to know if we meet the criteria is from the electric logs. That's step one. And even if the criteria are met, the well has to be tested." He looked at Al and then back to Kate and added, "We've been pretty lucky so far, but this whole thing is still a long shot."

———

That evening, D.L. pushed a button to adjust his bed to sit up and said to Kate, "Well, it's all going to be over soon."

She knew he was referring to the deadline tomorrow, but couldn't help thinking to herself that he could pass away within a matter of days. His condition seemed to deteriorate more each day.

She put her hand on his and replied, "I am going to be glad when this whole thing with Croft is over."

He cleared his throat, took a sip of water, and said, "There isn't much we can do at this point. It's out of our hands."

"I know, but I've been worried about Clay."

D.L. grinned and asked, "You love him, don't you?"

Kate didn't know how to respond.

He added, "I think you'll make a great couple."

"Have we...has it been that obvious?"

"Ramona has antennae for that sort of thing."

Kate grinned and replied, "We've both been concerned what everyone would think."

"Don't give a *damn* what anyone thinks."

"I know, but..."

"He's a good man, Kate. He's really shown what he's made of." He cleared his throat again and added, "I'm very proud of him."

"Me, too."

"No matter how this thing with Croft turns out, at least you'll have each other."

Tears began rolling down Kate's cheeks.

D.L. hugged her.

She laid her head on his chest and felt a sense of relief.

CHAPTER 35

Time had flown so quickly, Kate thought to herself while she sat at her desk. Only an hour and a half before the deadline.

Her neck was tight and her stomach was upset from several cups of coffee. She realized she had passed the pick-me-up caffeine stage to becoming hyper when she caught herself looking at her watch every fifteen or twenty minutes since noon.

She pulled a mirror and brush from her purse and looked at herself. Her bloodshot eyes were puffy and dark-circled. She tried to comb out her limp, tangled hair, but soon gave up. Out of frustration, she threw the brush back into her purse.

She thought about giving D.L. a call to update him on what she knew, but then realized he probably knew as much, if not more, than she did. When she called around two o'clock he had told her he didn't want to know anything until the well reached total depth. "Nothing else matters", he said. "You're only going to worry yourself sick thinking about it."

She thought about calling Haley, who could give birth any day. She wanted to check to make sure the helicopter was standing by at the ranch to rush her to the hospital, but knew Ramona had everything under control.

The intercom on her phone buzzed and her secretary said, "Kate, Monique Croft is here to see you."

Kate thought she had misunderstood and asked, "Who?"

"Monique Croft. Are you available?"

What was Monique doing here? she thought to herself. What could she possibly want? Could Ram have sent her to deliver some sort of message? She answered, "Yes. Show her in."

Kate stood, fluffed her hair, and walked around her desk.

Monique entered the open doorway.

Kate extended her hand and said, "Hello, Monique. It's been a long time. What's it been, three years?"

Monique's gaunt and pale face, that no doubt had been through a few plastic surgeries, turned to a combination grin and snarl. She didn't shake Kate's hand and said, "This is not a social visit."

"What can I do for you?" she asked and then saw that Monique was carrying a thick black binder.

Monique walked to the couch, sat down, and placed the binder on the table in front of her.

Kate sat in the chair across from her. She noticed Monique's huge diamond ring on her wedding finger and a diamond-studded tennis bracelet on her right wrist.

Monique reached into her Chanel purse, pulled out a gold cigarette holder and lighter and asked, "Mind if I smoke?"

Before Kate could say she preferred she didn't, Monique lit the cigarette.

After taking a draw and exhaling, Monique said, "Ram always hated me smoking. That's probably why I do it so much these days."

Kate managed a smile.

Monique stared into Kate's eyes and then looked her over.

Kate felt even more uncomfortable.

Monique asked, "Were you ever in love with my husband? Or was it just a fling?"

Kate blushed and said, "I'm sure that's not why you're here," and looked at the binder to avoid eye contact.

Monique snickered and said, "My father...he wasn't the man everyone thought he was, you know."

Kate didn't respond.

Monique added, "My mother died when I was sixteen, and dear ol' *Daddy* decided he was going to protect me from that nasty world out there." She grinned and said, "He protected me all right."

Kate was stunned. Did her father sexually abuse her?

Monique continued, "I didn't even cry at his funeral. And you know what? I felt relieved...almost like being out of prison."

Kate didn't know how to respond.

Monique took another drag on her cigarette and chuckled, "Speaking of prison!" She slid the binder across the table and added, "Take a look at what Daddy dug up on your lover boy."

Kate looked at the binder, turned it around, and opened it. The first page was what appeared to be a brief chronology of business transactions between Croft, Russell Schultz with Manhattan Commerce Bank, and the Mercers.

Monique added, "My attorney tells me he's done all kinds of crooked deals that could put him behind bars for a long time."

Kate leafed through the binder. There were copies of checks, wire transfer receipts, and other documents.

Monique said, "Daddy was always good at digging up dirt on people."

Kate paused and then said, "There was a Detective, Elsa Tiller, who thought your father was blackmailing him."

"The black woman?"

Kate nodded, and said, "She's dead. She was murdered."

Monique's eyes widened.

Kate asked, "She suspected Ram was somehow behind your father's death." Kate pointed to the binder and said, "This could have been his motivation."

Monique appeared shaken. She rose from the couch, grabbed her purse and replied, "He hated my father –– almost as much as I did."

Kate paused and asked, "What do you want me to do with this?"

"Help me destroy him."

———

Kate rushed down the hallway with the binder in hand and asked Kitty, "Is Al in?"

Kitty was startled and replied, "He and Brock are at the attorneys'. Bert is down in the parking lot. He'll take you to the courthouse."

Kate realized she had to take matters into her own hands. She handed the binder to Kitty and said, "I need a copy of this right away."

Kitty looked at it.

Kate added, "And tell Bert to meet me out front. I need to pay a little visit to Mr. Croft."

———

Kate got off the elevator at Croft's offices. As she approached the receptionist, she turned and noticed Ram walking down the hallway in her direction. He was joking with three of his attorneys. But once he noticed her and looked at the binder in her hand, he turned pale. He tried to maintain his composure and asked with a grin, "And how can I help you, my dear?"

The men snickered.

Kate replied, "I'd like a few minutes."

Croft looked at his watch, smiled, and answered, "I was just on my way to a court date."

Kate held up a binder and said, "I think you're going to want to see what's in this."

Croft gulped. He looked at the men and said, "I'll catch up with you later."

The men left them standing in the hallway alone.

Ram's face turned angry. He asked, "What's the meaning of this? Is this another one of your stupid little tricks?"

Kate grinned and replied, "No, it's Jonas Truesdale's."

———

Croft did the best he could to hide his nervousness as he entered his office. He turned around before he reached his desk and said abruptly, "Now what the hell is this all about?"

Kate handed him the binder.

Croft hesitated and then grabbed it. He opened it and immediately recognized the first page. He searched for a response as he leafed through a few of the pages and asked, "Where did you get this?"

"Does it really matter?"

He didn't respond.

Kate asked, "Tiller knew Truesdale had something on you, but couldn't prove it. Is that why you had him killed?"

Croft looked at her and began to tremble. The idea of committing suicide entered his mind.

"Did you have Tiller killed, too?"

In a weak tone of voice, he asked, "You don't have any proof of that."

"Maybe so. But you'll be going to jail anyway, won't you?"

Croft had frozen.

Kate added, "Call off the Seahorse Canyon deal. We'll buy all your shares at thirty dollars and call it a day."

Ram turned his back on her. He walked to the window and looked out. He had lost, he thought to himself. The Drummonds have won again.

Kate said, "If you don't agree to my deal, I'll make sure this gets front page news."

Without turning around, he asked, "What assurances do I have that no one else knows about this?"

Kate paused and said, "You have my word," she said unconvincingly.

Croft turned around and said, "That's not good enough."

"It's going to have to be."

Ram figured she got the binder from Monique or from one of Truesdale's attorneys. What will happen if it's released, he thought to himself? He'll probably end up paying some ridiculous fine and go to some country club prison. As far as Truesdale's and Tiller's deaths, the only person who knows is Tran. He'll keep his mouth shut for more money. The important thing is to close the Drummond deal. Then I'll deal with all this afterwards.

He looked at Kate, who appeared to be shaken, and said, "Okay." He managed a grin and said, "You got a deal."

Kate looked relieved and said, "Call your attorneys and stop the hearing."

With a slight grin, he answered, "I'll tell them in person –- in the courtroom."

"Just pick up the phone and end all of this now!"

"May as well make it dramatic."

Kate's face reddened. She replied, "I've made several copies of this."

"I'm sure you have."

"I'm not bluffing, Ram! We have nothing to lose!"

He paused and said, "See you in court."

Clay noticed the concerned look on Tito's face as he entered the aft control room wearing a yellow rain jacket.

Tito looked up from the monitor showing the dynamic positioning thrusters and replied, "We're barely holding. Winds are close to seventy and seas are right at fifteen feet."

Due to the back and forth motion of the ship, Clay had to brace himself against a chair while he walked across the room. He reached Tito and leaned against the control console. His whole body ached, especially his ribs. He asked, "What's our depth?"

"Eleven thousand six hundred."

Clay looked at the clock on the far wall. He had lost his watch during his dive. It was four-thirty. Thirty minutes to the deadline. He said, "Okay. Let's stop. I'd like a few more hundred feet, but we're out of time."

Tito nodded and picked up a phone to contact the driller.

———

Kate entered the quiet courtroom after Bert Glover cleared a path through the last crowd of reporters in the hallway. She was glad Federal courts didn't allow cameras in the courtroom.

Rosenberg and Brock were seated at a table to the right of the Judge's bench. On the opposing side were Croft's battery of lawyers.

Against a wall, next to the door leading to the Judge's chambers, was a screen Kate guessed was twenty feet long and wide. Below it was a work station with three chairs. She figured that was where the three geologists responsible for interpreting the data were to sit.

Brock rose from his chair when he noticed she had arrived. He walked toward her and said, "They stopped drilling and should be ready to send the information by the deadline."

Kate managed a grin and looked around to see if Croft was in the courtroom. She didn't see him and then looked at the clock on the opposite wall from the monitor. Less than twenty minutes to the deadline.

She desperately wanted to tell Brock about the binder and her meeting with Croft, but his mind, of course, was elsewhere.

She and Bert followed Brock to the row behind Rosenberg and their attorneys and then took their seats.

———

Clay was seated in the aft control room watching Captain Ricci barking orders to move off the location. It'll all be over within fifteen minutes, he thought to himself.

Everyone had done the best they could. They had pushed the ship and crew beyond the limits. Now, it was up to a power greater than him to decide if all their efforts were worth it.

Suddenly, a door opened and a strong gust of wind blew papers around the room. Tito, and a young man named Kyle, the well-logging technician, entered. By the look on Tito's face, something terrible had happened.

Tito said, "The wireline isn't responding. We can't make the trans mission."

Clay's eyes widened. He exhaled a deep breath and asked Kyle, "Is it your equipment?"

The overweight man in his late twenties gulped and answered, "No, Mr. Drummond, I think...it's the connection to the riser."

Tito added, "There are two cables connected to one another." He looked at Kyle and asked, "Ours...the one hooked into the riser. What is it? Ten feet long?"

Kyle nodded.

Tito continued, "The two cables were screwed together. The threads probably got stripped."

Clay asked, "How would we re-attach 'em?"

Kyle answered, "I've got an adapter. You have to screw it onto the end of the cable connected to the riser and then screw the end of our cable into the other end."

Clay rose from his chair. He grimaced from the pain in his ribs, looked into Tito's eyes and said, "Let's get down there and take a look."

———

Ramsey Croft entered the courtroom with one of his attorneys. He walked down the center aisle and did the best he could to act relaxed and confident. As he passed the rows, the tense chatter behind him quieted. He felt relaxed and in control — almost euphoric. Yes, he was concerned about what was going to happen once the contents of Truesdale's binder were released, but he'd deal with that later.

He had seen Tran parked outside the courthouse in a news van. The satellite transmission would be intercepted and the data falsified. It was all arranged. He had won.

Croft approached the bench where Kate was seated. Rosenberg sat closest to the aisle, then Kate, Brock, and Bert Glover.

He stopped. The four of them turned and looked at him.

Croft looked at Kate and said, "Now comes the moment of truth, huh, Kate?"

Brock sprung from his seat. He was restrained by Bert and yelled, "Go to hell, Croft!"

Croft laughed and said, "Your grandfather is going to get there before me," and then took his seat across the aisle.

CHAPTER 36

Amidst the heavy wind and rain, Clay stood with Tito, Ricci, Kyle, and four crewmen watching the column of water plunge up and then down the sides of the riser below them. As suspected, the cables had been disconnected. The ten foot cable Tito had described earlier was luckily still attached to the riser, but it had to be retrieved from the water.

Clay looked at Kyle and asked, "Do you have the adapter?"

Kyle gripped a railing to make sure he didn't slip on the wet deck. He reached into his pocket, pulled out a six-inch, long metal nozzle, and handed it to Clay.

Clay stuck his index finger in both ends to feel the threads. He then looked at Tito and said, "We'll need a crescent wrench."

For the next few minutes, Clay and Tito discussed how they could accomplish the task. It was decided that the two of them would wear harnesses and be lowered down by ropes attached to separate pulleys. Tito will be suspended in midair while Clay would fish the cable out of the water and then be pulled up to Tito.

Clay wiped rain off the face of the watch he had borrowed from a crewman. They had less than ten minutes until the deadline. He turned to Captain Ricci and shouted over the sound of the rain pelting the deck, "Tell the Judge we have some minor technical difficulties and that the transmission is going to be delayed."

"How much more time do we need?" he asked.

"Just buy us as much as you can."

―――――

Kate felt her heart pounding more rapidly as Judge Burnhouse walked out of her chambers. The tall, lean, woman in her mid-sixties was known for her no-nonsense approach. According to D.L., she loved her cigars and Jack Daniels.

Everyone in the courtroom rose.

The Judge sat down and looked at the clock.

Five minutes to the deadline.

The three geologists took their seats in front of the large monitors while the bailiff approached the bench and whispered something to the Judge.

Burnhouse frowned. She addressed the audience and said, "There's a call from the Captain aboard the Global Explorer." She turned to a young man standing next to the geologists and asked, "Can we broadcast it on our sound system?"

The young man nodded and replied, "It'll take a couple of minutes."

Kate looked at Brock. She gripped his hand and then looked toward Croft who was talking with the only female attorney in the group. Was he telling her to call off the deal?

―――――

Clay hooked the end of a rope to his harness and looked down. Waves exploded against the sides of the moonpool and sent heavy sprays into the air.

He calculated the column of water rose and then dropped every twenty to twenty-five seconds. He knew he had to grab the cable quickly and hand it to Tito before the water rose again.

———

Kate looked at the clock on the wall. Two minutes after five o'clock.

Suddenly, there was static over the loudspeakers.

"This is Captain Ricci, your honor. I'm afraid there has been a minor technical problem. The transmission should come through in a few minutes."

The Judge looked at the clock. She leaned forward and spoke into a speaker box and replied, "Captain, you are already beyond the deadline."

Ricci paused and replied, "We just need a few moments, please."

Croft's lead attorney stood and asked, "May I address the court?"

Burnhouse nodded.

The attorney held up a document and said, "Our agreement stipulates that the deadline must be met at five o'clock, your honor. No exceptions."

Burnhouse angered slightly and replied, "I know what the agreement says, counselor." She said into the box, "Captain Ricci, what exactly is the problem?"

Croft's attorney yelled, "Your honor! The deadline is up! You cannot grant them any more time!"

Burnhouse put her hand over the speaker and said, "Sit down, counselor!"

"Your honor, there are no provisions in the agreement to grant an extension of time!"

"Sit down! Or I'll hold you in contempt!"

The lawyer turned around, looked at Croft, and sat down.

The Judge continued, "Captain Ricci. What is the problem?"

"We are in the process of reattaching a cable."

"How much time do you need?"

"It should be done soon."

"How many minutes?" she asked sharply.

Ricci said, "I don't know...maybe...it's being done now."

The Judge paused, looked at Croft's attorney, and said into the speaker, "You have until five-fifteen."

The attorney jumped from his seat, but was then restrained by two lawyers seated beside him.

———

Clay watched the water level drop rapidly. Not yet, he thought to himself. The timing had to be just right. Wait. Wait. Now!

He dove.

In mid-air, he realized the distance to the water was more than he anticipated. He plunged into the water, quickly resurfaced, and tried to get his bearings. The cable was on the other side of the riser. He swam to reach it. He spotted it. A few more strokes.

Suddenly, he felt a surge beneath him. The current began to swirl violently under him. One more stroke!

He grabbed the cable. It slipped from his hand. The water level began rising quickly. He reached for the cable again. He got it!

The water beneath him exploded. He became completely submerged. The undercurrent pushed him violently to one side. He was heading for the wall. He curled.

Suddenly, he felt a strong tug on his harness. He was lifted upward, but hit the wall first. He nearly dropped the cable.

The rope straightened out. He was jerked out of the water.

He looked up. Tito was being lowered down.

Clay held the cable in one hand and motioned for Tito to be lowered faster.

He pulled the nozzle from his pocket. Tito quickly began screwing the end of his cable into it. After three rotations, he used the wrench to tighten it.

It was Clay's turn. He began screwing his end in. One rotation. Two rotations. Half-way through the third, it was too hard to hand-tighten.

Tito handed him the wrench.

Clay looked down. The water level reached his feet. It swelled. A large wave crashed against the side of the wall. It hit Clay and Tito and knocked them off the side of the riser. The wrench dropped from Clay's hand.

The swirling undercurrent sucked Clay downward as the water level reached his chest. He was flung around the other side of the riser. He crashed against Tito and then felt his rope become tangled with his.

He looked up. Tito's rope had slipped from its pulley. The crewmen struggled to get it back on its track.

Clay and Tito crashed against the wall. The strong undercurrent swirled them around. They hit the wall on the other side of the riser.

Clay got a brief glimpse of Tito's face. Blood was running down the side of his mouth and the side of his head looked like it had caved in.

He grabbed Tito. He attempted to unhook the rope from Tito's harness to his. A wave washed over them and pushed them along the wall.

Tito moaned. Clay felt a tug. He held onto Tito's harness. They were lifted half-way out of the water. Tito was suspended below him

Another wave.

They were flung against the riser.

Clay lost his grip. He looked down. Tito was braced against the side of the riser. He looked at the tangled lines and then at Clay. He began to unhook his line.

Clay screamed, "No!"

Tito unhooked the rope from his harness.

Another wave hit. Clay was flung against a wall. His rope tugged violently. He was pulled out of the water. He realized that without Tito unhooking his rope, he could not have been reeled in.

Clay looked below in horror. Tito's limp body crashed against one side of the wall and then another. The water level plunged. He was sucked downward and disappeared into the deep.

———

Clay swung out over the deck and landed. He unhooked his harness, grabbed a walkie talkie from one of his crewmen, and screamed, "Kyle, come in! Kyle!"

One of the crewmen said, "He's probably on his way to the control room."

Clay spoke into the walkie talkie again and yelled, "Ricci...Ricci is Kyle with you?"

There was heavy static.

Suddenly, the walkie talkie made a crackling sound, but there was no response.

Clay threw the walkie talkie to the deck. He had to get to the aft control room.

The quickest way was by using the metal walkway. He looked above him and realized it would be difficult to cross it through the violent wind and rain. He didn't have a choice. He ran toward the set of stairs.

Before he reached the first of two levels, the gale force wind knocked him off his feet and nearly blew him off the stairs. He managed to grab a railing and began to slowly pull himself up. The rain felt like needles.

While holding the railing, he started to climb the steps, one by one. The ship was rocking back and forth. His whole body ached. Adrenaline kept him going.

He rounded the first set of stairs. He began to climb to the second level. The winds were stronger. Every step was a struggle.

He reached the walkway. The gusts were violent. He fell again and hugged the railing to avoid being blown off. There was no way he could make it across, he thought to himself. The winds were too strong.

As he sat there, the look in Tito's eyes before he unhooked his harness flashed through his mind. Tito gave his life to save him. He owed it to him to finish what they started.

With every ounce of strength he had left, Clay picked himself up and began to slowly make his way across the walkway.

———

Kate watched as the second hand hit the twelve. Exactly five-fifteen.

The Judge told the young man in charge of communications to contact the ship.

Croft's attorney stood and asked, in as restrained a manner as he could, "May I address the court, your Honor?"

Kate's heart was nearly pounding out of her chest.

The Judge paused and simply nodded.

The lawyer said, "We recognize that you have exercised some discretion in this matter, your Honor. But your self-imposed deadline is in contravention of the agreement. We implore you to stop this circus."

The Judge frowned and looked toward Rosenberg who had stood. She put her hand up as a gesture for him not to speak, looked back at Croft's attorney, and then said to the young man, "Hurry up and reach the ship!"

———

Clay had only a few more steps to go. Two crewmen held onto a railing at the end of the walkway and reached for him.

He felt faint. He took another step. A man grabbed his arm while the other man slipped his hand around Clay's belt and yanked him toward him. He made it!

Clay shook his head. He tried to regain his breath. The two crewmen rushed him to the aft control room.

Once he entered the control room, he heard, "Captain Ricci! This is Judge Burnhouse. Can you hear me? Captain Ricci!"

Clay looked at a speaker box next to the phone. Ricci was about to respond. Clay put his finger to his mouth.

Clay whispered, "What's going on with the transmission?"

Ricci stepped far enough away from the speaker so his conversation wouldn't be overheard and said, "No signal yet."

Clay walked toward the speaker phone and then pushed the 'OFF' button.

Ricci screamed, "What the hell are you doing?"

"Buying more time."

———

Kate fidgeted in her seat. She looked over at Croft who was clearly agitated by what was going on.

"Captain Ricci!" yelled the Judge into the microphone. "Captain Ricci, do you hear me?" She looked at the young technician and asked, "What happened?"

He answered, "We've lost the connection, your Honor."

"Get it back!"

Croft's attorney leapt from his chair.

The Judge pounded the gavel, stared at the lawyer, and said, "One more word out of your big mouth, counselor, and you'll be escorted to jail! Do you understand, Sir?"

The attorney reluctantly took his seat.

———

Clay felt faint, but mustered enough energy to grab Ricci's walkie talkie and yelled, "Kyle! Kyle! Come in!"

The phone rang.

Clay and Ricci looked at one another.

It rang again.

Suddenly, there was a crackling sound from the walkie-talkie.

"Okay!" said Kyle. "The transmission...it's going!"

In the middle of the third ring, Clay picked up the phone and said, "Judge Burnhouse, this is Clay Drummond."

———

Kate, and the entire courtroom, were stunned and listened intently to Clay.

Clay said, "The transmission is being relayed as we speak, your Honor. Thank you for your cooperation." The call was ended.

The Judge swiveled her chair around and looked at the large monitors.

———

Clay felt his knees buckle after he put the phone down. He reached for a chair. The ship swayed to one side. The chair slid across the floor. He began to fall. The two crewmen who rescued him on the walkway caught him and helped him to another chair.

———

Kate watched nervously as the color monitors blinked on and then off a few times until an enlarged electric log appeared. She looked at Brock's face for a reaction.

Brock's brow furrowed. He grabbed some papers from his briefcase, glanced at them, and then looked at the monitors.

Just as Kate was about to ask what it all meant, Brock said, "I don't understand! It doesn't make sense."

Rosenberg and the lawyers turned around.

He added, "Based on the mud-logging samples, there should be more net pay! I'm sure of it!"

"What do you mean?" asked Kate.

"The last samples showed we had at least five hundred feet. The log indicates only three hundred."

Kate asked, "We needed how much?"

"Eight hundred."

"What about the other stuff?"

Brock looked intently at the monitors and said, "The porosity is around, I'd say, fourteen percent. We needed twenty-six. The permeability...it had to be five hundred milli-darcies. We'd be lucky to have three hundred."

Kate numbed. She glanced in Croft's direction.

He was huddled with his attorneys and consultants. He then looked up and grinned at Kate.

She looked away.

People around Croft began to cheer and pat each other on the back.

Judge Burnhouse pounded the gavel and called for order.

―――――

Ten minutes later, the phone in the aft control room rang. Clay was still groggy despite the ship's medic making him sniff smelling salts.

He rose from his chair, grimaced from the pain in his ribs, and looked around the room. Captain Ricci, Auburn Puckett, and several crewmen stood silently. He looked at the speaker phone, pushed the button and said, "This is Clay Drummond."

"Mr. Drummond," replied the Judge, "The panel of three experts unanimously agree that the well does *not*, I repeat, does *not* meet the criteria outlined in the settlement agreement."

Clay heard clapping in the background.

The Judge slammed her gavel and yelled, "There will be no more outbursts in this courtroom!"

The room quickly grew silent again.

The Judge continued, "Under article three-point-five, subparagraph A, Mr. Croft has the right to exercise his purchase of the Drummond family shares as stipulated. Counselor?"

"Your Honor, my client will exercise his right."

There were cheers.

Clay ended the call. He looked at Ricci and Puckett and then at the stone-faced crewmen and said in a strained voice, "We did everything we could." He paused and added, "My father and the rest of our family thanks you."

For a moment, there was complete silence. Then, Captain Ricci began barking orders to head for shore.

CHAPTER 37

Kate waited with Brock, Al, and Bert before walking through the front doors of the courthouse. She knew they would be mauled by reporters outside and that everything was being broadcast live on the evening news.

She withdrew a written statement from her purse and then nodded to Bert.

He opened the doors.

The reporters jostled for position. They blurted out questions. Light bulbs flashed. Lights on TV cameras brightened.

Kate stepped up to several news microphones bunched together, tried to gather her composure, and said, "We would like to make a brief statement, please."

The noise of the crowd died down slightly.

She shouted again, "We would like to make a brief statement, please."

The crowd grew quieter.

Kate read from a single sheet of paper, "The settlement agreement for the purchase and sale of all of the Drummond family shares and those shares controlled by Mr. Ramsey Croft has finally reached an end. The Seahorse Canyon well was successfully drilled in the Gulf of

Mexico. However, it failed to meet certain technical criteria outlined in the agreement."

The crowd was hushed.

Kate added, "Mr. Ramsey Croft has exercised his option to purchase our family's shares pursuant to that agreement. She folded the paper and added, "This matter has been concluded."

Reporters shouted questions and pushed inward on the ropes. Several policemen restrained them.

Kate saw the limo pull up to the curb.

Al took her by the arm and escorted her. Brock and Bert led the way.

The reporters began yelling at someone coming out of the door.

Kate turned around. It was Croft and his attorneys.

Croft had a wide grin on his face and stepped up to the microphones. He raised his hand in an attempt to silence the reporters and then glanced at Kate.

Suddenly, there was a noisy commotion across the street. Curiously, a man driving a white news van with a satellite dish on top of it had pulled up onto the sidewalk and was trying frantically to leave the scene.

At first, Kate didn't think anything of it. She looked back at Croft. There was fear in his face.

She looked back at the van. The lettering on the side of the truck identifying it as a news van had peeled off and was hanging. And the driver was oriental! She recalled Clay saying that one of the men involved in the parking lot shooting was oriental!

Kate yelled to Brock, "Over there! That man!"

Brock looked across the street.

Kate screamed, "That's the man from the parking lot! The one who shot at Clay!"

Brock plowed through the crowd.

Bert followed.

Cameramen and reporters rushed toward the scene.

The man looked in horror as he saw Brock and Bert approach. He reached for something under his seat.

Brock opened the driver's side door. He grabbed the man and threw him to the pavement. A pistol with a silencer dropped out of his hand. Brock put his knee in Tran's chest. He pinned him to the ground and screamed, "Who are you? What are you doing here?"

The man grinned in defiance.

Cameras captured the action.

Kate pushed her way through the crowd.

Brock wound up and punched the man in the side of the face. Blood poured out of the side of his eye.

"What have you done?" shouted Brock.

Tran didn't respond.

Brock hit him two more times.

Blood sprayed from Tran's mouth. He put up his hand as a sign to stop and then murmured something.

"What? What did you say"

"Croft...the transmission..."

Brock looked up at the satellite dish and asked, "You tampered with it?"

Tran gulped and didn't say anything.

Brock punched him in the face.

Tran screamed, "Yes! Yes! And he killed the detective!"

Kate looked back at Croft. He was gone!

————

Kate, Brock, and Rosenberg and their attorneys re-entered the packed, noisy courtroom. Croft's lawyers were in a state of confusion.

Brock ushered Kate to the same row of benches where they had sat previously.

Rosenberg joined the attorneys at the front table.

The bailiff called for order. People began to take their seats and the chatter stopped.

Judge Burnhouse emerged from her chambers, took her seat, and pounded her gavel twice. She said, "Case one-seven-four-three-nine-Ramsey L. Croft versus D.L. Drummond, et al, is hereby reconvened." She looked at Croft's lead attorney. "Do you have any objections, counselor?"

Kate looked at the attorney. He was visibly shaken and said, "The court has... issued its opinion regarding the settlement agreement. Therefore, my client objects to this proceeding."

Burnhouse replied, "Your objection is noted." She looked at the other table and said, "Does the other side object?"

Rosenberg stood and said, "Your Honor, Ramsey Croft developed a scheme to intercept..."

"I was watching the news, Mr. Rosenberg," interrupted the Judge. "Do you object to reconvening this hearing?"

Al replied, "No, your Honor," and sat down.

The Judge looked back at Croft's attorneys and asked, "Where is your client?"

The lead attorney stood and answered, "We don't know."

Judge Burnhouse looked at the Deputy Sheriff standing to her left and asked, "He's not in custody, I take it?"

"No, your Honor. But an APB has been issued."

The Judge turned to the technician who had a bewildered look on his face and asked, "Can you please explain to me, Sir, how this...*foul play* was carried out?"

The young man replied, "It appears, your Honor, that the satellite signal was somehow intercepted and the information...the electric log data...was replaced with false information."

Brock whispered to Kate, "I knew something was wrong."

The Judge pondered the young man's answer and asked, "Do we need to re-contact the Explorer?"

"No, your Honor. We have the correct data. It's coming on screen now."

The Judge turned to the three experts and said, "Gentlemen, can you please take your seats."

The three men complied.

Kate looked at Brock.

He took some papers out of his briefcase.

Kate said to Brock, "I don't know if my heart can take much more of this."

Brock gently rubbed her hand.

The monitor blinked on and then off a few times.

The electric log data flashed onto the screen.

Kate looked at the expression on Brock's face for the results.

Brock's mouth gaped open.

"What?" Kate asked. "What?"

Brock looked at a sheet of paper he had pulled from his briefcase and then back to the monitor.

She asked, "Brock, what is it?"

With his eyes still glued to the monitor, he replied, "I...I don't believe it!"

Kate nudged him and asked, "Believe what?"

People in the courtroom began to chatter.

Brock looked at her with a wide smile and said, "It's off the charts! I mean...all three criteria have been met — by a long shot!"

Kate looked at the monitor and then back to him and asked, "Are you sure?"

"Positive!"

The Judge banged her gavel and yelled, "Order! There will be order in this courtroom!"

The talking subsided.

The Judge asked the three experts, "Gentlemen, have you reached a conclusion? Have the criteria been met?"

The three men spoke among themselves for a moment. One of them stood and said, "Yes, your Honor, they have."

Kate and Brock leapt from their seats and hugged one another.

The courtroom exploded with cheers.

The Judge pounded her gavel and called for order, but to no avail.

Rosenberg, with tears in his eyes, jumped from his seat, rushed back to where Kate and Brock were standing, and hugged them.

Finally, the noise began to subside and the Judge's gavel and voice grew louder.

Everyone began taking their seats again.

Judge Burnhouse looked in Rosenberg's direction and said, "Mr. Rosenberg, under Article three-point-five, Subparagraph A, D.L. Drummond, et al, has the right to exercise the option to purchase the shares controlled by Ramsey L. Croft, and related entities. What do you wish to do?"

Al was bubbling over with joy and said, "We will exercise our right, your Honor."

There was some clapping from the audience.

The Judge looked toward the back of the courtroom and it stopped. She glanced at the paperwork in front of her and said, "You do understand, Mr. Rosenberg, that the consummation of the stock transfer is contingent upon the testing of the well as stipulated in the agreement."

Brock yelled, "No problem, your Honor! No problem!"

The courtroom roared with laughter.

The Judge managed a grin, pounded her gavel, and said, "Court adjourned."

———

Kate looked straight into a news camera outside the courthouse and said, "The Seahorse Canyon well has easily surpassed all criteria outlined in the settlement agreement, and...," she looked at Brock and then back to the camera, "and we are extremely confident the testing of the well will also be successful."

The crowd erupted. Reporters shouted questions. Cameras flashed.

Kate smiled. Her eyes watered, and she shouted, "The D.L. Drummond Oilfield has the potential to be the largest producing oilfield in the Gulf of Mexico."

——

D.L. turned off the TV with the remote control from his bed and wipedtears from his eyes. He looked at the portrait of Victoria on her white horse that he brought from his study, clenched his fist, and said, "We did it, ol' girl! We did it!"

C H A P T E R 38

Three hours later, Kate left the party on the fifteenth floor, walked to her office, and sat behind her desk. She was lightheaded from the champagne.

She looked at her watch. It was nine-thirty. Clay should be arriving at the ranch within a half-hour.

Brock entered and said, "I spoke with Clay again."

By the expression on his face, Kate knew something was wrong.

"Tito is dead," he said. He closed the door behind him and added, "I don't know all the details, but he and Clay had to reattach a cable to make sure the transmission went through. He drowned in the process."

Kate was stunned. With tears streaming down her cheeks, she looked at a family photo of Tito, his wife, Elena, and their two daughters, and asked, "Does Ramona know yet?"

Brock nodded and replied, "Clay called Pops, and he told her."

They were quiet for a moment.

Brock broke the silence and said, "We need to catch the chopper out to the ranch before the storm gets worse."

―――――

Croft finally found the front gate leading to Four Oaks. He had been driving up and down the long country roads west of Houston in the heavy rain for the past two hours trying to come up with a plan to get out of the country...after he killed D.L.

The police were more than likely waiting for him at his jet hangar and have already staked out the airports. Hell, he thought to himself, his picture had probably been flashed on the eleven o'clock news.

Maybe I'll keep driving to Dallas. The police won't be looking for me there. No, I should keep going to Oklahoma or some other state and then charter a plane in the morning for Mexico. No, I can't do that. I don't have my passport. Canada? You don't need a passport to get into Canada. But what about money? I can't use my credit cards. They'll be able to track me down. I've got about a thousand dollars in cash. That should be enough until I get somewhere and have money wired to me from my Swiss accounts. Then I'll find a way to get a fake passport and get to Europe. I've got enough money stashed away to buy a new identity and live comfortably. No one will ever find me.

———

"I had Ramona taken into town to be with her sister," D.L. told Kate and Brock as they entered his bedroom. He sat up in bed, took a sip of water, and added, "And I'm sending Doc Bender over to see her. She's pretty broken up."

Kate walked to his bedside and put her hand on his arm.

D.L. wiped a tear from his eye and said, "That boy was like a son to me. He was a good man."

Kate replied, "We all loved him."

D.L. looked at Brock and said sternly, "You make sure his family is well taken care of."

Brock nodded and replied, "You don't have to worry about that, Pops."

There was a pause in the conversation.

D.L. glanced out the window and said, "The storm is really pickin' up."

Brock said, "We'll have fifty to sixty mile an hour winds."

D.L. pointed to the mantle above the fireplace and said, "For some reason that damn clock stopped. He turned to Brock and asked, "What time is it?"

Brock looked at his watch and replied, "Twenty past eleven."

"Has the ship made it back to Brownsville?" asked D.L.

"Should have by now, but I'll check."

D.L. looked into Kate's eyes and said, "Clay should be here any time now."

She smiled.

He added, "You ought to be proud of him."

"I am."

"I told you he'd come through, didn't I?"

Kate nodded.

D.L. looked over her shoulder at Brock and added, "And you."

Brock straightened up.

D.L. continued, "Everybody thought I was touched in the head about Seahorse Canyon. But I'll tell you this: Had you not come up with the idea in the first place, that sonofabitch Croft would have gotten control."

Brock blushed and replied, "But... it was Clay. He made it all happen."

D.L. grinned and realized that, under Clay's guidance, his grandson may be ready to run the company sooner than he thought.

———

Croft stuffed the pistol in the front of his trousers, climbed over the fence, and walked to the driveway leading to the house. In the distance, he saw that several lights inside the home had been turned on and the huge oak trees surrounding it were up-lighted. He also noticed a series of lights on the ground to the right of the house and figured they were landing lights around the helipad.

He sought shelter from the rain beneath the pecan trees and began walking. He wondered if there was any security he had to worry about. Were there cameras? Did D.L. have bodyguards? What about dogs? He pulled the gun from his pants, clicked the safety off, and quickened his pace.

About halfway up the driveway, he turned around and noticed that he had left his parking lights on. He stopped, thought about going back and turning them off, but decided not to and continued walking.

———

Clay looked out the rain-streaked window of the helicopter. The lights around the helipad at *Four Oaks* formed a perfect circle. It was good to be home.

Once the helicopter turned and began its descent, he noticed a truck loaded with hay bales parked next to the helipad. He figured the ranch hands had been feeding the cattle and stopped once the rains came.

The thought of selling his property in the Bahamas entered his mind. It was time to leave that way of life behind now and move back to the ranch. After all, someone would need to tend to the place after his father passed away. But he knew he couldn't do it single-handed and wondered if Kate would consider moving in?

He glanced out the window on the opposite side of the cabin. In the distance, he saw a car parked near the gate with its parking lights on. Someone must be having car trouble, he thought.

He looked back out the window nearest him and noticed the porch light come on. Kate and Brock walked out to the foot of the steps and looked up. Clay waved, but then realized the chopper was too high for them to see him.

Brock opened an umbrella. Kate rushed under it, and they began making their way toward the pad.

Clay couldn't wait to hold her in his arms.

The helicopter was rocked by a gale. The pilot maneuvered back on course and then touched down.

Clay quickly unbuckled his seatbelt.

The pilot - this time a man - turned around and said, "I'm going to take off, if that's okay, Mr. Drummond. I have to get this back to the airport for a maintenance overhaul."

Clay gave him a thumbs-up, slipped on a rain jacket, and opened the door.

When he stepped onto the ground, his knees nearly buckled. His entire body was sore, especially his ribs.

Kate and Brock shielded their faces from the heavy spray made by the helicopter's rotors.

Clay hunched over and limped his way toward them.

Kate waved and then rushed toward him.

They embraced and kissed deeply.

Kate said something, but he couldn't hear over the whining sound of the helicopter as it prepared to take off.

Clay put his arm around her and they began to walk toward Brock.

By the time they reached him, the chopper had lifted off, and the spray had nearly subsided.

Brock extended his hand.

Clay gave him a bear hug and said, "Your theory was sure as hell right!"

"You got it done, Clay!" he replied. "You!"

Clay smiled, but then saw something move from behind the truck. He looked more closely. It was Ramsey Croft! He was holding a gun!

Kate turned and saw Croft.

Brock stepped in between Croft and Kate in an attempt to shield her.

Croft pointed the gun at Clay's head, walked toward him and yelled, "You've won again, huh, Drummond?" He stopped within ten feet.

Croft was trembling. He couldn't hold the pistol steady.

Clay said, "It's over. Put the gun down. You'll never get away with this."

"Really?"

Clay took a step near him.

Croft screamed, "Don't!"

Clay backed off.

Suddenly, Brock lunged toward Croft.

Croft aimed and fired.

Kate screamed.

Brock grabbed his neck, stumbled, and fell to the ground.

Clay rushed at Croft.

Another shot was fired.

Clay flinched from the shot to his left shoulder. He swiped at the pistol with the back of his hand. The gun flew out of Croft's hand and skidded across the pavement.

Croft rushed toward it. He picked up the gun. He turned and fired.

The bullet ripped into Clay's leg.

Clay tackled him. They fell to the ground. The gun dropped out of Croft's hand.

Croft punched Clay on his shoulder wound. He wailed in pain.

Croft began to get up. Clay grabbed his ankle. Croft kicked him in the side of the head. He felt himself losing consciousness. Another kick to the head. Clay blacked out.

———

Kate was in a state of shock while she kneeled over Brock. His neck was bloodied. The bullet had nearly hit his jugular vein.

Brock mumbled, "I'm okay...I'm okay." He looked in the direction where Clay and Croft had been struggling.

Kate noticed his eyes widen. She looked up. Croft had picked up the pistol and was walking toward Clay.

―――――

Clay lay face down on the pavement. He managed to open his eyes. His vision was blurry. All he could see was a rear tire of the truck. He blinked his eyes a few times. His vision cleared. And then he saw a pitchfork leaning up against the side of the truck.

He heard footsteps in the rain puddles. He tried to move but couldn't. He heard the trigger cock back.

Croft said, "See you in hell, Drummond!"

Clay cringed.

Suddenly, he heard Croft scream. A shot was fired into the air. With all his strength, Clay rolled along the ground and looked up. Kate had jumped on Croft from behind. Her arms were wrapped around his neck. Croft tried frantically to get her off him.

Clay summoned everything he could. He crawled toward the truck. The pain in his leg throbbed. He felt the steady stream of blood pouring from it.

He reached for the back fender of the truck and began pulling himself up. He heard Croft yell, "You bitch!"

Clay pulled himself up. He supported himself on one leg and turned. Kate was still on Croft's back. She had begun scratching at his face.

Croft dropped the pistol. He elbowed Kate in the side. She kept clawing at his face. He elbowed her again. She screamed and fell to the ground.

Clay looked at the pitchfork leaning against the truck. Croft stepped toward the pistol laying on the ground. Clay grabbed the pitchfork. He raised it and lunged toward Croft. Croft turned. Clay thrust the pitchfork forward. The long needles cut into his stomach. Croft screamed. He began shivering and shaking uncontrollably. His eyes bulged.

Clay looked at Kate. She was motionless on the ground. He looked into Croft's eyes. He gripped the handle of the pitchfork more firmly. He drove the pitchfork deeper and upward. Blood poured out of Croft's mouth. He stumbled backward and fell to the pavement.

CHAPTER 39

Two weeks later, D.L. was sitting up in bed holding his great-grandson for the first time. Haley, Kate, and Kendra stood next to him while Clay sat uncomfortably in a chair in the corner of the room.

D.L. cleared his throat. He looked at Haley, who stroked Daniel's head, and said, "He's a fine lookin' boy. Have a bunch more."

Haley smiled and gently rubbed D.L.'s arm.

Brock entered the room. He still had a bandage on the side of his neck and said, half out-of-breath, "Sorry I'm late." He walked over to D.L.'s bedside and added, "All the well test data is in, Pops. The well flowed at over twenty-seven thousand barrels."

Kendra high-fived Brock.

The topic of discussion among the family for the past few days was whether the well would flow more than twenty thousand barrels per day, — the criteria that had to be met in the agreement with Croft.

Clay asked, "What about the direction of the field?"

Brock answered, "We've done some seismic, and we're ninety-nine percent sure that the well is near the most southerly end of it." He looked at D.L. and said, "In U.S. territorial waters, not Mexican."

D.L. smiled and replied, "Hell, I knew it all along."

Everyone laughed.

"Now," said D.L., "you're gonna have to break the deepwater production record."

Brock looked at Clay and said, "We'll do it, won't we Clay."

"Yup."

D.L. was quickly losing what little energy he had left.

Apparently, Haley noticed it and took Daniel from his arms.

He coughed and then looked at everyone's faces. He knew this would
be the last time he'd see them all together. He felt his eyes water. He
cleared his throat again and said, "I'm tired."

Everyone got the message and started to leave the room.

D.L. coughed again and said, "Clay. Kate. I'd like to talk to both of
you."

Haley and Kendra took turns kissing him on the forehead and then
walked toward the door.

D.L. noticed Brock was getting choked-up and he said, "Go on now,
take care of that family of yours."

Brock nodded, wiped a tear from his eye, and closed the door behind
him.

Clay grimaced when he rose from his chair. He limped to the side of
the bed, put his arm around Kate's waist and asked, "What is it, Dad?"

"I want the two of you to be the Trustees...manage everything, okay?
Rosenberg has done all the paperwork.

Clay and Kate looked at one another and then nodded.

In a low tone of voice, D.L. added, "Now...it's time...for me to go."
He pointed to the vial and a syringe on the table next to the bed. It was
filled with a liquid. The box next to it was labeled 'Morphine.' He said,
"I've led a good life," and tried to hold back the tears.

Kate began to weep. She put her hand on his.

D.L. said, "Please."

Kate looked at Clay.

Tears were streaming down Clay's face. He nodded.

Kate looked at the vial and syringe and then slowly reached for it. Her hand was shaking.

Clay leaned over and said, "I love you, Dad."

D.L. put his hand on Clay's arm and said, "I love you, son."

D.L. watched Kate insert the needle of the syringe into the vial and slowly drain the morphine. Once the syringe was half-full, she placed the vial back on the table.

Tears poured down her cheeks. She looked at Clay. He nodded again.

Kate inserted the needle into the I.V. and slowly pushed the plunger. The liquid dripped down the plastic tube inserted in D.L.'s arm.

After the syringe emptied, Kate and Clay held D.L.'s hands. He smiled at them, looked at the antique clock on the mantle above the fireplace that Victoria had given him on their fortieth wedding anniversary, and then closed his eyes.

The image of Victoria appeared. She was walking her white horse on the West Texas prairie where she and D.L. had first met. She smiled and waved.

AUTHOR'S NOTE

This book pays tribute to the early pioneers of the offshore oil industry and to today's men and women who continue to push themselves and deepwater technology to new frontiers. Industry insiders (especially engineers) will surely note the creative license I have taken with some of the cutting-edge technology. I beg your pardon and ask your forbearance. I hope I have fulfilled my pledge to entertain as well as educate a public that should know more about your fascinating industry.